BEYOND A REASONABLE DOUBT

A NOVEL

Gary E. Parker

Publishers Since 1798

THOMAS NELSON PUBLISHERS
Nashville • Atlanta • London • Vancouver

Published in Nashville, Tennessee, by Thomas Nelson, Inc., and distributed in Canada by Word Communications, Ltd., Richmond, British Columbia, and in the United Kingdom by Word (UK), Ltd., Milton Keynes, England.
Scripture quotations noted NKJV are from the NEW KING JAMES VERSION of the Bible. Copyright © 1979, 1980, 1982, Thomas Nelson, Inc., Publishers.
Scripture quotations noted NIV are taken from the HOLY BIBLE, NEW INTERNATIONAL VERSION ®. Copyright © 1973, 1978, 1984 by International Bible Society. Used by permission of Zondervan Bible Publishing House. All rights reserved.
The "NIV" and "New International Version" trademarks are registered in the United States Patent and Trademark Office by International Bible Society. Use of either trademark requires the permission of International Bible Society.

Library of Congress Cataloging-in-Publication Data

Parker, Gary E.
    Beyond a reasonable doubt / Gary E. Parker
        p.cm.
    ISBN 0-8407-4148-0 (pbk.)
      1. Clergy—United States—Fiction. I. Title
PS3566.A6784B48 1994
813'.54—dc2   93-50917
                                                          CIP

Printed in the United States of America
1 2 3 4 5 6 7 - 99 98 97 96 95 94

PART

I

WHY COMES TEMPTATION

BUT FOR A MAN TO MEET

AND MASTER AND MAKE CROUCH

BENEATH HIS FOOT

AND SO BE PEDESTALED IN TRIUMPH

Robert Browning

THERE HATH NO TEMPTATION

TAKEN YOU

BUT SUCH AS IS COMMON TO MAN;

BUT GOD IS FAITHFUL

AND WILL, WITH THE TEMPTATION

ALSO MAKE A WAY TO ESCAPE

St. Paul

CHAPTER

1

B urke Anderson liked to think of the hands he shook every Sunday as different types of food. The slightly sticky, puffy white ones were marshmallows; the scaly, calloused hands were pineapples; the bony ones, long and pointed were carrots; and the fat red hot ones were smoked hams. He could close his eyes and identify most of his people by their hands. He knew he could because he'd done it last Christmas at a party when someone had challenged him to try. He squeezed every hand offered to him today as his flock filed past—a multitude of hands connected to people, hands and people blending together, a mass of fingers and palms, a church full of hands, passing in rapid succession, slipped in and out of his, pistons.

Burke wanted to spend some time looking into the faces connected to the hands, but people were always in a rush and this Sunday was no exception. Once or twice he managed to hold to a hand for a second and feel the life of the person wearing it, but for the most part the hands pumped by him without pause.

Only the children and the old people broke the assembly line. Burke liked to hug the old ones of his church, those slump-shouldered elders who graced his life with time and wisdom. His hugs were gentle—his arms around fragile shoulders, squeezing them lightly.

He hugged some of the children, too, but most were too shy to allow it for long. So, he high-fived the cow-licked boys and patted the girls on the top of the head, careful not to crush a bow or muss any hair. He gave both the boys and the girls Tootsie Rolls every Sunday and they thanked him quickly as they rushed after the hands beckoning them to the car.

He followed this beloved ritual every week and nothing changed today. When everyone was out, he stepped back into the church, snapped off the lights in the sanctuary, walked back to his closet-sized office and locked the door. Walking out of the church, he glanced at his own hands—his hands were apples, smooth on the outside, but firm and solid. He winced as he clenched and unclenched his right fist. He had scraped it over the weekend.

Finished closing up, he hurried out, hopped into his blue Cavalier and drove home.

Stomping across the gray wood flooring of the parsonage porch, Burke pulled the house key from his pocket and called out loudly, "Biscuit!" He heard his retriever before he saw him, a rush of paws across pine straw and a series of short yips signaling his approach. Biscuit skidded to a halt beside him, dropped the newspaper at Burke's feet and reared up on hind legs to receive his cuddle. Burke didn't disappoint him. He stroked the golden throat of his dog and scratched behind his ears and enjoyed the foul breath as he grabbed the dog's stout head and shook it side to side.

"Ready to go running, boy?" Burke asked. Biscuit yipped his approval.

"Good, me too. Hang on a minute and I'll get ready." Burke picked the paper up and eased into the cool foyer of the white-framed Methodist Manse. Eagerly, he jerked off his tie, kicked off his black wingtips, stripped out of his pants and shirt and slipped into his jogging shorts. Savoring the moment, he fondled his new shoes as he pulled them from the box, a crisp pair of Reebok Racers, the top of the line. Almost 100 dollars they cost him, white with a thin blue line creasing the side of each shoe, a lightning bolt of prestige and excellence, a statement about the shoe and the wearer of the shoe.

Ten minutes later, after slipping his feet into the shoes and stretching his legs carefully, he pulled the red headband over his forehead and rushed outside, anxious to run, anxious for release. Biscuit joined him at the sidewalk and he slipped into an easy pace. He sang as he ran, raising his trained voice to the sky. The singing helped him relax.

Today it took him six miles to find his zone, six miles of slog, slog, slog, six miles of one foot in front of the other one, driving, searching for the crossover point, the line marking the divide between anxiety and relaxation, the line moving him from the pain of running to the pleasure of it.

Biscuit had long since deserted him, leaving to do what boy dogs do—wet on bushes and chase leaves falling from tired trees and look for girl dogs with mischief on their minds.

Almost 40 minutes after beginning, Burke crossed the line and held his place beyond it for almost 25 more, for four more miles of inner vision, time when his body and spirit fused.

As his feet pounded through the golden afternoon, he wondered—should he go back to see her? He wanted to see Carol Reese again, and for more than one reason. Obviously, her beauty attracted him. He wouldn't be normal if it didn't. With eyes the color of a blue jay's feathers and skin the texture of Irish coffee with half a cup of cream in it, what man wouldn't want to go back? Beyond her physical beauty, though, he wanted to see her again because he knew she needed help. Most important, he had sensed she wanted it.

She had left the invitation open, like she wanted him to come back and talk with her again. Why not go? He believed he could help her and the desire to make a spiritual difference in people's lives had served as the most crucial factor compelling him into ministry.

Striding faster, Burke made the decision. He would go—just as soon as he could get home and take a shower. He could drive there in about an hour. By 4:30 he could be there, if he hustled.

He sprinted the last half mile to the parsonage, the sweat puffing up on his body, his black hair matted beneath his headband.

Within 45 minutes he had showered, slugged down a quart of Gatorade, heated and eaten a pre-cooked chicken dinner, slipped into his favorite khakis and a Georgia Bulldog jersey, and jumped into his car, headed out of Cascade. He turned up the radio and rolled down the window as he hit the interstate, letting the cooling air of the last Sunday of October wash over his body. He thumped the steering wheel in time with the music and raised his rich baritone to sing along over the swoosh of the wind.

The thought of Carol Reese created swirls of emotion in him. She was dangerous, too sexy for a preacher. But she seemed vulnerable too—a little like a skittish kitten stranded in the middle of a busy highway. He tried to push her out of his mind as he drove, afraid he might turn around and go home if he lingered too long over his thoughts. She tempted him. And that scared him.

He turned the radio to the football game—the Falcons and the Cowboys—hoping it would occupy his thoughts. It didn't. Carol Reese kept reaching for him, smiling at him. Burke shifted in his seat, mindful of the flush he felt on his brow. The miles sped by. It was 4:20.

He turned left off I-85 just inside the Atlanta city limits and, within five minutes, crossed the speed bump at the guardhouse outside the Foxfire condominium complex. No guard greeted him this time. He parked two buildings past the covered pool and slammed the door of the car as he hopped out. A gray-haired woman, struggling to hang onto an energetic cocker spaniel nodded to him as he walked toward condominium 869.

Would she be home? He hadn't bothered to call first. Might be better if she wasn't.

He wiped his hands on the sides of his pants and pushed the doorbell, leaning into it, listening. He bent closer—the sounds of a stereo playing a classical piece he couldn't identify filtered through the wall. If her stereo was playing, she must be home. But, no answer to the bell. Pushing again, he swiveled his head out and back, then up, searching the sky. He still heard nothing from inside Reese's place. He shifted to his left and quickly peeked through the drapes. Shouldn't do that, but if he was brave enough to come back he might as well see it to a conclusion. A lamp burned on a marble-top table just inside the window. He knocked twice, a little boy's knock, scared and tentative. Silence. Bolder now, he rapped harder three times, thump, thump, thump. The door swung open as he hit it the third time. No one greeted him. Should he go in?

His eyes darted both ways—no one was watching. The dog had pulled the lady out of sight.

Burke noisily walked into the condominium. "Is anybody here?" he called. Only the stereo answered. He noted the tasteful decor of the entryway as he called out—crown molding edged the ceiling and a Waterford crystal bowl filled with blue and rose silk flowers graced a cherry writing desk. Funny, he hadn't noticed the furnishings Friday night. Four steps further and he entered the main area of the condominium, a combination den and living room, divided only by two Georgian columns, one on each side of the room. A tan, L-shaped leather sofa with its back toward the entrance sat in the center of the spacious area. Directly across from the couch sat the stereo, in the middle of an entertainment center stocked with the latest in electronic gadgetry.

Burke squinted his eyes, confused. Obviously, no one was home. He stood in the fading light for a second, then decided to leave Carol a note, telling her he had come. He looked around the room for a piece of paper to write his note and saw a pad under the telephone resting beside the stereo. He edged around the floor-length sofa to reach the pad.

He saw her hand first, turned palms up with fingers spread, like it was waiting for someone to drop a ball into it. Carol rested on her side, not quite in a fetal position, but close, one leg on top of the other, a running pose, two l's, one just below the other. Her short black skirt was pushed up to her thighs. Her other hand lay across her stomach like a belt and she clutched a tiny American flag in it.

Reese's eyes were closed, but her lips sagged open like a door ajar, leaving her insides exposed.

For a second Burke thought she was asleep, hoped she was asleep, then knew she wasn't. Her face was too puffy for sleep, puffy around the gaping lips, like someone had blown too much air into her. She was white too, at least six shades whiter than on Friday night. White as loaf bread—dead white.

As he stared, mesmerized, an ant crawled from the inside of her mouth, stopped at the corner where her lips met, looked around, then dropped to the hardwood floor under her head.

Numbed beyond feeling, Burke tilted his head and bent lower, studying her, comparing her to the bodies he'd visited in funeral homes. Those bodies were neat, dressed in black suits or linen dresses, wax bodies, mannequins with rouge on, with lips wired shut and just the hint of a smile creasing the faces.

He winced. Carol's face wore bruises instead of a smile. The bruises blotted her forehead above her eyes and a thin crust of dried blood stuck to her lower cheek and spread out in an almost triangular pattern on the ivory carpet.

Burke noticed the smell of the stale air for the first time—air like dirty diapers in a closet—air like death. The stench attacked his stomach and his stomach turned over, waking up his mind and body. Carol Reese was dead! He stumbled backward, tripping over the sofa, falling into it, his stomach rebelling, refusing to stay silent. He threw up—a thin sluice of rusty bile—and the stench of it mingled with the stench of two-day old death and brought water to his eyes. In the same second he heard a pop in his head and his nose started bleeding. The red current spilled over his chin and mixed with the torrent from his throat and both spurted to the floor and puddled by his feet.

Pinching his nose and swallowing frantically, he fought for control of the volcano spewing inside. He wiped the spittle off his mouth with the back of his hand, raised his eyes from the body and struggled to think. Dead? Since when? Dear God, I was with this woman Friday night. She looks like she's been dead at least a day, maybe more. Maybe since Friday night.

He shut his eyes and sucked air through clenched teeth and forced himself to breathe it out slowly through his mouth. Like the former cross-country runner he was, he calmed himself through deep breathing, focusing on the blinking numbers of his digital watch. Two minutes passed as he slowed his heart and tried to think.

Feeling the nose bleed clotting, he peeked back at the body lying at his feet. Even death couldn't steal her beauty. He jumped like a teenager caught peeping through a window as the phone rang. The telephone jangled again. The loud sound in the quiet of the apartment sounded like alarm bells going off and Burke heard the alarm and jerked himself out of shock.

Someone calling her! What if the caller came to see her? With him there.

Frightened into action, Burke sprang from the sofa and fled the apartment. He sprinted to his car, popped it over the speed bumps of the complex, out of the gate and back onto the interstate. Pounding the steering wheel with his fist as he sped back toward Cascade, he thought back to Friday, to his birthday, a birthday only one person had remembered, one person he hadn't seen in over two years. . . .

CHAPTER

2

F riday! The baked beans from the squat red can and the Oscar Mayer wiener, blanketed in wheat bread and covered with mayonnaise, stuck to the roof of his mouth like Georgia clay stuck to his boots after a rain. Nothing tasted good. His spirits had dropped as the sun did and now both were dark. Burke wasn't usually so moody, but today he had a reason.

Today he turned 28 and everyone had forgotten his birthday. He had waited all day for a call from his mom and dad in Birmingham, or from his older brother in nearby Atlanta, but the phone never rang.

To make matters worse, no one in his church had congratulated him either. Earlier, eating breakfast at Edith's Coffee and Grill with what seemed like half the male population of Cascade, Burke waited for one of the boys to poke fun at him like they did everyone else. No one did.

Disappointed, he walked over to Chicken George's barber shop. Chicken, famous because he had just one ear and because people said he talked the other one off his own head, started jabbering the minute Burke sat down. Two other men, farmers by the looks of their faded blue overalls and lace-up brogans, sat in the shop with George, nodding appreciatively at Chicken's constant conversation.

"Morning, Preacher," Chicken said. "Sorry I missed church yesterday. Had my wife's folks in from Athens." Off he went, his tongue snipping in time with his scissors, clipping off the words and dropping them onto Burke's shoulders and ears with the same lack of thought he used in cutting his hair.

Burke listened, hoping Chicken would remember his birthday. Chicken usually kept up with such things. Kept a calendar marked with the birthdays of the important people in his life in the drawer with his clippers. He had shown the calendar to Burke one morning, on a day similar to this one, and bragged about it to him.

"Preacher, I've got seven brothers and three sisters, six children and nine grandchildren. Never missed a birthday in their lives. Always send them five dollars and a handwritten note. Figure if I don't forget them, then they won't forget me."

Today, he forgot Burke and everyone else did too. Burke went home early and tried to read but found no comfort in his book. The drawbacks of pastoring a rural church swelled up and pushed the joys of it away. Loneliness wrapped its frigid fingers around his neck and choked him.

He walked out and back from the porch to his bedroom, reading awhile and brooding awhile. On the porch he stared wistfully down the street, like a boy waiting for a friend to come home. He whistled several times for Biscuit, but it was dark and Biscuit was too busy with his night life to answer to a curfew.

Burke waited for the unfriendly day to end. Finally it did, the sun falling off slowly, its pink streaks holding onto the horizon like thin fingers clinging to a ledge.

Now, he sat alone, eating his meager supper. "What the heck," he thought as he tossed the last knuckle of the hotdog onto the plate. "I'll clean up the dishes, watch a little television, and go to bed. No use prolonging the misery."

Burke pushed back from the table and stood up. He heard the doorbell ring and, surprised, crossed the room to see who it was. Peeping through the hand-sewn white lace curtains, he made out the block-like frame of a familiar figure. He opened the door and his mouth dropped open as he saw Walt Litske, his former best friend and college roommate, standing on the porch.

Burke stammered, "Good gracious, Walt, is that really you?"

"You bet your first child it is," bellowed Walt, extending a huge paw and grasping Burke's much smaller hand in his. "How ya doing?"

"I'm still kickin'," said Burke, "Come on in." Burke opened his arms and hugged his pal as they stepped inside the house, still gaping at each other.

"How long's it been since I saw you?" Burke asked, a huge grin playing on his face.

"Two years since I saw you, but more like five since we really talked," said Walt.

Burke led his buddy to the kitchen, staring at him, amazed again at his square-jawed shape, rhino-like proportions, and shiny bald head. That's what the sports reporters had tagged him—the Polish Rhino. He motioned for Walt to sit down at the table with him and he obliged.

"Yeah, I saw you in Atlanta about two years ago, didn't I? I was there for a Conference on Alcohol Abuse, meeting at the Ramada."

Walt laughed. "You can bet your favorite dog I wasn't in that conference. But I might've been one of the guys you preachers were talking about."

The chuckle died out and Walt gulped a washtub full of air into his massive chest. Burke watched Walt's red face, a face redder than he remembered, redder than it should be, a face heated from a furnace inside, his eyes blue amethysts in the center of the fire. Walt leaned forward in the kitchen chair. "Do you remember when we first met, Burke?"

"Sure, man, how could I forget? I met you in the athletic study hall. You were one of the football players I tutored that fall. Your academic adviser told me you would be trouble."

"Was I?"

"No, not that I remember. In fact, your advisor missed it completely. You did fine."

Walt looked down at his feet. "I was so scared I had to."

"Scared? Are you kiddin' me? The Polish Rhino wasn't scared of anything!"

"The Polish Rhino wasn't, but Walt Litske was."

Burke, stunned for a second by his friend's honesty, asked gently, "What scared you, Walt?"

Walt scratched his stomach with a huge paw. "Well, Preach, you know, the possibility of failure. I wanted to play ball and I knew bad grades could keep me from it. So I studied. My teachers in high school told me I was smart, but I'd never tried."

"Until you went to college."

"Yeah, until I went to college and met you." Walt stared at Burke, challenging him to disagree.

Burke obliged. "I didn't have much to do with it."

"You're kidding me! You had everything to do with it. You made me envious."

Burke sputtered, "Envious? No way!"

"Yeah, envious. You made A's and you knew what you wanted. You were under control and I never felt like I was."

Burke tried to read Walt's mind. Walt had spent most of his college time chasing coeds and sucking the foam off beers. It didn't seem right for him to tell Burke so much now, not after they'd gone their separate ways. But he knew Walt wanted to talk and he decided to go with Walt's flow.

"I can't believe you ever felt jealous of me. I felt it was the other way around. You raised all kinds of mischief while I played it serious. You were free to rout and rave. . . . No chains on you."

"Oh, I wore a few chains," countered Walt.

"Like what?"

"Like the image I had to uphold. That I was such a bad dude. How do you think the boys of Georgia would have felt if they knew their Polish linebacker carried a B average onto the field with him every week? Or that he got so scared before a test he couldn't sleep the night before? They'd have a bad time with that one. Not sleeping before a game is fine, but before a test—no way."

Burke stood up, walked to the refrigerator, pulled out two Cokes, picked up a bottle opener and snapped off the caps. He handed one to Walt and sat back down, straddling the vinyl chair.

"How in the world did we ever become best friends, Walt? We were so different."

Shrugging as he swigged off the Coke, Walt said, "They say opposites attract. Maybe that was it. Maybe we just needed something the other offered. I needed your help with my grades and I figured the best way to get it was to get an apartment with you."

"And your offer to pay for it sure made it easy on me."

"Actually, my rich pappy paid for it, Preach. Didn't cost me a dime. Besides, your dad had recently had a heart attack, right?"

Burke sighed, the frightening memories punching their heads up again. "Yeah, the year before. Had to give up his job at the textile plant. Money was tight, that's for sure."

"So we helped each other."

"In more ways than one." Burke remembered their symbiotic relationship. "Maybe we fed off each other's excesses. I gained a perverse excitement through you and you gained a little stability through me."

"I guess that's one way of saying it. I never exactly figured it out. Just seemed like we fit each other, like those white birds that sit on the backs of cattle out in Texas, eating the bugs and ticks off 'em. The birds keep a full stomach and the cows get relief from the bugs."

"And I'm the white bird?"

"You pick 'em any way you want." Walt patted his watermelon-shaped stomach and grinned. "But if I was callin' it, I'd say I was definitely more of the big bull than you."

Burke didn't argue the point. Though not frail, standing a thin hair short of six feet, and weighing in at a well-toned 170 pounds, he didn't scare many people with his bulk. Sitting across from his jumbo-sized friend, he lowered his eyes, dealing again with his feelings of physical inadequacy, remembering he was an epileptic—a psychomotor epileptic, one who didn't suffer spells often—the last one over 10 years ago, but one who still suffered from the anxiety and the shame of the blackouts that accompanied his seizures. He never knew how long those blackouts would last nor what he would do during one of them. Thankfully, medication had controlled his affliction. But medicine hadn't controlled his fear.

He turned his thoughts back to the conversation with Walt.

"I don't know if I'm the white bird or not, but I have to admit I'm not the big bull. Some of my church members think I'm full of big bull sometimes, but I haven't heard anyone say I am one."

Walt leaned back in his chair, twisting his weight on its flamingo legs, dancing the chair on the tiled floor, chancing a spill. "Do you remember our nicknames?"

Burke's eyes crinkled and smiled. "How can I forget 'em? Neon and Freon. One of your girlfriends gave 'em to us our freshman year. The music major. She said you were bright lights and I was cool air."

"She was right, you know. I was hot and crazy back then. Remember when I jumped out of that dorm room from the second floor?"

Burke remembered. "You were drunk as a sailor on shore leave. I'm just glad you had sense enough to put a mattress on the ground before you jumped."

Walt doubled over with laughter. "I didn't put any mattress out, never crossed my mind. Some drinkin' buddy saved my life with that mattress and I still don't know who to thank for it."

"Good heavens, Walt, I'd never do anything so outrageous," Burke said.

"No, guess not. That's why she called you Freon."

"Was I that bad, Walt, that stiff?"

"Well, I'm not the one to ask. I suppose, compared to me, you were. You focused too much. You know, your studies and all. You just seemed a tad tense for a college student."

Burke furrowed his brow. "Seems like I've always been that way. Extra serious. My dad always told me 'Anything worth doing is worth doing right.' So, in college I thought I should study, you know, do it right."

"No one can say that you didn't. All A's, if my recollection is correct."

Shrugging, Burke said. "Yep, and few dates and little fun, if my recollection is correct."

"Yeah, well, you did keep your distance from the girls, didn't you?"

"Arm's length. While you grabbed dates like they were halfbacks trying to run past you on the football field."

"Amen to that, Pope. My image again. The boys in the dorms used to brag I squeezed for flesh wherever I found it. Couldn't let anyone prove those boys wrong, now, could I?"

"Suppose not." Burke rubbed his forehead, thinking hard. The two were talking on a level unknown to them, even during their closest times as roommates. They'd been too young and too scared to talk like this in college. He was glad they could do it tonight.

Walt gently interrupted the quiet which had fallen over the room. "What happened to Neon and Freon, Burke? They were such good friends. Why didn't we stay in touch?"

"I don't know." Burke rubbed his eyes. "It just happened. We drifted apart like most people do, even though they promise they won't. Time carried us away, down different paths. Circumstances and interests shifted, can't blame anybody really. Before we knew it, everything changed. You went to play for the Falcons, I entered divinity school at Wesley Methodist, and we didn't have much in common anymore. So, we moved on, away from each other."

"But we were still in the same town, right in Atlanta," Walt said, frustration raising his voice an octave.

"That's true," Burke said, his mood shifting downward with Walt's. "I watched you play, kept up with you through the sports page. But the deeper I got into my studies, the less anything else mattered."

Burke tried to make up. "I called you when you hurt your knee."

"You did? I didn't know."

"I left a message at the Falcons' office. Told them to tell you I called. I hated to see you get hurt."

"Not half as much as I did," snorted Walt. "I was cruisin' till then. Three years with the Falcons, second team All-Pro linebacker the second year, up for a new contract and primed for a Gillette shaver commercial. Saints alive, man, I was about to become a star!" Walt paused and sucked down a drink of Coke and started again. "Then that offensive tackle clipped me from behind and buckled my knee. Everything fell apart. I became landfill material overnight."

"I'm sorry, Walt" said Burke, pressing his lips together in a tight crease. "I wish I'd visited you. But I didn't think it would make much difference. I hadn't seen you for almost three years and you never seemed to need me. I always thought I was the one who needed you, that you were pretty much indestructible."

With a quick shake of his head, Walt grimaced, "Burke, for a guy who's supposed to be so smart, you couldn't find your backside with both hands and a flashlight sometimes. When I got hurt everybody deserted me! My teammates treated me like a contagious disease. The Falcons paid the rest of my salary for the season and my medical bills, but the minute they saw I couldn't come back, they dropped me like a dead cat. I was a 265 pound rhino with a bad addiction to stardom and a knee that couldn't carry him to the rocking chair. Man, it was over in a hurry."

Burke squeezed the neck of his drink bottle and apologized. "I just lost track, Walt. Didn't mean to, it just happened."

Walt waved off the apology. "Forget it," he said. "We've both made a few mistakes in the last few years. I'm just glad to see you tonight."

Suddenly, as if reaching a decision, Walt slapped his thighs with his racket-sized hands and bounced up from the table. "Well, all that's behind us. No need to sit around and groan about the past. Time to get on with the affairs of the evening."

Burke stood, too, curious. "Just what are the affairs of the evening? We've talked so much you haven't told me why you drove forty miles to see me on a Friday night."

"Maybe I came to see if you're taking good care of your flock."

"I doubt that, Walt. Quit dodging the subject. What are you doing here?"

A smile slashed Walt's face, a knife slice from one earlobe to the next. "Let me put it this way," he said. "My date cancelled on me and I found myself unattached. So, I decided to try something different and I figured visiting a Methodist pastor was about as 'different' as it gets. Besides," he shrugged, "it is your birthday, isn't it?"

Stunned, Burke mumbled, "I can't believe you're the only one who remembered."

"Yeah, I remembered and I took a chance you'd be home reading *Fifty-Four Ways to Grow a Giant Church and Start a Television Ministry.* Looks like I was right!" Walt threw his arm around Burke's shoulders and steered him toward the door. "Come with me, Preach, I'm going to take you away from all of this." He waved his free hand, dismissing the entire house. "I have a present for you. . . . But you'll have to come with me to Atlanta to get it."

Burke started to protest, to say it was too late for him to run off to Atlanta. But he changed his mind and decided to go. He'd kept himself under wraps too long. A night out with an old friend was just the tonic he needed to perk him up. He unhooked himself from Walt's towing arm and grabbed his wallet and a beige windbreaker. Quickly he trailed Walt out the door and climbed into his black Mercedes.

The CD player blared the words of an old song as Burke snuggled himself into the plush leather seats. "Celebrate, celebrate, dance to the music," the vocalist urged. "I haven't heard that for awhile," Burke said.

"Still a good one," said Walt.

"Yeah, at least tonight it is."

"You still a teetotaler?" asked Walt.

"Yep," said Burke, "but tonight . . . maybe not. What you got?"

"Beer or Jim Beam. Take your choice. Beer's in the cooler in the back. And here," Walt reached under his seat, "is the Beam."

"Let me see that," said Burke. He took the bottle from Walt, twisted off the top and smelled the hot cut of the alcohol. He remembered one of the reasons why he didn't drink. He hated the taste of the stuff. And he'd seen it rip too many lives into shreds. He clutched the bottle to his chest, but didn't drink from it. He sighed, closed his eyes and allowed the sound of the music and the warmth of the car's heater to wash over his nerves. He and Walt both stopped talking, as if by mutual agreement to let the other think. He opened the car window and caught a whiff of freshly mown grass and the smell carried him to other places and to simpler times—to sunny days in Alabama, to boyhood freedoms without the lead weights of adulthood he now carried around. Right now he yearned for those days.

He rolled the bottle of liquor in his hands, feeling the smoothness of its neck and sides. Seductively, the bottle beckoned to him, seemed to speak to him. Make friends, it said. Let me soothe your frayed nerves. I can do it. Just this one night. Just one drink. You'll like it, I know you will.

Burke twisted the top back onto the bottle and dropped it under his seat and stared out the window. The sleek car chewed up the miles.

Within the hour, Walt slowed the car and turned into the front gate of the Foxfire condominium complex. A sleepy-eyed guard with a too-short blue tie and rumpled uniform stuck his head out the guard-house window.

"Evenin' fellows," yawned the guard. "Anything I can do for you?"

"No, sir," Walt said. "Just here to visit a friend." Flashing a driver's license for the guard's inspection, Walt moved across the speed bumps and eased his way toward the Williamsburg-styled condos.

The creaky guard chewed the stump of his cigar and watched the Mercedes drive past.

"Help me find 869," Walt urged Burke as they neared the first building. "I think it's the third building past the pool. I wasn't in the best shape to remember the last time I came."

Burke jarred himself from his introspection. "What're we doing here, Walt? You taking me to some insane party like you did in college? You know those bashes are out of my league. The moment someone asks me what I do for a living, I'll either have to lie or admit I'm a minister. Either way, somebody gets embarrassed."

"Just pipe down, Pope, and help me find the building," chided Walt. "And no, it's not a party. Not for me anyway. Be patient and don't jump to so many conclusions. Isn't patience one of the things you religious guys are supposed to practice?"

Burke clammed up. Through the glare of the headlights, Walt spotted the number. Pulling into the driveway, he killed the engine and turned to Burke. "Okay, Bishop. This is your night. Follow me."

Burke surrendered to Walt's insistence. Whatever Walt had in mind couldn't be changed now. He had to play along, if only to satisfy his own curiosity. He followed Walt's choppy steps to the door, listening to the scattered crickets singing from the green hedges hunched by the sidewalk.

Walt punched the doorbell. A second later a light flicked on inside. In conspiratorial tones, Walt half giggled, "Burke, my pet, do I have a surprise for you!"

With his whisper dying on the air like autumn leaves falling on red clay soil, Walt paused. The door opened. The shadows fell across her face. The light from the hallway cast a sharp glow on her right side.

Burke, lonely from the forlorn day, peeked into the shadows. His heart jumped inside him, a child leaping to grab a toy it has always wanted but has never been allowed to receive.

Somehow, he knew this girl. He had met her in other times, in other places. He saw her from a distance then—in dreams which always obscured her face. He watched her in those dreams and reached out for her and ached for her in those tormented moments between the closet of sleep and the open door of wakefulness. She crawled around inside him in that half-moon world, scratching her initials on his insides with her presence but never allowing him to meet her or to touch. She always escaped him when he chased her and stayed one arm-length beyond him.

Now, his dream stood in front of him and studied him with jagged eyes cutting through him and causing him to freeze.

Walt's voice made the dream real. He gave it a name. "Carol, I want you to meet the friend I told you about this afternoon. He's a good kid. He just needs to relax a bit tonight. It's his birthday and old Walt, his long-forgotten friend, was the only one who remembered. Be gentle with him."

Finishing his instructions, Walt turned with the quickness of the All-American linebacker he had once been and sprinted to his car. Sliding into the driver's seat just as Burke caught on, Walt hung his head out the window and chuckled loudly, "Carol, one more thing, don't ask him what he does for a living. See you in the morning, Father Burke. Here's one birthday present I don't think you're ever going to forget."

Stunned by the emotion stirred by Carol's eyes, Burke stood open-mouthed on the stoop. He wanted to protest, to chase after his friend, to run from the claws which he sensed were raking at him.

But, he also wanted to stay, to give those claws a chance to catch him, to draw blood, to mark him with the scratch which would assure him he was a man and a good one at that.

Unable to run from the claws, he waited for them to reach for him. And they did.

CHAPTER

3

C arol Reese stepped back from the door and invited Burke inside with a sweep of her hand. "Come on in, birthday boy, and we'll have ourselves a party."

Not knowing what else to do, Burke stepped across the threshold into the apartment.

Carol, taking him by the hand like a mother escorting a frightened child across a six-lane intersection, ushered him to a low-backed sofa. "Sit down and relax," she encouraged. "You look a little tense." She stood over him as he sat down. "Want a drink?" she asked. "The bar is open."

Burke rolled his eyes up at her. "A glass of water will be fine," he said, "but nothing else."

She turned to walk away from him but he stopped her, "Could I use your phone for a minute? I need to call a cab."

"You're not staying?" she asked, moving on into the kitchen.

"No, I can't." Burke rubbed his hands on his pant legs and watched her.

"Why not, don't like the company?" She stuck out her lower lip and pretended to pout as she threw ice cubes into a glass and sprayed water over them.

"No, that's not the problem."

"Then what's the matter? Walt told me you were a friend and he wanted to do something special for you. And," she laughed like one with inside knowledge, "I'm definitely something special."

"I'm sure you are," Burke said, wondering how to squeeze out of this without anyone knowing it and without hurting this woman's feelings.

Carol didn't give him time to puzzle out an answer. Gliding back over, she handed him his water, plopped down beside him, kicked off her shoes, pulled her feet under her and propped her head on the back edge of the sofa.

"Tell me how you know Walt. You two don't seem to fit together somehow."

Burke grinned and his dimples jumped onto his cheeks. "No, we don't fit together at all. You see, I'm, . . . well, I'm a minister. I . . ."

Carol burst into laughter, cutting him off. "You're a minister! That Walt knows how to buy the perfect gift, doesn't he?"

"You didn't know?" said Burke.

"Heavens no!" She regained her composure for a moment. "How could I?"

"I thought Walt might've told you. I pastor a church in Cascade. If my church members saw me here they would fire me in a second. You're one birthday present I can't accept."

"Why not?" Carol raised her eyebrows mischievously. "I'm yours whether you're a minister or not. I'm an equal opportunity employee. I don't discriminate against anyone—except the poor."

"You mean my occupation doesn't change anything for you?"

"Not at all," said Carol, reaching over and rubbing her fingers down the side of his face. "I don't live by the normal rules. I live by my own standards and they're not based on the self-righteous tripe I hear from most preachers."

Burke blanched. Carol changed her tone and lowered her hand from his cheek. "I'm not saying all preachers are like that, but you've got to admit a lot of them don't seem to practice what they preach. I figure I bring more joy into people's lives than some ministers do. I make men happy and by doing that I figure I make some wives a little happier too. . . . Besides," and here she stared at Burke defiantly, "at least I'm not saying one thing to people and then doing another behind their backs. Anyway," Carol concluded, "I'm just practicing a little bit of the 'love your neighbor' philosophy the church is always encouraging."

The color in his face rose like capped steam in a radiator. He couldn't let her blanket condemnation of ministers stand, but he didn't want to offend her either. "Sounds like you've learned just one side of the story," he said. "Not all ministers act so irresponsibly."

"All I know have."

Burke heard grief in her voice and wondered what caused it.

"You sound bitter, Carol" He gave her an opening and she took it.

"I guess you could say that."

"Want to talk about it?"

"Why should I?"

"'Cause I'll listen if you do."

She steepled her fingers together, considering his offer. "Let me put it this way—I haven't seen much love from God or anyone else. My father walked out on me and Mom while I was still in pigtails, said he had to find himself. Then, when I was 14 one of Mom's boyfriends helped himself to me while she lay passed out drunk in her bedroom twenty feet away. Since then, I've taken care of myself."

Carol's eyes glazed over. "When you've had that much garbage dumped down your throat you tend to get a little cynical about God and your fellow human beings."

Burke watched the anger capture her eyes and make prisoners of them. She turned and faced him directly. "Look Mr. . . . ."

"Anderson," he said. "Burke."

"Look, Burke, I don't have anything against you. But I don't want you to preach to me."

"It's O.K.," said Burke, sympathetic to her hurt. "Life doesn't always make sense. Believe me, I know how insane it can get, how things can chop you up inside and leave you in little pieces. But, that's just one side of it. We can't forget the good side, can we? The people who live out their faith with love and kindness? The ones who make God visible?"

Carol didn't say anything for a second. Staring at her face, Burke sensed she hadn't really heard him. Her mind seemed to have moved away, to have chosen another tangent. His eyes met Carol's and she didn't flinch. Instead, her face evolved as the anger stole away on slender feet and a look he sensed was lust charged in. Her eyes woke up and danced and her body followed their lead—she emerged from the shell of the hurt and angry child and turned into a night cat in heat.

Burke gulped as Carol challenged him again, this time physically. He tried to catch his breath and failed. He gasped, his lungs plunging into oxygen debt the instant the temptation of the holy seduction struck her. He tried to cough, but his throat refused to cooperate. He struggled to get up and run, but his legs faltered.

As if in an out-of-body experience, Burke watched Carol's arms encircle his neck as she bent toward him. His eyes disconnected themselves from his conscience and took on a life of their own, peering downward toward her throat and the beauty beyond. His eyes lingered over a gold locket lying over the top button of her blue silk blouse.

Round, like a child's tea saucer, the locket had a smooth back and a heart engraved on the front. It rose and fell, surging upward and downward with the quick inhale and exhale of her lungs.

Her breath seared his cheek and he responded. He lifted his eyes and saw her moving her face toward his—lips red and full, wet and open. The kiss which exploded against him shook away the last chink in his resolve. If this was sin, then God help him, he wanted to enjoy its pleasure.

Burke heard his conscience collapse, a dam pushed over by pounding water as Carol took control. Pushing him backward on the divan, she pulled his jacket off and tugged at the buttons of his shirt. Her hands burned into his chest and urged him to respond in kind. In a fever-induced trance he reached to answer. He touched her face first, cradling the smooth skin, framing her chin with his fingers. Downward he moved his hands, exploring southward, to her neck, fondling the locket, rolling it over frontward and backward, surprised it felt cool to the touch. Cool, like he had been all these years. Holding back his normal urges, struggling to stay pure, suffering through the ridicule of friends, sacrificing for the God he loved.

Sacrificing. Even as he pulled Carol closer and closer, the word fought its way to the surface. Burke reached for the word—a drowning man lunging for the only life jacket—the rescue bobbing on the top of a heaving sea. He grabbed for the word and held onto it for the salvation it offered.

Sacrifice. Although his fingers slipped as Carol squirmed eagerly against him, his heart firmly clenched the word and his hands pulled it to his chest, close and safe.

Sacrifice. He floated to the surface now and the sea began to calm and he could breathe again.

Sacrifice. Jesus had sacrificed. Though he had seen seductions of all kinds, he had refused each one as it threatened him. The sharp claws had reached for him, too, but he had sacrificed and survived.

Burke felt the claws release his body. They unhooked his flesh and he saw them, blood red, retract. Though they had scratched their quarry, they had not killed it. He pushed Carol away and sputtered out his embarrassment, "I can't, it's not right. I'm not condemning you. It's just not the time for me."

Jumping from the cushions of the sofa, he grabbed his jacket and moved quickly toward the door. Unnoticed, his pocket Bible dropped from his jacket and lodged behind the sofa folds.

With his hand on the door handle he took a final look at Carol and said, "Don't think it's you. It's me, my belief, I can't destroy that. It means too much to me."

"Don't worry, Burke." Carol said, perched on the edge of the couch, stunned by his sudden decision. "I just wanted your birthday to be special. You're the first one who ever refused. You're the one I won't forget."

* * * * *

As the door slammed, Carol slumped back, suddenly tired and lonely. She shook her head at his refusal, analyzing the turn of events. An expert with men, she knew it wasn't a lack of maleness that caused Burke to flee. No, something stronger controlled him. Whatever it was, it was new to her. All her life men had desperately sought to seduce her. Tonight she had tried to seduce a man and he had refused her advances.

The tears which climbed unbidden to her eyes surprised her. She stuck out her tongue and tasted the salty drops cascading to the top of her lips. She wished she had met a man like Burke earlier; she wished all men treated her with his gentle tenderness; she wished his God did exist and loved her.

Leaning back, she felt an unfamiliar lump jamming her and she reached down and pulled Burke's Bible from the corner of the divan. For the first time since the seventh grade, Carol opened a Bible. Randomly, she turned its pages and her eyes fell on words from the book of John. She read:

Then the Scribes and Pharisees brought to Him a woman caught in adultery. And when they had set her in the midst, they said to Him, "Teacher, this woman was caught in adultery, in the very act. Now Moses, in the law, commanded us that such should be stoned. But what do You say?" This they said, testing Him, that they might have something of which to accuse Him. But Jesus stooped down and wrote on the ground with His finger, as though He did not hear.

So when they continued asking Him, He raised Himself up and said to them, "He who is without sin among you, let him throw a stone at her first." And again He stooped down and wrote on the ground. Then those who heard it, being convicted by their conscience, went out one by one, beginning with the oldest even to the last. And Jesus was left alone, and the woman standing in the midst. When Jesus had raised Himself up and saw no one but the woman, He said to her, "Woman, where are those accusers of yours? Has no one condemned you?"

She said, "No one, Lord."

And Jesus said to her, "Neither do I condemn you; go and sin no more.

John 8:3–11   NKJV

Carol brushed away the tears as she read on.

* * * * *

Outside, Burke stopped to look back. The lights from Carol's condominium winked at him. His pulse quickened as his instincts warned him, "You'd better move fast. Temptations don't stay beaten long. They come back, and quickly, if you don't run from them." But, how beautiful she is! What could be wrong with enjoying that beauty?

Standing exposed under the streetlight beside the curb, Burke suddenly caught the sharp whiff of onions. He remembered the last time he'd smelled onions this strong—when he was sixteen. He hated that smell, hated it because it taunted him, warned him, reminded him of his epilepsy, of a tragic day ten years ago, of an impending seizure, of a blackout, of pain and maybe death.

Burke croaked out a high-pitched prayer.

"Please, Lord, not here, not now! Not after ten years." Burke glanced at his watch: 11:04. He had to remember . . . had to remember . . . as he passed out.

CHAPTER

4

T he Cascade exit sign beckoned Burke back into the present, to Sunday afternoon, to a harsh reality—Carol Reese was dead. He glanced at his watch and calculated the time he had left her apartment Friday—around 11. Between then and now, someone had killed her.

Who? He considered the possibilities.

Walt? He's never been too stable. Maybe he came back later to see how his plan had turned out, got into an argument, hit her, killed her accidentally.

Maybe Carol tried to blackmail a wealthy client and he put a contract out on her to protect his identity. . . . A thief maybe. It wouldn't be the first time a robber had murdered. What about drugs? Was Carol a user? A dealer, furious over an unpaid account, gained his pound of flesh. A jealous lover? Carol could certainly inspire that. He wanted her to stop working. She refused and he decided he preferred her dead rather than shared.

His mind bounced around like a silver ball in a pinball machine. *Should I call the police? Tell them I was there Friday, but left about 11? Wait a minute! How can I explain even being in Carol's apartment? My church members won't believe I didn't have sex with her. But what about Walt? Won't he vouch for my story? Maybe, but not necessarily. Walt might be the killer. No, can't go forward, not yet. Have to keep quiet, bide my time, see what happens next.*

The hair on his arms stood to attention at his next thought and he tried pushing it away. It insisted though, forcing its way in—a rude intruder, reminding him—you're a suspect too. You've got motive and opportunity.

He pulled into his driveway and hurried into the house. He

perched himself on the edge of his recliner and switched on the television set, wondering if anyone had discovered Reese.

They had.

The spit-shined profile of Les Atkinson, chief anchor for WATL, filled the screen. Burke stood up and paced as he watched.

Atkinson began, "For the second time in two weeks a call girl has been murdered in northeast Atlanta. Tragically, I am again standing outside an expensive condo in northeast Atlanta to report the death of another woman. According to sketchy accounts, police at the Peachtree Street Station received an anonymous phone call 30 minutes ago telling them a homicide had occurred sometime Friday evening. The caller directed the police to a specific condominium in the Foxfire complex and immediately hung up."

Burke watched Atkinson pause like the slick professional he was. He seemed to give his audience a chance to digest this first bite of information and to admire his Redford-like profile. After the necessary count of two, he continued.

"Acting on this tip, two detectives from the Atlanta Investigation Squad, Lieutenants Mays and Broadus, entered the unlocked condominium with search warrants and discovered the body of a woman approximately 25 years old."

The camera switched beyond Atkinson to an ambulance and a sheet-draped stretcher. The camera's eye zoomed in for a tighter shot of the dead girl's body and probed it like a hungry dog pushing its nose at a trash can.

* * * * *

Off camera, Atkinson pointed to his production chief sitting in a white van a few feet from him. The assistant nodded, still propping a car phone to his ear. An official at the Peachtree Street Police Precinct listened on the other end. The production chief wanted just one thing—information to give Atkinson the edge on everybody else. He wanted the angle desperately and he wanted it fast. So, he offered a high price for it.

"Look, let's not tap-dance around with this one," he said. "We're only on the air for another minute or so and I need to hear what you've got. We've worked together before and we can do it again if you produce."

"What'cha offering?" the nameless cop bargained. He didn't do this often—about once a year or so. But, on the really hot cases he liked to pick up a few extra bucks by cooperating with the highest bidder.

"I'm not offering a dime until I hear the information," countered Atkinson's assistant, his patience oozing away as the seconds ticked off.

"I could lose my job over this," insisted the informant.

The reporter cut to the bottom line. "O.K., listen up, I don't have time to pick nose hairs here. I'll give you $5,000 if Les uses it on the air right now! Spit it out or I'll buy it from someone else."

"Agreed," said the source, hurriedly dismissing his chances of a higher bid. "Here's what I've got. The police found a Bible under the girl's hip. The Bible has a name engraved on it and it's not hers. We think the name on that Bible is the name of the best suspect. We're moving now to get a warrant to pick him up."

Scribbling furiously, Atkinson's man closed off his informant, "Gotta run. Your check will be deposited as usual." Jerking himself out of the seat and dropping the phone as he moved, he rushed to Atkinson and held up the message.

Back on camera, Atkinson's okra-slick voice slipped words over the picture of the body being lifted into the ambulance behind him. "Though an autopsy will determine the precise cause of death, the woman apparently died from a series of fierce blows to the head, resulting in a cerebral hemorrhage and death.

As Atkinson talked, Jackie Broadus, one of the detectives assigned to the homicide, walked within earshot. Atkinson called out, "Lieutenant Broadus, could you take a moment for us?"

Broadus' elegant frame flowed into view—a tall and pretty woman, towering at least six inches higher than Atkinson. Atkinson grinned into the camera, congratulating himself for getting Broadus on screen. Atkinson stretched the microphone up to her lips, "Lieutenant, can I ask you a few questions about the victim?"

"Sure, you can ask," said Broadus, casually flipping her black bangs out of her eyes with her hand.

Atkinson ignored her sarcasm. "First, can you give us the identity of the deceased? Second, was she a prostitute like the other recent victim? Have you found any specific clues you can share with our viewers? Do the police have any suspects?"

In an ice water voice, Broadus said, "We have identified the body from a driver's license found in the apartment, but we cannot release the name until we notify the relatives and they make a final identification. Her occupation is unknown. We've no definite suspects, but we have enough preliminary reports to start our investigation."

Broadus turned toward Atkinson, her aristocratic profile to the camera. "That's all I can say. We'll keep the public informed as developments warrant." She pivoted sharply and moved beyond camera view.

Atkinson, dwarfed by her presence, stepped back into the center of the frame and paused strategically as he reached over and took a slip of white paper from his assistant. He read the note and switched gears.

"I need our station to hold for one more moment. My production chief has just handed me a note which bears our attention. According to our sources, detective Jackie Broadus, who just spoke to me, found a pocket-sized Bible with a name inscribed on its cover on the floor near the body of the deceased woman. Our source couldn't divulge the name on the Bible, but the police are moving right now to obtain a search warrant so they can pick up the suspect. In the opinion of our source, the person who owns this black, leather-bound Bible ranks as a prime suspect in the death of this woman and possibly of the other woman recently killed as well."

* * * * *

Atkinson's lips were still moving but Burke no longer heard him. Like a punch drunk fighter, already numb from too many blows to the head, he lurched up from his seat, stumbled to his bedroom and picked up his windbreaker from the chair where he'd dropped it Friday night. He rummaged through its pockets, looking for his Bible—it wasn't there. He collapsed onto the bed and lay transfixed, a mounted animal on a wall, inanimate, resigning himself to the fates. He hadn't missed his Bible until now. Didn't know he'd dropped it. After all, it wasn't his preaching Bible and he hadn't used it over the weekend. Now, the police had found it and they were coming for him.

Numbly, Burke reviewed the last two hours. How fast life changes. He felt an earthquake shaking inside him causing demons to escape from the bleak places where dark fears lurked, from the caverns of the heart where doubts were born. Doubts about God and the way that life should unfold. Why should this happen to him? Why should it happen to Carol Reese? Why should it happen to anyone? The questions hung in the air like blades of grass tossed up by someone testing the strength of the wind. Then with no answering breeze to hold them aloft, they fell heavily to the ground.

Burke stared down at his chest and watched his heart beating through his shirt. He tried to clear his mind, scrambling for answers to the questions banging around in his head.

He rubbed the top of his right hand, touching the torn skin and fresh scabs forming on his knuckles and noticed again the soreness in his wrist. *What happened while I was blacked out? Over an hour I can't remember. Can't recall much even after I regained consciousness. Staggered to the interstate, caught a ride with a teenager driving a pickup, made it home, fell into bed and slept most of Saturday morning. Worked on my sermon Saturday afternoon, then went to bed early.*

Burke thought of Walt again. Frantically, he picked up the phone by his bed, pulled his address book from the top drawer of his nightstand and turned it to the L's, hoping the number was still correct. It wasn't. A computerized voice informed him, "The number you have dialed has been changed or disconnected. For further assistance, call your operator or dial information."

He tried the operator. She gave him a second number. He called it, but it was changed or disconnected too. He wasn't surprised. Walt wasn't to be found.

Burke chewed on the inside of his lower lip, wondering what Walt would say if the cops connected him to Reese and called him in for questioning. He trusted Walt to keep his name a secret unless he had to give it to prove his own innocence. But, his fingerprints were surely on the glass Carol gave him and on the locket she was wearing. He wondered if forensic experts could lift fingerprints from flesh. The sleepy guard might identify him and if he couldn't, the teenager who drove him home surely could. His hand was busted up—he didn't know how he'd managed that. The police were moving to obtain a warrant to arrest him on suspicion of murder.

He calculated. Stay and try to prove his innocence? Or, run and try to find Walt and get some answers?

Innocence will be almost impossible to prove. Running, though, points even more to guilt. But not many options. With so many preachers messing up, one more will just seem normal. Have to run, not sure where, but have to run . . . to find Walt, force him to tell the truth.

His decision made, Burke yanked himself off the bed, hauled a suitcase from the closet and filled it with basic necessities—underwear, toiletries, an electric razor, two pairs of jeans, one pair of sweat pants, athletic shorts, a favorite flannel shirt, two wool sweaters, and the same jacket he had worn Friday.

Off his desk he grabbed the picture of his mom, dad, and older brother taken at Christmas two years ago. With a lump in his throat the size of a goldfinch, Burke wondered if he would ever go home for Christmas again.

He looked around—what else would he need? His address book, an Atlanta Braves baseball cap, and a checkbook topped off the uneven stack he threw into the Samsonite. He pulled his new shoes from under the bed and held them to his chest. A runner since the seventh grade, a sport an epileptic could do alone, Burke slipped the cherished shoes into his suitcase.

The odds and ends jumbled together forced a smile to his pinched face. How strange—when forced to choose what he really needed to survive, it boiled down to such an odd conglomeration of stuff. In normal times—he smiled grimly, noting he was already thinking in terms of the past—he wouldn't have thought he could live with so little. Now, though, what he owned didn't matter much. Survival counted, and a person didn't need fancy clothes, or electronic gadgets, or antique furniture to survive. A couple of pairs of jeans, a jacket, a shirt or two, and a toothbrush would do just fine.

With his booty shoved into the suitcase, Burke hustled to the door and opened it. He whistled. This time Biscuit heard him and scurried across the porch to wait on the other side of the screen as Burke turned for a last look at his home. He soaked in everything—the yellowing lace curtains on the windows; the carpet, stained by the spills and drippings of the 14 children and three preachers before him; the 98-year-old mahogany dining room table with the big scratch in the middle; the fireplace mantle boxed on the corners with brass sconces and bearing in the center the manse's official Bible.

Burke walked over and placed his right hand on the Bible. If not for a Bible, he wouldn't be running. What would his mom think when she heard that the Bible she gave her son at his seminary graduation had been found in a dead prostitute's apartment? Maybe she already knew.

He wanted to blame the Bible . . . or God . . . or himself. *I need to blame somebody*, he thought. But, he couldn't blame the Bible and he couldn't blame himself. He hadn't known what Walt had in mind when he drove him to Carol's. He couldn't blame God either, could he? God didn't want this to happen, did He? If God wanted this, then God wanted death. That couldn't be, could it? But if God didn't want it, then what? God didn't want it but couldn't do anything to stop it? What kind of a God was that? Not much of one. A false one, a puny God, a bare skeleton with no muscle to stop the bully who knocked people into death. That was no God at all. No God. No God! Could he accept that?

No, he didn't think so. That made it all even more hopeless. If no God, then no hope at all. Not for him or anyone else.

Too much to settle now. Only thing to do now is run. If God exists, God will help. If God exists and if God cares. If! His whole life depended on If. Or did it? If God didn't exist, he had no one but himself.

Burke patted the broad pages of the Bible, then lifted his suitcase from the floor. His lower lip trembled as the pain of the day hit him. He remembered the day he left home for college. Life was never the same after that. His room shrank while he was away and he filled it up too much when he returned from Athens to spend weekends with his folks. College cut the umbilical cord and sometimes, when he was alone, he could still feel its swollen throb.

He trudged out of the parsonage, grabbed Biscuit by the collar and pushed out again from a womb—from the womb of the church, from the protection of his Methodist shelter, from the womb of the known into the mystery of the unknown. He felt like a child slipping through the birth canal, certain only of the security it was leaving and not at all happy about the prospects of what it would face. Burke closed the door. And, like a borning child, he cried.

PART

II

MAN'S MOST VALUABLE TRAIT

IS A JUDICIOUS SENSE OF

WHAT NOT TO BELIEVE

Euripides

DEAR FRIENDS, DO NOT BELIEVE

EVERY SPIRIT,

BUT TEST THE SPIRITS TO SEE WHETHER THEY

ARE FROM GOD

BECAUSE MANY FALSE PROPHETS HAVE GONE

OUT INTO THE WORLD.

St. John

CHAPTER

5

Burke pointed his Cavalier out of the gravel driveway of 207 Swans Lane. He drove cautiously and took stock. He knew from watching cop shows what a suspect needed first—a place to lay low—a hideout where no one would look for him. He motored past the Dairy Twister, the outer boundary of Cascade. *Where can I hide? Get a chance to think, find someone who will listen to me? Believe me? Can't go to the family—the police will check them first. Where?*

Burke reeled each possibility through his mind like clothes in a dryer. Watching the pieces turn before him, Burke caught a glimpse of an odd piece tumbling by. He watched for it again. There it was—a possible fit. He reached over and patted Biscuit on the head. "What'cha think, boy? Cody Stimson? A twenty-year-old single man—no complications with a family. Not well known in the community, just moved to Cascade a few weeks ago. Not connected with me in any public way. A few people know I helped him find a job and he's visited with me several times. But nobody knows he's a recovering heroin addict, released two months ago from Atlanta Correctional. Even though he's attended church once or twice, no one will tie us together. What'cha think?"

Biscuit whined, still uncertain. Burke decided it fit better than anything else he could imagine. No one would look for him at Cody's. Of course, Cody might not help him. But maybe he would.

Burke let out the breath he'd held since leaving the parsonage and followed the left fork of Highway 53 past the Little League ballpark on the outskirts of Cascade. This old route slithered for 17 miles through a sea of pine trees, red clay fields, and kudzu-covered countryside until it ran into Interstate 85.

Burke wasn't going the full 17 miles to the interstate. Cody's place was a garage apartment on the way. Thankful he had a first step, Burke sagged back into his seat. He wanted to sleep and dream and forget. Unfortunately, he couldn't sleep—not yet. And his nightmare was real. No wakefulness would remove it.

Six miles out of Cascade he slowed as he passed the last post of a barbed wire fence running along the right side of the road. He strained his eyes, searching for an abandoned car on the left which served as a final marker for his turn.

Within moments, the car appeared. Burke scanned it as he passed—a peaceful corpse sitting in the center of an open field. He turned left past the car and inched his way through the curtain which had slammed the anvil of blackness down on Cascade. There it was! A stone-block building with *Rembert's Painting and Remodeling* tattooed across its front. Burke held his breath. Was Cody home? Would he believe him? Would he hide him?

Peering through the inky dark as he pulled into the grass-infested driveway and shut off the car engine, Burke raised his eyes toward the second floor of the ramshackle dwelling. A yellowish light dripped out of the first window on the right. Whispering, "Stay," he left Biscuit in the car and stepped out. He smelled motor oil and saw a dented navy pickup by the stairwell of the apartment. He stepped past the wounded truck and tiptoed up the creaky stairs and knocked on the door. Within seconds it opened.

Cody, sporting a three-day-growth of beard, wasn't expecting company. "Pastor?" he started with surprise.

Burke held up his hand. "Yeah, it's me, Cody. Can I talk with you for a few minutes."

"Well, uh, sure, come on inside," Cody said as he stepped back to let Burke in the narrow door. "But I got to tell you, I'm not ready for no company, the place is a mess."

Burke scanned the bare walls of the apartment as he entered the tiny space. Nothing on them but smudges. No pictures, just blank white paint. More like a cell block than an apartment. Not much bigger either—two rooms, neither much larger than a bathroom, and a bathroom smaller than most closets he'd seen. One cheap vinyl couch leaned wearily against the wall under the window and a plain rocker kept it company. A skinny rug that was once yellow, but now looked more brown than anything else, completed the decor of what would charitably be called a living area. One half of the room contained a waist-tall refrigerator, a gas stove, and a barrel turned over with a piece of plywood on top, acting as an eating table. Canned goods and two or three paper sacks rested on top of the scratchy table and a garbage can bulging with trash sat beside it. Burke smelled the oil from the truck downstairs infiltrating the walls.

Cody waved at the room. "Not much to look at, but at least it's paid for."

"It's better than the dorm room I had at college," said Burke, trying to put him at ease.

Cody gestured toward the couch and Burke took a seat. Cody backed into the rocker and offered his excuses. "Pastor, I know I've missed church recently, but I can explain. I've worked three straight Saturdays for over 14 hours for Mr. Rembert and I've been flat wore out. I'm sorry."

Burke vigorously shook his head. "No, Cody, I'm not here to gripe at you 'cause you missed church. I wish it was as simple as that, but I'm afraid it's not."

Cody smoothed down the brown ponytail hanging on the back of his neck and tried again. "What's the problem, Pastor? I'm clean and haven't missed any of my probation meetings. Has somebody accused me of something?"

"No, nothing like that, Cody. My visit has nothing to do with you."

Cody leaned toward Burke, turned his palms upward and asked, "What gives, then? I'm glad to see you, but you didn't ride way out here just to say hello."

Burke's hands shook as he pushed them together to steady himself. He stared at Cody, an unlikely ally, an ex-con wearing a cheap earring and sporting a tattoo on his left forearm which read, "Hell Ain't a Bad Word." How could he tell Cody? How could he tell anyone the Atlanta police were looking for him as a suspect for murder? Just thinking it made it sound ludicrous, impossible. But he had to tell someone. It wasn't like he could keep it a secret anyway. By now the whole town of Cascade might know. Even if the police hadn't released his name, he knew the media would discover it soon enough. Burke began slowly. "Cody, what I'm about to tell you will be hard for you to accept. It's even hard for me to accept and I know it's true. I want you to wait until I've finished before you say anything."

Burke wiped his brow and poured out his confession. "Friday night I was sitting at home finishing supper. It was my birthday."

Cody started to interrupt, but Burke stopped him with a wave of the hand. "Don't say anything. I need to get this out. The doorbell rang and when I answered it I found an old friend, a friend I hadn't seen for two years, at the door."

In the next ten minutes Burke regurgitated the details of the last two days. As he talked he fastened his eyes on Cody's face. Like a confused storm blowing in with alternating moments of cloud and sun crossing over the ground, Cody's face shifted as the story progressed. A twinge of a smile crossed his lips as Burke mentioned the gift Walt prepared for him. A scowl replaced the sun as he outlined the temptation which almost overpowered him. The sun peeked out again when Burke described his flight from the apartment. The scowl returned for a final visit as Burke recounted the news of the afternoon.

"I found her dead, Cody! The same girl I met Friday. She's dead and the police think I killed her."

Cody scratched his fuzzy chin. "I can see how they would," he said. "You were in her apartment. They found your Bible there. Even people who know you will wonder about that. Even if they don't think you killed her, they'll want to know what you were doing there in the first place. It don't look good."

"No, it doesn't," agreed Burke sadly. "I'm finished as a minister. Even if I get off the murder charge, no one'll believe I didn't have sex with that woman."

"What about this guy Walt? Won't he vouch for your story?"

"He might, but what if he killed her? If he did, he won't come forward to help me and I can't wait around to see what he will or won't say. I tried to call him, but his number is disconnected."

Burke stopped and stared at the dingy wall of the apartment. He knew Cody didn't own much. A used color television, a 1979 Pontiac Firebird his uncle gave him when he left prison, a couch bought at a garage sale, three pairs of jeans and a few shirts—flannel checks for winter and collarless tee shirts for summer. He couldn't lose much materially by sticking his neck out.

But, he was free after two horror-filled years in jail and he was straight—off drugs and out of prison. Harboring a fugitive could cost him his freedom. The courts would have little patience with an ex-con assisting a murder suspect. They might even accuse him of being an accomplice.

Burke hesitated to ask, but he had no choice. His words poured out in a gush, "Cody, I hate to ask you this, but I don't know what else to do. I need a place to stay for a day or two until I can figure something out. Could I possibly stay here? I realize it's risky for you and I'll understand if you say no. But, I couldn't think of anywhere else where the police wouldn't look for me."

Burke took another deep breath and wiped his hands on his thighs. It was done, the secret was out, and someone else knew his story. What would Cody do with it?

Burke watched as the sun came out again on Cody's face. His next words soothed Burke's frayed nerves. "Pastor, several weeks ago I walked into your office off the street and asked you for help. You took me home with you, fed me a meal, let me spend the night in your house. The next day you called Mr. Rembert and asked him to give me a job. I don't know yet about a lot of the stuff you preach. I'm not sure I can swallow all of that. But when I needed a friend you were there for me." Cody stood up, put his hands in his back pockets, and spoke quietly. "Yeah, you can stay here. Fact is, I'm honored you thought of me when you needed a friend. You just tell me what you want me to do and I'll do my best."

Thankful to the point of giddiness, Burke shoved his hand toward Cody, needing some physical gesture to seal the decision. Cody grabbed it for a second, noticed the scratched and swollen knuckles, and then, embarrassed, dropped it and stared down at his bare feet.

"What happened to your hand?" he asked.

Burke glanced away. He hadn't told Cody about his blackout and the 70 missing minutes. Though asking Cody to hide him, he hadn't leveled with him. Trapped in a corner of his own making, Burke whispered his regrets. "I fell, Cody. You don't know this, but I'm an epileptic. I haven't had an attack in ten years, until Friday night. I guess my adrenalin level got so high it short-circuited my brain cells or something. Anyway, as I left the woman's apartment, it hit me and I passed out and I must've landed on my hand."

With head still bowed, Burke continued. "If you're going to help me you need to know one more thing." He raised his head and searched Cody's eyes, pleading with him to understand and not to judge.

"Cody, I was out for over an hour. With my kind of epilepsy a person can blank out for fairly long periods of time. They're like sleepwalkers while they're out—zombies who can function but don't know what they're doing. When I woke up, I was several hundred feet from where I fell."

"You mean you got up and moved, but don't remember doing it?"

"Yeah."

Cody pressed, "And you don't know what happened in those minutes?"

"No, Cody, I don't."

"How'd you get home?"

"I hitchhiked. As well as I can remember I staggered to the interstate. It's less than a half mile from the condo. I caught a ride from a teenager in a pickup truck. He let me out at the Cascade exit and I ran home from there. That's all I can remember."

Cody squinted at Burke and glanced at his torn knuckles again. Then he nodded and walked away and stared out his only window. He swiveled around and asked, "Preacher, do you think you killed that woman?"

Silence creaked through the shoe-box room. "Cody, I've been asking myself that question all afternoon. I know anyone can kill under the right circumstances. In a war or to protect someone I loved I would do whatever was necessary. Yeah, I *could* have killed that girl. But, *did* I kill her? That's what you really want to know, isn't it?"

"Yeah, Preacher, that's what I really want to know."

Burke squeezed his eyes shut and rubbed his hands across the thighs of his pants, stalling, afraid to face Cody's question. Finally, he said, "I can't answer you with certainty. When I black out I don't have any control over myself. I've tried all day to jog my memory, to push out whatever happened in those missing minutes. Sometimes, when I black out I remember later what I did. But other times I don't recall a thing. My head hurts from trying to force it today. I can't let myself believe I killed her, but I can't tell you for sure I didn't."

Now it was Cody's turn to hesitate. But he didn't. Instead, he trudged across the narrow room, eased himself back into the rocker beside the sad sofa, and began to move back and forth, back and forth, using the motion to steady his fractured nerves. Burke crouched on the divan and waited. Cody stopped rocking and said, "You're asking me to have faith in you, aren't you, Preacher?"

"I suppose I am," said Burke.

Cody rocked again. "Well, I don't know much about faith. But I do know about fear and I do know about needing somebody to believe in you. I've had the cops after me too—three different times before I turned 20. They came with their guns pulled and they slapped handcuffs on my wrists and they threw me in jail with grown men. I don't want anybody to go through that if I can help it. You can stay here as long as you want."

Burke slumped back against the couch. Although it was barely 9 o'clock, he was exhausted. He wanted rest but knew sleep was impossible. He heard a buzz in his ears and his arms and legs were twitchy, like he'd run beyond his endurance and the muscles were rebelling.

"Cody?" he asked timidly.

"Yeah?"

"What's prison like?"

"Don't even think it, Preacher."

Burke raised up. "I can't help but think it, Cody."

Cody shook his head. "I'd rather not talk about it."

Suddenly Burke understood and he hated himself for pressing but he couldn't let it drop. Not knowing and imagining was worse than knowing and fearing. "I'm sorry, Cody, I know it's not fair to ask you to dredge up bad memories, but I've got to know. I've never even visited a jail! I don't think I could survive it. What's it like? You've got to tell me!"

Cody pulled at his ponytail, fluffing it out as he answered. "What's hell like, Preacher?"

"I'm not sure," said Burke, confused. "I . . . I guess it's like your worst nightmare."

Cody laughed sadly, "Well, Preacher, I have been to prison. And I suspect it's a lot like hell."

Burke, too scared to push the curtain back any further, let it drop. The two men talked on, into the night, talked about tomorrow, about yesterday, about a lot of yesterdays, about everything but prison, talked until the moon dropped beyond the trees and the frogs stopped croaking, talked until they both dropped off to sleep, Burke on the weary couch and Cody upright in the rocker.

CHAPTER

6

T he news staff of the *Atlanta Independent* gathered their coffee cups and Tab cans and headed into the conference room at the end of the main hallway. An oblong mahogany table dominated the room. Stan Wraps, managing editor of the paper for 32 years, slouched at the head of the table. Cigarette smoke curled from the ashtray beside his right hand, an ashtray which had stayed empty for over ten months, but filled tonight with half a dozen smoldering butts.

Behind his shag-carpet eyebrows, Wraps' mind churned with worry. He mentally replayed the phone call he'd received at 9:35 A.M. from Nelson Steadman, the man who had given him his first job in the newspaper business and the only man who frightened him. Steadman, the 90-year-old patriarch of southern journalism and the co-founder of the *Independent*, had given him a bleak report.

"Stan, this is Nelson."

Out of reflex, Stan had risen from his normal slouch, as if Nelson had stepped into the room.

"Nelson, what a surprise. How ya doing this morning?"

"Not worth spit. I'm old and I don't like it. But I didn't call to talk about my health. I'm worried about the paper—you know the figures. Our circulation's off by 16 percent since the first of the year and that puts us close to the red line."

Wraps grunted back, "Look, Nelson, sure I know the figures. What I don't know is what to do about them. People don't read newspapers much anymore. Not quick enough or colorful enough for them." Wraps rubbed his forehead, trying to scrape away the sad truth.

Newspapers couldn't compete unless they went after the underbelly like television and the tabloids. But, Stan rebelled against the cash for trash method of journalism. He liked his news plain and, most important, he liked it verified. He told every new reporter he interviewed, "Get it straight and get it confirmed. Otherwise, don't print it."

Nelson interrupted his musings. "Don't give me the stock answer, Stan. Right now, I need a prescription, not a diagnosis. The bottom line is pokin' me in the keester and we've got to find a way to make a profit or you can start looking for a cemetery to bury a proud old paper."

Like a man washing out his mouth after flossing, Wraps spat out the words, "Nelson, all we can do is compete with the tabloids. If we don't spice things up, we're dead meat on a stick."

Nelson's voice softened. "Repulsive, huh?"

"As ugly as road kill." Wraps, resigned to the reality, was already calculating a date in early spring to announce his retirement. "I'll get out the yellow paper, Nelson. Let's see if that'll help."

Nelson signed off, "Do the best you can, Stan. And, Stan."

"Yeah?"

"Don't let them see you sweat. At least you know quality journalism when you see it. Not many do these days. Talk to you soon."

With Nelson's call still fresh, Wraps had convened the session to decide Monday's layout. He moved around the table, calling on the editors to suggest leads. The national editor said, "The President is headed to Europe for the Economic Summit."

"A lot of puff, but not much substance," said Wraps.

The state editor, Linda Brighten, piped in "I think we've got something better right here. Senator Raymond Steele is battling the League of Professional Educators over the banning of books. Seems the Senator finds some of them objectionable."

Wraps nodded for her to go on.

"It's got local appeal," she said.

"Don't tell us the obvious," growled Wraps.

Wraps liked Brighten. She wasn't much to look at with hair the color and density of rat's fur and a complexion which looked like a picked-over pizza, but he had long since passed the age when he cared much about a person's appearance. As long as his people produced good stories he didn't care if they were ugly enough to frighten small dogs, which Brighten could probably do he decided, looking at her.

Brighten continued as he stared at her. "It's a conflict between two powerful groups, the Senator's ultraconservative constituency and the more moderate LPE. A good fight sells a lot of papers these days and the Senator is always colorful copy."

"What else we got?" asked Wraps. If nothing else stood out, they could go with the headline *Senator Seeks to Ban Salinger*, but he hoped they wouldn't. He needed something with more sizzle.

The city editor, Randy Fontly, pointed his pen at Stan. "The story with the best hook is the murder of this Reese girl."

Stan listened to Fontly. Though he was a hard drinker, with the red nose, blood-streaked eyes and sagging skin to prove it, Fontly churned out stories at a pace younger reporters seldom matched.

"We get dead prostitute stories all the time," objected Brighten, defending her turf. "Nothing fresh in that."

"No, there's not if that was all there was to it," countered Fontly, scratching his veined nose. "But we don't see many prostitute murders with a young preacher being sought as the chief suspect."

Confident of his footing, Fontly paused to let the information marinate. In this room everyone received the same chance to sell his story in the process of decision. But, if the editors reached no consensus, Wraps called the winning hand.

Fontly knew Brighten wouldn't back down; he saw others at the table who supported her.

Brighten jumped back in, "My story broadens the interest beyond Atlanta, into the state, even the nation. Senator Steele always stirs up the emotion."

"Yeah, you either love him or hate him," said Wraps.

Fontly glanced at Wraps and tried to read him. Wraps stared back. Fontly had actually worked at the *Independent* 16 months longer than Stan. The two shared a lot of history—went back to the days when a reporter was always a man, when he carried a number-two pencil behind his ear and a brown pad in his front pocket, and when he would chase an ambulance or a squad car to the Sahara Desert if it took him to a story.

The way Fontly measured it, he and Stan wouldn't chase too many more stories together. If his bad liver didn't kill him soon, retirement would; he defended his ground.

"Stan, this preacher and prostitute story hits people in two places—in the gut and in the groin. It's got state appeal and national appeal if we play it right. We don't gain a thing running another Steele-the-conservative-senator piece. He's always against something—nothing new there. But this preacher story has the two things everybody wants to read about—sex and death. We can slam dunk everybody in town with this if you let me run with it." He flipped his pen onto the table with a dramatic flourish and stopped.

With an unusual forcefulness, Wraps rocked suddenly forward in his swivel chair, pounded his fist on the table and said, "Go with the prostitute's murder. I want two-inch bold headlines. I want the sex angle played big and I want the religious angle emphasized. Dig out everything you can about the preacher."

Fontly raised his hand and grunted, "The police haven't released his name, Stan."

Like a pit bull watching his dinner bowl being pulled from under his nose, Wraps turned on Fontly. "Look, Randy, you sold me on this garbage, so get me the name. I won't stand for any excuses. I want the name printed with the story tomorrow morning. Get on the phones, touch your sources, pay them if you have to. I want this paper to print that preacher's name before anyone else. If we don't, you can all stick your number twos where the sun don't shine cause you won't be using them anymore for this rag of a paper. Now, get on it." He twirled his chair around and left his staff staring at his back.

The editors headed for their workstations, like hot dog wrappers scattering in the wind at a ball game. Wraps sat still for a second and waited for them to disperse. When he thought they were all gone, he turned slowly around. To his surprise, one person stood silently by the door, watching him intently. She spoke to him like she was in a cemetery and afraid of disturbing the dead.

"Mr. Wraps?"

"That's me."

She took a step closer to him, "Could I talk with you for a moment?"

Wraps started rocking his chair, hoping to remember something about the girl. He vaguely recalled she wrote human interest stories for the Sunday edition but that was as far as his memory went.

"Sure," he said, "I've got a second. What's up?"

"Uh, Mr. Wraps, I'm Debbi Meyer. I've only been at the paper a few months and I don't know exactly how to say this . . ."

"Just spit it out," he groused. "I do have a second, but I don't have time for mumblers."

"Well," she stammered, "I uh, get the feeling we want to portray the minister as the killer of this prostitute."

"That's right. We do. Any objection?"

Interested now, Wraps checked Meyer over. About 5' 4" he guessed, hair the color of beach sand and eyes as green as an empty Coke bottle. She watched Wraps' eyes widen as he inspected her.

"Not really an objection, so much as a concern," she answered. "Shouldn't we wait to get more information before we assume he's guilty?"

"Sure we should, Miss Meyer. But, we can't always do what we should, can we? We'll use the word *alleged* when we refer to the minister. We'll call him a 'suspect' for murder, not a murderer."

"I know that," objected Debbi. "But, we're determining his guilt before he has a chance to prove himself innocent. Think of what this will look like to the people in his church."

"Aren't you forgetting one thing?" cautioned Wraps.

"What's that?"

"Chances are he is guilty. It won't matter what it looks like if he is, and the facts as we know them don't leave much choice but to believe he killed her."

"I know what it looks like," she said, not giving ground. "But we should give him the assumption of innocence until the courts prove otherwise. Isn't that our constitutional right?"

"Look, Miss. . . ."

"Meyer," Debbie reminded him. "Debbie Meyer. I've just been here eleven months."

"Yes, Miss Meyer, I know that's our constitutional right, but— " Wraps stopped, suddenly shamed by a rookie reporter who seemed to care about journalistic integrity as much as he once did. He reversed his cynical response. "Look, Miss Meyer, why don't you tell me what you think we should do."

"Great!" she said. "I do have one idea."

"Somehow I knew you would. Spit it out," he said. A wry grin creased his face.

"We go on with the story as planned on the front page. Puff it up, big and sordid. Draw attention to the preacher and prostitute angle as much as possible. Let Randy run with it. Then, on the editorial page, let someone write an opinion that cuts against the grain of what we're carrying on the front. Let the editorial say we have jumped to a danger-ous conclusion. Let the opinion piece argue with the methods of our own newspaper. The editorial says we should assume this minister innocent and refrain judgment until the system concludes its work. Use it to play up the human side of this preacher and the grief this will cause if he's proven innocent later. Let it remind people that what they say about others often marks that person for life, whether true or not. Use the editorial page to remind folks of the Constitution's protection of all of us—that we're innocent until proven guilty."

Her green eyes glowed. Meyer sped on. "We can carry the scandal and criticize the method at the same time! It'll carry punch for the paper and it might just do some good too."

She stopped, out of breath like a filly given the freedom to run through a pasture unsaddled.

"That's a good speech, Miss Meyer. Just answer me one thing. Who do you propose to write this editorial? You've figured out everything else."

Meyer held back her urgent desire to hug him.

"Mr. Wraps, could I do it?"

He smiled. "Somehow I figured you'd ask that. Why not? You're the one who suggested it. Just bring me a piece of copy you've written in the last month. I should at least read something you've done before I turn you loose on the editorial page." He waved his hand, dismissing her.

Meyer pivoted smartly to leave, then peeked back at Wraps as she reached the door. "I'll get something right to you, Mr. Wraps. And I'll check everything with you before it prints. You won't be sorry for this, I promise you."

Watching her gymnast-like figure rush away, Wraps slumped back into his chair. He shook his head, "I must be gettin' old not to have noticed her."

* * * * *

Three offices down, Randy Fontly was sweating and the webbed streaks of red in his nose grew larger with every minute. He needed a name to make his story fly in the morning edition and he was willing to do anything to get it.

He dialed a private number. The voice which answered on the other end belonged to a public figure—to police chief Frank Conners. Conners and Fontly went back even further than Fontly and Wraps. They had shared much together—like the Marine Corps and a bloody hill in Korea named 871. They still shared things—things like excessive drinking, a dislike of modern ways, and a predilection toward younger women. When they could find them. When they could buy them.

"Evening, Frank, Fontly here. Can you talk a minute?"

"For your ears only, Randy?"

"Yeah, it's my private line."

"What'cha need?"

"I expect you can guess."

"Let's pretend I can't."

"I need the preacher's name, Frank."

"You know that's confidential. We haven't even picked him up yet."

"I know, Frank, but Stan's pushing me hard on this one. The paper's not doing too well and I suspect old man Steadman is stepping on Stan to perk things up. He left me no choice but to call you. You know I wouldn't do it unless I absolutely had to."

"Sure, Randy. Sure. I don't guess it'll hurt anybody. The way I see it, some other reporter is probably paying off one of my office cops for the name tonight anyway. Just like they did for the information about the Bible. You might as well get it for free. Just protect your sources, my friend."

"You can count on that, Frank."

"I know I can, little buddy, got a pencil?"

"Always."

"O.K., here goes. The name on the Bible is Burke Anderson. We've tracked down his address. It's 2-0-7 S-w-a-n-s Lane in Cascade, about forty miles out. Anderson pastors the Methodist church there."

Fontly scribbled furiously as he listened. Finished, he laughed, "Drinks are on me Friday night."

"You bet they are, buddy. For the next year of Friday nights."

"I think I've found your price."

"Maybe so," said Conners.

* * * * *

Dropping the phone back into its cradle, Conners squeezed his 250 pounds into his seat. He wiped a ridge of sticky sweat off his chin and looked down at a blue, leather-bound book filled with 51 names and numbers of the rich and famous of Atlanta lying on his desk. The book contained one especially scary name—Senator Raymond Steele.

Conners wasn't giving that information to anyone. Not until he could figure out what to do with it. With only three years left before retirement, he didn't want to make an enemy of Raymond Steele. No one wanted to get on the hit list of the man who controlled Georgia and wouldn't hesitate to destroy anyone who threatened him. No, Frank would keep this name to himself. No need for the public to know this.

CHAPTER

7

The unmarked squad car gobbled up the highway stripes as it moved through the slipstream of the silvery night, headed toward 207 Swans Lane in Cascade. It had taken Jackie Broadus and Avery Mays over two hours to track down a county judge and convince him to sign a probable cause search warrant so they could search Anderson's house. Early Sunday evenings made the old maxim "the wheels of justice grind slowly" far too true for their liking. Both of them were hot. Broadus expressed her anger.

"Look, Mays, if Anderson did kill Reese that pea-brained judge has given him enough lead time to be in Jamaica getting a tan by now."

Mays shifted but said nothing. Broadus continued her griping. "And Atkinson told him he'd better get his ticket. I wish I knew which one of Atlanta's finest leaked the information about the Bible."

Mays grunted. "Spilt milk."

Broadus stayed steamed. "Doesn't it toast you when some desk cop sells information and hurts our chance to make a good arrest?"

"Sure it does, but no amount of griping will change it. That's the system, so why get your insides in an uproar over it? Let's just get where we're going and take it from there." Mays lapsed back into silence. Broadus recognized the signs—nothing she could say would rile him.

Her partner, 58-year-old Avery Mays, slumped beside her. His posture matched his clothing—saggy and tired looking. He wore old ties—as wide as tablecloths and equally as colorful. Jackie knew Mays dressed this way deliberately so he could stay out of the headlines. As a man who treated words like most people treat diamonds—like rare and valuable jewels which shouldn't be wasted or thrown away care-lessly—Mays detested headlines.

Once, in the first year of their partnership, she asked him point blank; "Why don't you speak out more?"

With what amounted to a short lesson from a disgusted teacher, he replied, "I'm only going to say this once. 'A policeman with an open mouth is usually a policeman with a closed mind and an empty head.'"

So, people left Mays alone. Reporters tended to overlook brown paper sacks and that's the way Mays looked to those who knew no better.

Tonight, Broadus and Mays worked as they often did—with few words—letting the facts and semi-facts and supposed facts rattle about in their minds like pennies in a tin can, without any definite beginning or ending.

Broadus always spoke first, tossing out a theory or a hunch for Mays to digest. He listened quietly, sometimes feigning sleep while she talked. Then, when she finished, he answered in one of two ways—either punching a hole in her balloon by finding a flaw in her reasoning or blowing air into it when he approved. Occasionally, when she came up empty he sent up a balloon himself—watching and listening to test her reaction.

Both of them were single—Mays because his wife of 22 years had walked in one Tuesday in February four years ago and told him bluntly, "I have cancer. The doctor says I'll live until August if I don't take chemotherapy. I might make Christmas if I do."

Deciding together to refuse the debilitating treatment, Theresa died in July and left her devastated husband in silence.

Jackie's explanation for her singleness took a more complicated route. Mike, her dentist ex-husband, never understood why a former beauty queen and honors graduate from Georgia Southern wanted a career in law enforcement. Their seven-year marriage started souring the fourth night after their honeymoon when Jackie left at 11 P.M. to begin her night shift on the streets.

The next evening he suggested: "Why don't you give up your career? I make more than enough money for us to live well. My mom never worked a day in her life and I never knew a happier woman."

"I'm not your mother and you know that," said Jackie. "You knew what I wanted to do when you married me. We'll have to learn to work together with our careers."

To his credit, Mike tried. For seven years. But, he wanted children immediately and Jackie wasn't ready yet. It wasn't that she didn't want children. She did, and she often suffered pangs of guilt that she didn't have any yet. Her own mom had happily poured her whole life into raising seven little ones and Jackie admired her stamina and humor as she did it, but Jackie wanted a career too. She wanted it all and believed that one day she would get her fill of her dangerous work and walk away from it and birth her babies. But Mike wanted those children immediately. She kept saying "not yet." Finally, he grew tired of waiting and of coming home at the end of the day to an empty house.

So, he left and Jackie let him go. She was married to her job for now anyway. She loved the odd combination of thrill and drudgery which police work brought. Whether waiting in the back of a camera-filled van to take a picture of a suspect or charging gun first through a blocked door to make an arrest, Jackie thrived on the beat.

She turned and glanced at Mays. "I don't expect much trouble picking this guy up, do you? His sheet makes him look pretty harmless."

"An exemplary citizen," said Mays.

"A minister serving his first church, an expert in four languages, almost a 4.0 student at the university, lead baritone in the chancel choir. Not even a speeding ticket. Not exactly your profile for a murderer," said Broadus.

"You know better, Jackie," warned Mays. "It's the one we don't suspect who always gives us the most trouble."

"I know," she said, "but this guy just doesn't seem the type."

"I never knew there was a type. If you find one let me know. Then I can get out of police work."

Jackie tried to picture Anderson and his friends and family. What would they think? She and Mays would interview most of them.

"Do you think he'll have an alibi?" she asked.

"No reason to worry about it until we get there."

The car's flashing blue light warned other motorists to let them pass. Jackie didn't use the siren—people pulled over without it.

"What do you think?"

"'Bout what?" He stayed nonchalant.

"Is it as cut and dried as it seems?"

"You know it's almost always cut and dried. It's the rare case that doesn't solve itself."

"Yeah," she agreed. "But those are the ones that get the publicity."

"And they're the ones where we earn our money."

Mays fell silent again. Broadus pressed him. "So, you think this Burke Anderson did it?"

Mays raised himself and ticked off what they already knew. "We have a Bible with his name on it. That places him in her apartment. So, he had opportunity."

"Maybe he gave her the Bible somewhere else, at a church service or something," countered Jackie. "Maybe she was religious."

"That's possible. But that blue book filled with men's names we found in her nightstand didn't look like a directory of the men's choir to me."

"She could've found the Bible."

"That's true. But why would she pick it up and take it home with her? If it proves that she was a prostitute, and I would bet my first grandchild she was, it doesn't make much sense for her to keep it. And why was it found so close to her—under her hip?"

"Maybe she was reading it before she died." Jackie knew her arguments sounded weak. Detectives didn't see too many prostitutes getting religion.

Mays aimed and fired at this point. "'LADY OF THE EVENING GETS SAVED.' Makes a nice headline. And the tease line would be, 'Reading a Bible She Found Just Before Death.'"

"Sounds like the *National Informant*," admitted Jackie.

"And that's like wrestling," said Mays. "We all watch it, but we know it's not true."

The Cascade exit blinked at her from the highway sign and she slowed down and turned right. Five minutes later she steered down Swans Lane. The smell of wood smoke filled her nose—crisp air had fallen over northeast Georgia and someone had started their fireplace. She shivered—chilled by the cool air, by the stimulant of a murder to solve, by her loneliness.

The numbers over the doors of the neat houses stared out at them as they passed, looking them over, as curious about the slow moving car as it was about them. *"There."* She and Mays spotted it simultaneously—the Methodist Manse.

"It's dark," Broadus said.

"Yeah, empty dark."

CHAPTER

8

Broadus and Mays spent over an hour sorting through the parsonage in Cascade. While waiting for the forensic crew from the police lab, they walked from room to room, not touching anything, just browsing, getting a feel for the place. A row of purple violets bloomed in a window box over the kitchen sink. Four old pairs of running shoes lined the floor in the bedroom closet. A computer sat like a square-eyed sentinel in a book-lined study.

"I didn't think we would find him here, did you, Mays?"

"I wasn't sure either way."

"He must've seen Atkinson on television."

"Whoa, woman," cautioned Mays. "Aren't you jumping to conclusions?"

"You mean, since he's not here, I'm assuming he's guilty and has run."

"Bingo."

Jackie developed Mays' point for him. "He could be visiting with friends or watching a movie. It's possible he hasn't even heard about the murder."

Mays nodded and Jackie continued. "We can stake out the place and see if he comes back."

Mays punched her bubble. "I don't think he'll be coming back. In fact, I think our suspect has heard about the murder and has checked out of the church hotel."

Confused, Jackie sputtered, "But you just cautioned me about reaching quick conclusions! Aren't you being a little hasty yourself? How do you know he won't stroll in the front door any minute?"

Mays turned and walked into the bathroom connected to the master bedroom. Entering the pale blue square, he pointed toward the lavoratory. "Notice anything unusual?"

She inspected the sink. "No toiletries."

"Exactly. Either young Anderson's spending the night with friends or he's heard about our homicide and has decided we're after him. I'm choosing the second option."

Jackie bowed to her partner. Mays often noticed details she missed. Her gift, to tie the strands of facts together and to reach conclusions based on those facts, complemented his exactly. She was the creative thinker; he was the bean counter.

Stepping out of the narrow bathroom and back into the living area, they heard the front door open. A pack of white-coated technicians bustled into the room, donning their rubber gloves and beginning the inch by inch sweep of the house. Broadus and Mays watched them for a few minutes, following them as the workers spread out ant-like through the house, their antennae darting side to side, testing the air, probing for the scent of a killer. They watched them dust the brass knob of the front door, pull hair follicles from the drain in the bathroom sink, and stuff shoes and books from his closet and bedroom into plastic bags.

"What's the motive?" asked Jackie, her interest in the mundane process waning.

Mays barely looked at her. "You tell me."

"He buys her services. She decides to earn more than her $500.00 per hour. She tries to blackmail him."

"So to shut her up, he beats the literal life out of her."

"Maybe killing her was an accident. Until we get the autopsy report, we won't know exactly how she died."

"Yeah. He *accidentally* hit her five or six times according to the preliminary accounts."

"However it happened, she's still dead," Jackie said.

"Absolutely," said Mays, turning from her and following the lab crew into the kitchen. She trailed after him, not wanting to wait alone in the bedroom of a preacher who might also be a killer.

* * * * *

Two hundred miles away a black and white patrol car ground to a halt. Two uniformed officers crawled out and walked to the front porch of a Cape Cod sandbox home owned by Mr. and Mrs. Thomas Anderson, proud parents of two boys: Richard, an accounting executive in

Atlanta, and Burke, a "preacher boy" serving in the Lord's vineyard in Cascade.

Tom and Thelma Anderson had often joked that Richard would earn enough money to pay their way into a nursing home when they reached their old age and Burke would earn enough merit to pave their way into heaven when their days in the nursing home wore out. Either way, they noted to their friends, their boys had all the fronts covered.

They had tried to raise both boys the same way, but looking back, they saw they'd failed to do so. Religious people to the core, and conservative Methodist religious at that, Tom and Thelma tried to measure out equal doses of love and law. As the firstborn, though, Richard received a bit more of the law than Burke did.

Tom and Thelma figured that's what made Richard reject his faith when he went off to college. The way Tom said it later, "A boy forced to eat cabbage all his life will probably leave the cabbage on his plate when he grows too old for his parents to make him eat it."

Richard gave up both cabbage and religion as soon as he matriculated to the University of Georgia. So far, he hadn't decided he needed either one as a staple in his diet.

Burke, on the other hand, genuinely liked cabbage and religion. Maybe because his mother and father learned a lesson or two about how to serve both of them before he came along. No longer force-feeding the vegetable or the religion, they simply left a little of both on his plate for investigation. He found the taste of both to his liking. In fact, his taste for cabbage and faith actually outgrew the love his mom and dad had for them.

His love of faith culminated in the summer of his sixteenth year at a youth retreat. On a Friday night that August he found himself sitting by a bonfire under Georgia pines staring into the canopy of a star-studded sky. Along with 26 other teenagers, he had just heard a young preacher of considerable charisma issue a divine challenge. The challenge called him to "take up his cross and follow Jesus."

As the stars blinked at him, Burke decided to accept that challenge. Like the man who had issued it to him, he wanted to serve God with his whole life.

At lunch that Sunday, he told his parents. At first, Tom and Thelma were a little skeptical. They thought the emotional nature of the retreat might have overly swayed their son. But, they decided to wait and see, assuring Burke of their support even as they waited.

His resolve never wavered and, true to their word, Tom and

Thelma stood with him. No one could say Tom and Thelma weren't supportive of their boys.

Officer 675 knocked on the solid oak door. Inside, Tom dropped his newspaper, kicked down the footrest of his recliner, eased into his bedroom slippers and tugged himself to the door. Opening it slightly, the sight of the two officers woke him up.

"Are you Mr. Tom Anderson?" questioned badge number 675.

"That's me," he said. "Can I help you officers?"

"Could we come in for a moment, Mr. Anderson?"

Tom hesitated, then said, "You got some I.D.?" 675 flashed his wallet picture and badge number at him.

Stepping aside to let 675 and 971 enter, Tom arched his eyebrows and shrugged his shoulders toward his wife. She rested in a tan recliner that matched Tom's and tugged repeatedly on the hem of her blue cotton dress, trying to make sure her legs were covered.

"Has there been an accident or something?" she asked nervously, pushing her dress down over her knees.

"No, ma'am," 675 replied. "But I need to know when you last saw your son Burke."

Tom stayed cautious. "Why do you need to know that, officer? We don't mind answering your questions, but not until we know why you're asking them."

"Maybe we'd better sit down," commanded officer 971.

Tom sat down beside Thelma and pointed to the sofa for the police. He listened to 971 as he intoned, "We're looking for your son in connection with a homicide this past Friday night in Atlanta. A young woman was killed and your son's Bible was found in the apartment with the slain woman."

If the officer had taken an ice pick and plunged it into their eyes, he couldn't have hurt Tom and Thelma more. Thelma reacted outwardly—wrapping her arms across her billowy chest and uttering a high-pitched squawk; she rocked backward, sticking against the recliner like sticky gum thrown against a wall.

Tom stayed outwardly calm. "Officer, I'm sure some mistake has been made. Burke's a minister. He couldn't kill anyone."

971 and 675 knew the scenario by heart. 675 picked up the good guy's lines this time. Reversing the parts of good guy and bad guy made the work more interesting.

"We're not saying he did kill anyone," soothed 675. "We just need to ask him a few questions. If he has a strong alibi, he walks—scott free."

"But," and here 971 interjected the tough line, "we did find his Bible in the girl's apartment and he's not home in Cascade. Our folks in Atlanta checked an hour or so ago."

Thelma stared at the pale green walls of the den, her eyes unfocused. Then she spoke. "I gave him the Bible for his graduation. He kept it in his pocket all the time."

Tom reached over and picked her limp hand off her bosom.

"Don't worry, sweetheart. I'm sure there's been a big mistake. We'll find Burke and he'll explain everything."

Twisting toward 675 and 971, Tom sighed and said, "Ask us whatever you want to know. We'll help any way we can."

675 started to run through his list. "When did you last see your son?"

"About six weeks ago. We drove over to Cascade to be with him for the weekend. It was over 100 degrees that day."

"When did you talk to him last?"

"Two weeks ago, on a Sunday night. We have an agreement. He calls the first and third weeks and we call the second and fourth."

"Did you call him this weekend?"

"Yes, we did, but he wasn't home."

"When did you try to call?"

"Friday night—that was his birthday. We planned to call earlier, but Thelma's sister fell Friday afternoon and broke her ankle. We went to the hospital with her; we're the only ones to look out for her. We didn't get back until about 10."

Tom stopped and waited for the next question.

971 jumped in, "So you tried to call him Friday night but couldn't get him?"

"That's right."

Like a child caught writing on a wall with a red crayon, Tom caught the implication of his answer. "I don't think I should say anything else," he said. "Not without a lawyer present. We want to help you, but we don't want to hurt our boy. He couldn't do this and anyone who knows him will tell you he couldn't."

Mrs. Anderson interrupted. "Who was the girl?"

"I can't tell you her name, ma'am," offered 675. "We're still trying to contact her parents and, until we do, we won't identify her."

"Was she Burke's girlfriend?"

"We just don't know." Looking toward 971 and shaking his head slightly, 675 took pity on Mrs. Anderson. No reason to tell her Reese was a hooker. He watched her tug at her dress hem again, modestly keeping it over her calves, and he held back his tawdry information. She'd learn it soon enough. He stood to leave and 971 followed him.

"Case detectives will contact you soon. In the meantime, please contact us if your son tries to call you. We just want to question him. If he's innocent like you say he is, then the best thing he can do is give himself up and let justice take its course."

With hats in hand the two badges swung open the screen door and stepped outside into the apple-crisp air. Relieved the dirty work was over, they pulled open the car doors and crawled inside. The wheels crunched gravel as they drove away and 675 pulled off his glasses to clean them.

"Those folks would've dropped dead from a heart attack if we'd told them the girl was a prostitute."

971 agreed. "I'm not surprised. I never met a mama who didn't believe her boy was innocent."

675 nodded, "I hope I never do."

* * * * *

Burke's mama stood at the window watching the police car slip into the dark. Without turning around she said, "He couldn't do that, you know, not our boy."

Tom joined her at the curtains and the two stood side by side like brick pillars guarding a driveway. They always stood together in tough times—when Thelma suffered her miscarriage between Richard and Burke, when their two-year-old daughter died, when the doctors sliced Tom open for triple-by-pass surgery during Burke's first year of college . . .

They stood together again. Putting his warm hand on her shoulder, Tom bent down and kissed her on the cheek.

"No, not our boy, Thelma, not our boy."

CHAPTER
9

Burke snapped to consciousness, flopped off the couch and looked around frantically, then remembered where he was. A dream had startled him awake, a dream he'd suffered often on Saturday nights, but never with as much power as tonight.

The dream was always the same. He stood behind the pulpit, holding his Bible high in the air—a torch lighting the way for his people. The people watched him intently, glued to his movements with their eyes, listening to his captivating words. He basked in their attention, strutting, preening, gesturing grandly.

Halfway through his preaching, he noticed an oval-faced little girl sitting on the third row laughing at him through piano key teeth. She pointed her right index finger at him from behind her hymnal. He looked down to see the object of her mirth. He was goose-bump naked before a whole church full of people. Shame and guilt and fear lanced through him like hot lava burning through a mountain, leaving charred remains in its wake.

Pulling the Bible from the air, he spread its holy pages and tried to stretch them over his shame. He ran from the pulpit with the Bible as his only cover and slammed the door, shutting off the derisive laughter.

He always woke up here.

Tonight, a new person had invaded the dream. Sitting on the third row, beside the laughing girl, was a woman. She stared at him, but she wasn't laughing. She listened. He couldn't quite make out her face, but he knew who she was.

Thankful the dream had ended, Burke moved carefully to get up, twisting his neck and raising his arms over his head to stretch out the numbness. He ran his tongue over his teeth and scraped away the night's sour residue. He looked out the window and saw a sliver of sun stretching its face over a group of skinny clouds near the horizon. He glanced at his watch—6:18. Not his usual hour to get up, but this was no usual day.

He called out to Cody as he padded toward the bathroom. No answer. He peeked into the only bedroom in the apartment and saw it was empty. Alarms sounded in his head. Where was Cody? Had he gone to the police? No, he didn't think so. Even if he did, he couldn't do anything about it.

Resigned, Burke stepped into the bathroom and pulled his tooth-brush and comb from his suitcase. He washed his face with warm water and soap, brushed through his thick black hair and scrubbed his teeth.

Finishing up, he heard the twist of the front door handle. He stopped breathing as he peeped around the bathroom door and watched Cody step inside. Biscuit trailed behind him wagging his tail at the sight of Burke. Burke walked out of the bathroom and squatted down as Biscuit padded over to accept the hug Burke gave him. "Sit," he said. Biscuit obeyed immediately.

"Thanks for getting him out of the car," he said to Cody.

"He was pretty happy about it, I can tell you that." Cody walked to the table and dropped a sack full of groceries and a newspaper down on it. Burke followed him. "Glad you're back," he said. "Thought for a minute you went to turn me in."

"No, not that," said Cody. "I don't keep much food here and I went to the Quick Stop at the interstate to pick up a few things. I bought some milk and cereal for breakfast, plus some dogfood for your friend. Hope that'll be O.K."

"Yeah, that'll be fine. I don't eat much breakfast."

Pulling out two folding chairs from the closet and a couple of bowls and spoons from the cabinet by the stove, the two men sat down to eat. Biscuit slipped under Burke's legs and lay down as Cody tossed a newspaper across the table to Burke.

Burke took it, rolled the rubber band off, and stared down at the glaring headline: **PREACHER SOUGHT IN PROSTITUTE'S MUR-DER.**

He dropped his spoon by his cereal bowl and gobbled up the story with his eyes.

"Atlanta police are searching for Burke Anderson, the 28-year-old minister of the First Methodist Church in Cascade, Georgia, in connection with the beating death of Carol Reese. Believed to be an upper bracket call girl for

Atlanta's elite, Reese was killed sometime Friday night. Authorities found her. . . ."

Although the story continued onto the next page, Burke stopped reading. Biting his lip, he slumped forward. His worst fear was realized. Reporters—the by-line said Randy Fontly in this case—had squeezed his name from the police department and printed it.

Everyone knew—his church members, his mom and dad in Birmingham, his brother in Atlanta and his professors at Wesley Methodist. He glanced at Cody. "Have you read this?"

"Yep. First thing. Didn't surprise me a bit. These guys get paid to dig up what they can. Your name's part of the story."

Burke picked up the paper carefully, like he was pulling soiled paper from the bottom of a bird cage, and read the rest of the article before speaking again. "I wonder how many people read the *Independent*."

"I don't know, couple hundred thousand I guess, maybe even a million or more," said Cody, shrugging his shoulders.

Burke smiled ruefully. "I've always wanted to be famous, but this isn't exactly how I planned it to happen."

"Get it anyway you can," said Cody, joining in the sport.

"Well, at least they didn't print a picture," said Burke. "Other than the people who already know me, I'm still only a name. That'll help while I figure out what to do."

Cody perked up. "I've been thinking about that, Preacher. What'cha got in mind? You can't prove your innocence sitting around here."

Burke grunted and shifted in his seat, flexing his tired muscles. "You're right, Cody. I can't. I've got to find Walt. That's my only hope. If I can find him I think I'll get some answers. At least he can back my story."

"How do you plan to do that?"

"That's all I've been thinking about," said Burke, chewing the side of his left cheek from the inside. "I think it's a safe bet Walt and Carol were intimate—if you get my drift."

Cody nodded.

Burke continued, "If they were, then I suspect Reese kept a record of it. I've read that professional women like Reese usually protect themselves by keeping the names and numbers of their clients hidden somewhere."

Cody scrunched his forehead, following Burke's thought. "If she did then she might have Walt's number and address listed!"

"Absolutely. Only one problem left to solve. How do we find her list if she actually had one?"

Hopefully, Cody offered, "Only one place to look— her condominium. But, wouldn't the police have already found it?"

"You tell me; you're the one with the experience with the police."

"I don't know. The police tear a place apart pretty well when they're looking for something. And, if we thought of a list, you know they thought of it too."

"So you think they probably found the file if one actually exists?" asked Burke.

"No, I'm not saying that necessarily. Sometimes they do and sometimes they don't. Back before I went to prison I stayed for a few weeks with a coke dealer. One day the cops busted down the door, shoved us against the wall, and ripped out all the sheet rock looking for drugs. The place wasn't fit for *Home and Garden* when they finished, I can tell you that. But they didn't find a thing. My bud had hidden the stuff inside the monitor of his computer and nobody looked there. If Reese hid her list well, it might be right where she left it."

"So we need to know if she had a list."

"And whether or not the police found it if she did."

The conversation stopped and they sat still, trapped at a dead end. Burke licked his lips and wiped his hands on his pants legs. He heard his blood thumping a slow rhythm, then he heard it stop, then start again. He stared down at the table and the front page of the paper stared back. His eyes stopped on the teaser— Presumed Guilty. Editorial on page 16."

Licking his thumb, he turned the pages. The inset picture of Debbie Meyer pointed him to the opinion. Pausing for only an instant to appraise her looks, Burke searched hurriedly through her editorial.

By now most of you have already read the front page story in this paper chronicling the death of Carol Reese and the search for Burke Anderson in connection with this homicide. If not, please turn to page one and check out the thorough job our reporters have done in ferreting out the supposed facts of this grisly case.

In reading this account you will notice we have carefully used the words "alleged" and "suspect" when referring to Burke Anderson, the minister sought in this case. Our lawyers tell us to list him this way or face a possible slander suit if he is later proven innocent.

As you read this story, you'll see we make a pretty good case against Reverend Anderson. The data points to him as a guilty man. The

Reverend Anderson might have fallen. In the words of his church, he might have sinned. In the words of our laws, he might have murdered.

Looking at the facts as we now have them, I figure he's guilty like most of you probably do. I, however, don't want to stack the case any worse against him. Randy Fontly, our chief reporter on this story, has managed that pretty well. Instead, I want to remind everyone that no matter what it looks like, no matter how this newspaper paints it for you, Reverend Anderson deserves more than an assumption of guilt. The same laws that make us use the word "suspect" also demand that we assume "innocent until proven guilty."

I know that's hard to do. It's easier to make snap decisions and reach certain judgments. But, don't be taken in by sharp commentators and anxious police, desperately searching for a killer. Hold out for our law. The Reverend Burke Anderson is innocent right now. Until proven guilty, he is innocent. Don't forget that. It might be you the next time.

Finished with the column, Burke leaned over Meyer's picture and admired her attractive features. She had high cheekbones, full lips and a cute button nose, even on the less-than-flattering newsprint.

Staring at her face, Burke saw it—a road cutting through the dead end, a road with potholes in it to be sure, with steep shoulders and slick spots, a road with treacherous corners—but it was the only road he saw and he knew he had to try it.

He handed the paper to Cody.

"Read this."

He chewed on a thumbnail while Cody read, barely daring to breathe. Finished, Cody dropped the paper and stared back.

"What'cha think?" Burke asked.

"Sounds like she's either real idealistic or real cynical. Could be either. But if she believes what she writes, then you have at least one person who hasn't automatically assumed you're guilty."

Cody stopped and watched the corners of Burke's mouth turn up slightly and he knew Burke saw more in the article than he did. "What?" he asked impatiently. "I can see something churning around. What's the plan?"

Burke swallowed a saucer full of air. "Do you think this woman would help me?"

"The woman who wrote this editorial?" Cody's voice rejected the possibility. "Are you kiddin'? Harboring a suspect is dangerous business. She could end up in jail."

"I don't want her to harbor me," countered Burke. "Just to give me information about Walt."

Cody pressed his argument. "Tell me why she should. I'm on your side, but I don't see any reason for her to stick her neck out for you."

"You are," Burke said.

"Yeah, but that's 'cause you did so much for me I couldn't turn you down. If you hadn't helped me I wouldn't have taken you in. That's the way life is. This is a 'you scratch my back and I'll scratch your back' world, and you know it as well as I do."

Though Burke hated to admit it, he agreed with Cody. Most people helped others only if something was in it for them. Cody was right—Meyer might help him, but only if he convinced her she could gain something from it.

A new wrinkle crawled onto his brow. What did he have to offer her? Only one thing came to mind. His story. He floated the idea to Cody. "What if I promised her the whole story, Cody? My visit with Carol; the temptation; the flight back to Cascade; the fear of being a suspect; the agony of loved ones disappointed. What if I offered her an exclusive on the whole mess? Would that bait her enough to get her to help me?"

Cody nodded his head, slowly warming to the idea. "It's possible. After all, she is a reporter. If you can convince her you can give her a story no one else has, she might buy it no matter if you're guilty. Yeah, I say it's worth a try."

Burke looked at his watch. Almost 8 A.M! With a fresh optimism, he jumped from his chair. "Where's the phone book?"

"Don't have one."

"Don't have one? Why not?" Burke's voice rose in frustration.

"You don't need a book if you don't own a phone," said Cody. "Better watch those assumptions, Preacher, they can get you in a lot of trouble. But, don't worry. We'll call from the pay phone at the Quick Stop off the interstate."

CHAPTER

10

Burke borrowed some clothes from Cody and changed, turning in his button-down blue oxford shirt for a green and navy flannel job, and his khaki trousers for blue jeans with holes in both knees. Cody walked into the room where he was dressing and handed him a red, paint-splattered baseball cap. Burke took it, shoved it onto his head, and moved to the bathroom mirror to survey his unshaven face and change of clothing. He pulled the hat down further over his eyes. "If it's true that clothes make the person, then what do these make me?" he asked.

"They make you a face in the crowd," said Cody, satisfied with Burke's outfit. "Ready to go ask a girl for a date?"

"As ready as I'm gonna be."

A minute later they parked Burke's car out of sight behind a clump of kudzu-covered trees and climbed into Cody's battered pickup. Biscuit hopped into the back and pointed his nose toward Highway 53. As they rattled the five miles to the Quick Stop, Burke kept swiveling his neck in a circle like a terrorized crane, watching for traffic. Not even the bumpy ride, though, could shake Debbi Meyer out of his mind.

"Wonder what kind of person Meyer is," he said.

"Hard to tell from a picture," said Cody. "But she sounds fair. Otherwise she wouldn't have given you the benefit of the doubt in her editorial. "

"She could fake it for the story," cautioned Burke.

"Sure she could, but either way what she said helps you more than it hurts you. The motive doesn't matter much, does it?"

"Guess not," said Burke.

For a moment both of them were quiet, listening to the truck tires spinning on the blacktop. Cody broke the silence. "Preacher, I hope you don't mind me asking, but something's been tuggin' at me. Why didn't you tell the folks in Cascade you were epileptic?"

Burke shrugged. "I never deliberately kept it a secret. But I hadn't had an attack for over ten years and didn't see any need to tell. I didn't want folks to think I was looking for some kind of special treatment and I didn't want them feeling awkward around me, waiting on me to fall over and froth at the mouth."

"I guess it can scare people, can't it?"

"Sure it can. Most of us stay away from what scares us. So people shun epileptics."

"What causes it?"

"It's a neurological disease. The electric current in the brain gets fouled up somehow and the message the brain sends to the body gets confused. So the body shuts down."

"With convulsions."

"Yeah, some with convulsions. Others with blackouts. The body keeps functioning, but the mind loses track of what the body is doing."

"That's how you react?"

"Yeah, I don't convulse. I black out."

Cody smiled. "I guess being alone with a gorgeous girl eager to please was too much excitement for a pure-hearted preacher."

Burke smiled too. "You're wrong about this pure-hearted preacher. I reacted to Carol Reese like any man would."

"But you didn't follow through," said Cody.

"No, I didn't."

"Why not?"

"I don't know. Lots of reasons I guess. I didn't want to feel guilty later. I didn't want to disappoint other people. Didn't want to displease God. All of that."

"'Cause you didn't think it was right?"

"Yeah, 'cause I didn't think it was right."

"Preacher, you've got scruples," Cody said, not a little pleased.

"Yeah, I do," said Burke. "But, like everybody else, I sometimes wish I didn't."

Silence fell again. Burke stared out the window at the roadside as it slid by, a roadside cluttered with broken beer bottles and brown paper sacks. He spotted an old tire, split on one side, and a dead racoon—crushed and red and covered with flies busy about their business.

Turning left past the highway overpass, Cody pulled into the paved driveway of the Quick Stop and parked by a gray fence, headed outward.

Burke's heart pounded. He stepped from the running board of the truck, shoved his hat down further on his head and scurried to the pay phone, hanging like a birdhouse to the side of the brick building. Biscuit jumped out of the back and followed him.

Burke reached for the phone book. Finding the number, he called Meyer at home: 565-1286. An answering machine lilted the message. "Hello, in case you couldn't guess, this is an answering machine. If you want to talk to a real person, you'll need to leave a name and number. I'll call back as soon as possible. You know what to do. BZZZZZZZZZZZZZZZ."

Burke automatically liked her style. Bouncy, unique and a little humor. Not a bad sign. He shook his head, indicating his lack of success to Cody, who sat in the truck with the motor running. He looked up her work number and punched it into the dial: 514-7783.

"*Atlanta Independent*. May I help you?" queried the receptionist.

Burke nervously croaked out a response. "Could I speak with Debbi Meyer, please."

"Just a moment, sir, let me see if she's here this morning."

Burke reached down and patted Biscuit on the head, then bit off a piece of thumbnail as he waited. A spritely voice cracked across the line, "This is Debbi Meyer."

Time to lay the cards on the table. "Miss Meyer, are you the lady who wrote the editorial in this morning's *Independent?*"

"Yes, I am. How can I help you?" She sounded warm, even inviting.

"Miss Meyer," said Burke, "I hope we can help each other. Are you in a private place?"

On the other end, Debbi paused. Tired from an all-night search for information on Burke Anderson, Debbi wanted nothing more than to rush home, scald herself with a shower and collapse across some crisp sheets. But, she heard something in this caller's voice and it gave her reason to pay attention.

"Yes, I'm alone. How can I help you?"

Burke gushed the words out, a geyser spewing into the air. "Miss Meyer, this is Burke Anderson and I'm asking you not to hang up but to listen to me 'cause I think we can help each other and I want to talk with you privately."

Burke never knew, of course, that a shotgun exploded in Debbi's mind. But he did hear an intake of breath from Debbi's end. He imagined a stunned look on her face. For a brief second, Meyer said nothing. Burke bit his thumbnail into the quick and winced as a thin point of blood rose on it. Time slowed and stopped. Death and life ran together.

"I'm listening," Meyer said at last.

"Miss Meyer, I didn't kill Carol Reese. If you believe what you wrote this morning, then I ask you to believe me and withhold judgment until the courts do their work."

"I'm willing to reserve judgment," she said.

"I wanted to prove my innocence but didn't think I could. So, I ran. Now I need help to prove I didn't kill that girl."

"Why are you calling me?"

"Because your editorial made me think you might help me."

"Why would I do that, Reverend Anderson? It's a crime to aid a suspected murderer."

Burke measured his words carefully, gaining more confidence the longer Meyer stayed on the line. "Miss Meyer, what if I promised you the full story of what happened in Carol Reese's condominium last Friday in exchange for your assistance? You get a story every other reporter in the state would kill for and you prove your editorial was the right response to all of this."

"What information do you want, and what makes you think I can get it for you?"

"Miss Meyer, the media seem to have sources of information most people don't. Mr. Fontly, for example, gathered some information which wasn't yet public for this morning's edition. I know you have methods to get what you need. You have access to computer files; you know people in high places on the police force; you pay for some information, too, I suspect."

Debbie interrupted, "If I already have all this, then why should I help you? Won't I eventually find out everything I want without you?"

"Maybe. But, you might not do it before someone else does. I'm offering you an exclusive, the first crack at my story. Even if it turns out I'm guilty, you still have the inside report. Isn't that what all reporters want? I'm willing to give that to you in return for some information I can't get myself."

Burke's chest heaved—in and out, like a jackhammer, fast and hard, edging him toward hyperventilation as he waited for her answer. Finally, she swung the door open. "What do you need from me if I agree to help you?"

Burke heard both curiosity and ambition charge into her voice. Now, he was the one who paused. Don't give her too much, he thought. A smart girl like her might piece the puzzle together and not even need you. Don't tell her about Walt. Don't tell her about the possibility of a client list in Carol's condo. Not yet, anyway. Not until you know if you can trust her. But, don't run her off, either. You need to hook her, but not give her so much slack she'll run off and break the line.

He said, "Miss Meyer, I don't want to say any more right now. What I would like to do is meet with you privately. I'll give you everything you ask for then. Can we set up a meeting?"

She paused again, then said, "Reverend Anderson, I think I can do that. But, I won't come alone. In the last three weeks the police have found two different girls in Atlanta with their skulls cracked and I don't plan to add my name to the list. I want to bring my city editor with me."

Burke grimaced, not liking her counter offer. But, he saw no alternative. "O.K.," he said, "but we meet in the place and at the time I designate."

"Agreed."

"O.K. You got a pen?"

"I'm a reporter, remember?"

"Yeah, right. Tonight at 10:00 drive out I-85 to the Highway 29 exit. Get off there and turn left across the overpass. Just past the bridge you'll see a chimney standing in the field to the left. Park the car, get out and go to the chimney. I won't be there, but a friend will meet you and bring you to me."

"Reverend Anderson, what if something goes wrong? Is there a number where I can reach you?"

"If something goes wrong I'll get back in touch with you. See you tonight."

He hung up, scratched his grinning dog on the head and turned toward Cody, giving him the thumbs up. Back in the pickup a second later, Burke rested his head against the window, suddenly exhausted. "What if this doesn't work, Cody?" he asked. "It seems so far-fetched."

"Can't worry about the what-if's, Preacher. At least you've got a chance. She's going to listen to you."

"She says she will, but what's to keep her from bringing the police?"

"Can't answer that either. We'll just have to wait and see."

Burke raised his head and wiped his palms off on his pants. "I wonder what's happening in Cascade."

Cody grunted and drove on, back to his apartment, back to safety, back to wait.

CHAPTER

11

The phones in Cascade started ringing early Monday morning. The word fanned out exponentially—one telling two and two telling four and four telling eight until everyone was having a hard time finding someone they could tell who hadn't already heard the story. Nothing disappointed the 2,847 people in Cascade quite so much as having the story of the decade to tell but being unable to find anyone who hadn't already heard it. The six A.M. crowd at Edith's Coffee and Grill caught wind of the news first. Men met here every morning except Sunday to swap the latest scores, stories and jokes. If the fellas at Edith's hadn't heard it yet, then it probably hadn't happened. And, if nothing worth telling hadn't happened, the boys at Edith's weren't above making up a story or two. Other than coffee, conversation flowed best at Edith's.

Today, no one needed to make up anything. The minute Mayor Tom Stacy walked his stooped five feet, eight inches under the jingling bells hanging over Edith's door and perched himself at the bar, she poked the *Independent* under his nose.

"Mayor Stacy," she said, "you'll want to read this."

"What'cha got, Edith?" Stacy asked, "Don't bother me with reading; give it to me in words.

"You haven't seen the paper yet?"

"No, Edith, I haven't. You know I can't see nothin' till I've swallowed at least two cups of coffee. Now, get me my coffee before you stick some fool paper in my face."

Refusing to let his gruffness put her off, Edith said, "I don't think it'll take two cups to get you awake today, Mayor Stacy. Not after you read this headline."

Stacy flipped open the folded paper and scanned the headline. He snickered, then dropped the paper. "What's the big deal, Edith? Another preacher caught with his pants down. Not the first time. Won't be the last, neither. Now get me my coffee or I'll take my business to the 7-ll."

"Don't you think this is a little more than a preacher caught in the sack with a prostitute?" asked Edith.

"Yeah, I guess so. A *murdered* prostitute does make this sadder than those others. But, they'll catch the guy soon enough."

Edith slapped her order pad on the orange tiled bar and fumed, "Good gracious, Mayor, either you really aren't awake or you can't read. Pay attention to more than the headline!"

Stacy groaned as he slipped off his glasses and pulled the paper closer.

Edith chomped her gum as she watched the Mayor read. Edith liked the Mayor. Had to. As the richest man in town and the head of every organization of any importance, Mayor Stacy ran Cascade like the gentle dictator he was. But the dictator took on a defeated look as he read. Each word of the story cut another wrinkle into his furrowed brow. He looked suddenly frail to Edith, an old man hunched over the bar— frayed at the edges, like a pair of socks with holes in the toes and heels. Though not given to much religion herself, Edith hated to see the Mayor shrink like this, hated to see such scandal in her town. This wouldn't help anybody.

She kept staring at him as the bell jangled again and six men shuffled to the two tables in the corner and called out for service. She ignored them, still chewing her gum and waiting.

"You O.K., Mayor?" she asked.

He didn't take his eyes from the editorial. He sat still, like a dead animal on the yellow line of a highway. Then, slowly placing the paper on the bar like he was afraid he might break it, Stacy slid his knobby hands up the sides of his face and buried his eyes in his palms.

He whispered, "We just never know, do we?"

"There's no way we can, Mayor."

"I checked him out, you know. Before we accepted his appointment from the conference. I called his professors at the seminary. They told me he was bright. Said he was capable, dependable. Shows how wrong even the smartest can be."

Stacy rubbed his eyes, hooked his glasses back over his ears and stood up to go. "I've got work to do. People to call. Damage to control.

Plans to make. Edith, just skip my coffee and toast. I don't feel much like eating today. I'll see you tomorrow."

As the Mayor trudged out the door he passed under the mounted head of the 12-point buck Edith's husband had shot last fall. The deer looked innocent hanging there, innocent and dead. The Mayor had lost his innocence long ago. But, he'd never looked dead before—not until today.

Edith watched him duck into his car before she moved over to the corner where six of her regulars were cussing her slow service. She tossed the paper into the middle of the table.

"You guys seen this yet?"

* * * * *

By 8 A.M. everybody in Cascade who wasn't out of town or stretched out in the Hillview Cemetery had either read the paper or heard the news on the phone. Everybody had their theories about how it happened.

One group of women, several of them members of First Methodist, congregated in the parking lot of Cascade's grocery store to talk about the scandal.

"I bet you he's been seeing this girl for a long time," offered Margie Whitson. Margie stood in the center of the bunch like a skinny flagpole surrounded by saluting troops, plucking at her pink curlers. She was used to everyone listening to her or at least pretending to do so. Her money and good works demanded attention. She had the ability to talk without ever stopping to draw breath. This gift gave her a leg up on monopolizing a conversation and she liked to take advantage of it.

She pointed her needle-thin fingers at the bouquet of ladies gazing at her and took a running start on a sentence. "Living just two houses down from the Reverend like I do, I want to tell you I have more than a passing knowledge of what goes on over there. You can believe me when I tell you Burke Anderson didn't comport himself like a preacher cause I saw him cut his grass without his shirt on and he never dated church girls either. And worst of all, I noticed every time I looked out the window at the parsonage—did you know I hand-made those drapes in the living room?—that he didn't get home before midnight on most nights and it always bothered me he didn't keep some decent hours. He probably went to her place every Friday night and—"

"She probably wanted money from him," said Shelley Ricks.

Margie winced at the interruption. Ricks was two times her size, but when it came to influence size didn't matter. She wasn't even sure Shelley belonged to their group. Usually she didn't, but scandal makes strange allies. Shelly's faith was normally too passionate, too rigid for this circle of the gentler sex and she didn't consort with them and they responded in kind. But today everything seemed different. Margie remembered Shelly's abusive, alcoholic husband and blamed him for Shelly's anger so when she walked by in the parking lot, Margie beckoned her to join them. Even now she elected to pass over the interruption and make Ricks a part of the group, "Money, eh? You think so?"

"Yeah, I do," said Ricks.

"You've been just as dissatisfied with the Reverend Anderson as we have, haven't you?"

Ricks pursed her bird-like lips, hugged her grocery bag to her ample bosom and measured her words. "Well, I don't know that dissatisfied's quite the word. I just wanted him to get a little deeper into the Word. Spend more time with doctrine. He tended to give us too much milk and not enough solid food."

Margie nodded for Ricks to continue. Ricks looked at the curious faces of the circle of ladies.

"I expect he paid her a pretty penny," she said.

"No doubt about that," said Margie, sticking her finger in her ear, scratching it out. "Wonder how he killed her?"

"Maybe he didn't." The shaky voice sounded from the edge of the group and the cluster in the middle turned as one head to see its owner. Mrs. Barbara Metcalf was the shy and polite wife of Bill Metcalf, owner of the gas station that sat in the forks of the two main roads running through Cascade.

Margie let the drama build. "You think not, Barbara?"

Barbara looked around the circle. "I'm not sure, either way," she said, her clear voice firming up. "Maybe he did, maybe he didn't. But I do know this—all this talk don't change it either way. Until we know, we ought to keep idle chatter to a minimum, don't you think?"

A couple of women nodded in her direction.

Ricks tried to head off the interruption. "Paper said the girl died from blows to the head. Reverend Anderson must have gotten awfully mad to hit her that hard."

No one else said anything for several moments. During the silence bad pictures danced in Margie's mind. Of the preacher with a prostitute, committing adultery, sinning. Getting angry, incensed. With his fist hardened, striking out, killing her. She shook her head and pursed her lips. Suddenly Barbara pivoted and walked to her car. Margie understood. It wasn't Barbara's way to force her opinions on anyone.

"I saw him mad once," Margie said, reaching for their attention again.

"When?" asked Ricks.

"The day the board of elders refused to let Alcoholic's Anonymous use our church fellowship hall for their meetings."

"What happened?"

"I was standing outside the door of the library where the elders were meeting. When they finished, he stormed out and went into his office. Didn't even speak to me as he walked by. Just slammed the door to his study. I could see him through the glass panes in his door. He took his fist and pounded it down against a book on his desk. Then he sat down and put his face in his hands."

Shelley listened with awe. "You'll need to tell this to the police, you know."

"I already figured on doing that," said Margie, patting her curlers with her hands. "But, I got to tell you, I won't get much pleasure in it." She licked her lips.

* * * * *

Broadus and Mays were driving as fast as they could to get to Margie and to everyone else in Cascade. Both were thinking about the briefing they'd just finished in the conference room back at Peachtree Precinct.

They knew Frank Conners was edgy. He had chewed on his unlit pipe as he exhorted them, his drum-heavy chest heaving and his thick neck straining out of the collar of his white starched shirt. The shirt was already clinging to his back and shoulders from sweat.

He had stretched his six feet, three inch body over the front of his desk and given it to them straight. "I'm getting it from all sides on this one, gang. The black community is angry because the newspapers gave so little play to the first murder. They say nobody paid any attention until a white girl bought it. Plus, the governor called a few minutes ago. Said we need to tie this one up before the holidays start. Seems like homicides cause a downturn in tourist traffic and our good governor wants to keep those customers headed to Atlanta for Thanksgiving and Christmas. We need an arrest fast."

Conners settled back into his chair and yielded the floor to Broadus. "Give us the what-we-know-so-far."

Jackie filled them in point by point. "We've placed Burke Anderson at the scene through fingerprints. Plus, we found a shirt in his closet with type A blood on it and that matches the blood found on Reese's living room floor. Hair found in his drain at home matches a hair found in her sofa. Plus, we have the Bible with his name on it."

"What about the flag?" The question came from the back, from one of the uniformed patrolmen.

"Not sure about that yet," said Jackie.

"Maybe a God and country killer," offered Conners.

"Maybe," nodded Broadus, "But all that's still speculation. Anderson's the guy we're looking for until something better turns up."

"Don't think we'll find anything better." Conners stood up. "Let's get to it."

Mays and Broadus had followed his advice and were getting to it now. They pulled into the gravel-covered parking lot of Cascade's gas station, unfolded themselves from their seats, and crunched over toward two men seated on wooden chairs, just outside the open door of the station.

Bill Metcalf, the raisin-faced, 72-year-old owner of the two-tank station, hoisted himself from his seat and shuffled halfway out to their car. Then, seeing they weren't parked within reach of a gas hose, he stopped and waited.

"Morning," offered Mays, extending his hand.

"Howdy," countered Metcalf, taking the hand limply, then dropping it. "What can I do for you?"

"You Mr. Metcalf?" asked Mays, pointing at the *Metcalf's Gas Station* sign hanging over the garage door.

"None other."

"Mr. Metcalf, I'm Lieutenant Mays and this is Lieutenant Broadus." Mays flashed Metcalf his badge. "We're investigating the death of a young woman in Atlanta Friday evening and a Reverend Anderson is a suspect. I suppose you've heard something about this already?"

"Yeah, I heard something about it." Metcalf spat a brown stream out of his mouth and it splattered on his brogans and barely missed Avery's black Hush Puppies.

"Do you know Reverend Anderson?" Jackie tried her luck.

"Yep. He's my preacher." He glanced down at Jackie's shoes, poised to spit again, but Jackie stood her ground.

"When was the last time you saw him?"

"Sunday morning, at church."

"Did you notice anything unusual about him Sunday?"

Metcalf hitched his hands under his overall straps and shook his head. "No, not really. Seemed fine to me. Preached a good sermon. Talked about Judas betraying Jesus. Said everyone had the potential for betrayal in them, that even someone close to Jesus could turn bad. Like Judas, like any one of us. Like you even. I shook his hand as I left."

"He didn't stop by here Sunday night?"

"I wouldn't know. I don't open on Sunday. Sunday's a day to go to church." The brown juice filled the corners of his mouth, ready to fire.

Jackie backed off a step.

"Mr. Metcalf, I'm glad you like your preacher. That's the way it should be. But, we did find a Bible with his name on it in the dead girl's apartment. I'm sure you can see why we need to talk to him. If he didn't do it, we need to find out who did. So, if you think of anything unusual you've seen since Friday just call me at this number. Collect."

* * * * *

Broadus handed Metcalf her card and wheeled to leave.

He watched her walk away. At least she wasn't pushy. Maybe he'd been too harsh, too suspicious. He flashed back to Friday night. He figured it wasn't important. But, who knew? Maybe it would help Reverend Anderson.

"Ma'am," he called.

Broadus pirouetted to him.

"I saw a black Mercedes drive through here about 8:30 Friday night headed downtown. Don't see too many of those here in Cascade. 'Bout thirty minutes later, it came back by, pointed toward the interstate. One man was in it headed in and two was in it headed out. I didn't look too close at the passengers. Paid more attention to the car than the fellas in it."

Jackie flicked her eyes at Avery. He was scribbling it all down.

"Can you tell us anything else, Mr. Metcalf? Any numbers or letters off the tag?"

"No, ma'am. Like I said, I just watched the car. It was a pretty thing. You think any of this is important?"

"We don't know yet, Mr. Metcalf. But, it could be, could be real important. Thanks for your cooperation and we'll get back in touch."

Avery lifted his pen and said, "Mr. Metcalf, one more thing. How about keeping this information about the Mercedes to yourself? No use giving these reporters any more ammunition than necessary, right?"

Metcalf lifted his hand and made a circle with his thumb and index finger, "A, O.K."

Broadus and Mays walked away.

Metcalf settled back into his creaky seat and watched the two detectives get in the patrol car and drive around the bend. He spat at a roach crawling over his boot and spoke to the man sitting beside him. "My preacher ain't guilty," he said. "I don't care what anyone says."

CHAPTER

12

B ill Metcalf's Gas and Grocery ran out of Dr. Pepper early on Monday morning as representatives of eight newspapers, five television stations, two church journals, 11 radio markets, and the *National Informant*, passed through his station yard.

They asked the same questions. Did he know Burke Anderson? When did he see him last? What kind of man is he? Where do you think he is? Do you think he killed her? How do you get to his house?

Metcalf didn't lose his patience until nearly 2:30, when Les Atkinson screeched into the dust-choked yard and blocked the gas tanks with his red, camera-filled van. Without asking permission, Atkinson's crew set up their equipment, strode like conquering soldiers into Metcalf's station office, stuck a mike to his mouth and flashed a spotlight into his eyes.

"Are you Mr. Metcalf?" Atkinson asked.

"Last time I checked I was."

"How well did you know the Reverend Anderson?"

Same old questions. Tired of answering them, but trying to act civil with these intruders, Metcalf grunted short responses to each one. He saw his answers weren't pleasing Atkinson. Good.

* * * * *

Atkinson refused to give up. He smiled—a paper doll, cut-out smile. Watching him, Bill had no doubt about the way he would portray the scene.

A gas station run by a red-neck old man, complete with two dusty pumps, a flop-eared dog lying on the steps, and two jars of pickled pig's feet sitting by the cash register offered enticing image potential. Bill could just hear Atkinson's introduction to the story.

"*The town of Cascade, a town time seems to have forgotten, woke up this morning (the picture of the dog asleep in front of the steps would strike just the right pose) and found a modern headline staring it in the face. The epidemic of scandal which has punched into the stomach of the Bible Belt in the last five years has struck again. This time, however, it's no big city preacher caught with his religion down. This time, it looks like what the Bible calls fornication and what the law calls murder has originated in Cascade, Georgia.*"

Atkinson said, "Mr. Metcalf, I know you've had a long day, but I need to ask you one more question. Why do you think your minister was in this woman's apartment and why did he kill her?"

Metcalf stretched his neck out of his shirt like a turtle stretching in the sun and stood up tall. He felt the sweat trickle down his back and wet his shirt. Between the hot lights of the cameras, the unending questions, and now this prima donna of a newsman, he'd had enough. God would forgive him.

"Look, Mister, nobody has proved anything yet about Reverend Anderson. Who do you think you are, pokin' your mikes into everybody's face and expecting us to bow down to you like you're some kind of king or something? You don't care about this town or Reverend Anderson or the girl either for that matter. You're just looking for something to excite folks. So, you assume things—about us and about Reverend Anderson. We don't need that. What we need to do is to wait. Don't try the Reverend on the T.V. screen. Let folks decide for themselves when we know the facts."

He flapped his arms like he was fighting off a swarm of bees and shooed Atkinson away. "Now, get out of my face before I lose my temper."

Atkinson grinned at his camerman and pulled his index finger across his throat. Cut. Quickly, they rolled up their cables, stowed their gear in the van and sprayed gravel as they pulled out of the yard.

Atkinson said, "Did you get the look on that guy's face?"

"Yeah. He could have chewed nails."

"That'll make a pretty good opening if we don't come up with anything better. We can show a backdrop of the station's gas pumps, slide into the picture of the sleeping dog, switch to sound and start, 'Not everyone in the backwoods village of Cascade believes their Reverend Burke Anderson is guilty of murder.'"

Atkinson continued his description as they headed toward the courthouse. "We can quote a couple of other Anderson supporters then go back to the facts which indicate his guilt. If we play it right, we can make Metcalf look like a naive old fool, taken in by a hypocrite preacher."

They parked the van in front of the square block building marked "Cascade Courthouse" and hopped out. Before leaving Atlanta, Atkinson had looked up Cascade in the Town and Municipalities Guide published by the state. He had found the information he wanted. Under Cascade he read, "POPULATION: 2,847; COMMUNITY STATUS: RURAL; CHIEF OCCUPATIONS: FARMING AND MERCHANT; MAYOR: THOMAS STACY; POINTS OF INTEREST: NONE REGISTERED.

Atkinson detested Cascade—it reminded him too much of home, a town with a different name but a similar M.O. in North Carolina. He hated the tree-lined streets, now gold and orange and red in the October afternoon, the hardware store filled with nails and chintz cloth and peppermint sticks and witch hazel, the men wearing brogans with mud stuck on them, the children riding their bikes on empty streets, the clothes flapping on the lines and smelling fresh in the air. He hated it because he'd grown up a poor white boy in a town like Cascade and he'd sworn as a child if he ever escaped, he'd never go back. His good looks and street-wise charm had provided him his escape, but the anger at the Cascades of the world had stayed.

He stepped through the glass doors of the courthouse and searched over the building with a trained eye. A lazy ceiling fan stirred the dry air of the unusually hot day. He smelled onions and hot dogs in an office nearby. He read *Government: By the People and for the People* over the archway of the inner hallway. From the left, he heard the sound of Southern Gospel swelling out. He poked his head inside this office.

A bored-looking secretary with a ridge of sweat rimming her upper lip looked up at him. Atkinson glanced at her name plate. He smiled politely and asked, "Ms. Legget, could you tell me where I can find the Mayor?"

Ms. Legget said, "I'll get him for you. Can I tell him who's asking for him?"

"Sure, I'm Les Atkinson, from WATL in Atlanta."

Her cow-like eyes widened. "I thought I recognized you, especially when you spoke to me. I'd remember that voice anywhere. Hold on right here, honey, I'll get the Mayor for you."

Ms. Legget patted her beehive hair as she swished out of the room. Within minutes, she swished back in, her legs rubbing against each other as she walked. Stacy followed her. Atkinson sized him up. Age lines snaked from the Mayor's eyes like the grain in oak wood. His hair was pasty white.

Atkinson decided to take the compassionate approach. They shook hands and sat down in two straight-backed wooden chairs sitting in Ms. Legget's office. Ms. Legget stood over them for a second, but Stacy flicked his hand at her and she moved off down the hallway.

Stacy said, "I'm not surprised you're here, Mr. Atkinson. Lots of reporters are crawling through Cascade today. This sure is a mess, isn't it?"

"Can't argue with that," said Atkinson. "And I hate to butt in on all the confusion and hurt you must be feeling, but I've got a job to do. I want to look at this from the standpoint of the community, you know, get the human angle. See how something like this upsets a town."

Atkinson furrowed his brow and feigned concern. "Since you're the mayor you can probably give me some insight into what the folks of Cascade think."

Stacy stared at the floor and said nothing.

Atkinson tried again. "Aren't you a member of Anderson's church?"

"Yeah," said Stacy.

"I guess it's pretty disheartening."

"You could say that."

Atkinson plowed ahead. "Mr. Stacy, how do you think the folks of Cascade are reacting to this?"

Stacy raised his head, took off his glasses, and wiped off the lenses with a brown handkerchief. "Everyone reacts differently. Folks tend to believe what they want to believe. Reverend Anderson hasn't been here but about two years so we don't know him too well. That's part of the problem. Plus, he was single. Lots of people didn't like that too much, myself included. Thought we needed a more settled man. Looks like maybe we were right."

"So you tend to think he did it?"

"I don't want to pass judgment too fast. Even if he didn't kill her, he sure was in her apartment. Either way, it looks bad."

Atkinson noticed the sweat stains spreading further and further under Stacy's arms, wet half-moons supporting his armpits and soaking his white shirt.

"Mr. Stacy, I have just one more question. As a member of Reverend Anderson's congregation, what do you think the church will do about this?"

Stacy pushed his glasses back onto his nose and shoved the handkerchief into a shirt pocket. "That's a question I've tried to avoid all day. I've thought about doing nothing. Waiting might clear up a lot of mysteries. But, who knows how long it might take to find Burke? Then, when he does turn up, how long will it take to prove his guilt or innocence? So, we really can't wait. Over 50 people already called me today, wanting me to do something."

"Even if it's wrong and he's innocent?"

"Yeah, even if it's wrong and he's innocent."

"What about advice from someone else? Don't the Methodists have guidelines for this kind of thing?"

"I don't expect anyone would have guidelines for this kind of thing, but I suspect they could give us some advice. But I hate to throw it into their laps. That's too easy. We should handle our own problems. Besides, I'm the guy who got us into this mess."

Surprised, Atkinson asked, "How's that Mayor?"

"Well, it's like this. If I had thrown my weight against Burke at the beginning, like I thought I should, the church would never have accepted his appointment. But I let it pass. So, I'll have to find a way to control the damage."

Stacy's voice dropped lower. "I'm sure the conference will review whatever we do, but I suspect they'll accept our recommendation. We'll have a meeting of the congregation and decide what action to take."

"Any idea when this meeting will take place?"

Stacy didn't hesitate. "Tonight. Cascade's pretty small. We can get in touch with everyone fairly easily. No use putting this off any longer than necessary."

Slapping his knees as he stood slowly to his feet, Stacy stuck out his right hand. Atkinson took it. It seemed cooler now than ten minutes ago. Firmer. More controlled.

"Do you know what time?"

"At 7:30. You plan to come?"

"Do you mind?"

"Not at all."

"O.K. I'll see you in a few hours." Atkinson couldn't wait. A church full of sad-eyed Methodists. It didn't get any better than that.

CHAPTER

13

T he hours passed slowly for Burke while he waited for Cody to come home from work. Noon stretched into three and three reluctantly moved off stage for five. Late afternoon shadows gradually took over. Finally, like a dying man desperately holding to life, the longest Monday of Burke's life gave up and breathed its last. Cody drove up in the early darkness.

"I've fixed a couple of hamburgers for you," Burke said to him as he entered the apartment.

"Good. I'm hungry."

"A hard day at work?"

"Not too bad. What about you?"

"I've had easier."

"I expect so."

"What's going on in town?"

"Man, you wouldn't believe it. The place is crawling with police and reporters. You're a hot topic."

"I'm sure of that. Did you see any church members?"

"Yeah, a few."

"How are they taking all this?"

"I'm not sure. The Mayor has called a church meeting for 7:30 tonight. He wants the church to talk things over. Rumor has it Shelley Ricks and Margie Whitson want them to vote you out as pastor."

Burke shook his head. "That doesn't surprise me a bit. Those two have chewed on me ever since I got here." Burke glanced at his watch and made a quick decision. "Cody, I'm going to that meeting."

"Yeah, Preacher, and I'm Elvis Presley in hiding," Cody laughed. "How do you figure to do that?"

"You said the meeting was for 7:30?"

"Yeah, so?"

"So, I get there before anyone else and climb up to the attic. There's an air conditioning vent right behind the pulpit. I can crack it a little and get a clear view of the whole sanctuary."

"Isn't that a little risky?"

"Maybe, a little. But I'm not going to sit around here and wait to hear what happens. If they're going to vote me out, then I want to see their faces when they do it."

"It's your show, Preacher." said Cody, "Mind if I tag along?"

"You sure you want to?"

"Why not? I've come this far. Let's go to church."

Cody wolfed down his hamburgers and they piled into his truck. With Burke lying prone in the seat, the two drove the twenty minutes it took to reach the middle of Cascade. Cody pulled his pickup into a parking lot adjacent to the church yard. Burke raised up, glanced around, pushed his hat over his eyes and hustled to the back door of the dark church. A twist of a key and they were inside. They crept up the back stairs into the attic. Burke located the air vent and loosened it with a screwdriver, then sat down with Cody and waited.

They barely beat the crowd. Within fifteen minutes cars pulled up outside. Burke walked to a dusty window at the front of the attic and watched the crowd gathering below. As he unlocked the window and pulled it open, the squeak sounded like a siren going off, but no one noticed.

He heard Bill Metcalf talking to Stacy. "How can we make any type of decision? We don't know anything for sure yet."

"No, we don't. But just knowing Burke was in that woman's condominium is enough for us to act."

"What do you mean by 'act'? We can't do anything against Burke unless he's here to explain. That Bible could have gotten there in a thousand different ways."

Bill's voice got louder and Burke whispered to Cody, "Bill's got a short fuse."

The Mayor tried to soothe him. "Bill, don't get riled at me. You can defend Burke in a few minutes. I don't think anybody's made up their mind yet. I know I haven't. Let's just see what happens." The two men walked side by side into the church.

Burke spotted a white van pulling up. He recognized Les Atkinson.

Everyone else did too and they straightened up as the T.V. anchor strutted past them with his production crew, headed into the church to set up their lights and test their mikes.

Shelley Ricks and Margie Whitson came next. Whitson had Ricks by the elbow, ushering her up the sidewalk. People quit talking as the two passed.

"Looks like a Bible under Ricks' arm," said Burke.

"Yeah, and a knife in her purse," said Cody. "Too bad she uses a Bible as a club and not a comfort."

Whitson puffed out her chest and squared her shoulders as she marched in. Time to do battle. The congregation trailed behind her and Ricks and the church filled up. Burke and Cody shifted to a sitting position and peered like peeping Toms through the loosened vent into the sanctuary.

They stared at the back of Stacy's head as he stepped to the pulpit and called the meeting to order. Everyone quietened. Even the babies shut down their whimpering.

"Friends, I want to convene us into conference," said the Mayor. "We all know why we're here tonight. A terrible situation brings us here. Our preacher is being accused of a vicious crime. We don't know all the facts. But this is one of those situations when we can't wait to know all the facts. Many of you called me today telling me we should get together and talk. So, that's why we're here. Before anyone says anything, though, we need to pray."

Two hundred heads bowed automatically, chin to chest, and eyes slammed shut. A few coughed nervously. Others took deep breaths, fanning their runaway heartbeats.

"Bill Metcalf, will you lead us in our prayer?"

Bill raised himself up and began. "Lord Jesus, we come to you tonight upset and confused. We want to do the right thing for your kingdom and for Reverend Anderson. But, it's hard to know what the right thing is. We know you don't condone sin. And it looks like our preacher got himself into something sinful. But, we also know you're a God who forgives us when we sin. And we all do sin, Lord. Thank you for forgiving us when we do. Help us know how to be forgiving toward Reverend Anderson and help us know how to stand against sin so a watching world will know we don't condone wrongdoing. In Jesus' name, we pray. Amen."

A chorus of gentle Amens echoed Bill's.

From his perch above, Burke breathed a sigh of thankfulness for Bill and watched Stacy step back to the pulpit and hug it. Sweat glistened on Stacy's forehead. "Friends, we're going to open the floor for discussion. We want to know what you think and what you want to do."

Like a bull fired out of a chute, Ricks leaped to her feet. "Mayor Stacy, could I speak?"

"Yes, of course, Mrs. Ricks."

All eyes rested on Shelly.

"Mayor, I've been praying about this since I heard the news this morning. I even called several of my friends in Athens where I lived before and asked them to pray with me. This afternoon I broke through to the Lord and He gave me this verse to share with the church."

Shelly glanced around, then said, "These verses come from I Thessalonians, Chapter 4, verses 3-7 NIV. The Lord gave it to me because it applies to our situation tonight. Listen to this. 'It is God's will ... that you should avoid sexual immorality; that each of you should learn to control his own body in a way that is holy and honorable, not in passionate lust like the heathen, who do not know God. ... The Lord will punish men for all such sins, as we have already told you and warned you. For God did not call us to be impure, but to live a holy life.'"

Shelly held up her Bible and said, "Mayor Stacy, we pretty much know that Reverend Anderson went to that poor woman's apartment last Friday. It's obvious what he was doing there. If we don't speak out tonight against this kind of activity, the whole state of Georgia will think we don't care that our preacher was involved with a prostitute." She gathered her anger and spewed out the words, "I move that we dismiss Mr. Anderson as our pastor. That way everyone will see we stand firm against sin."

The congregation buzzed immediately at Ricks' words. Burke could see that her sudden motion had swept them away. They saw a bandwagon moving and didn't want to miss it.

Stacy rapped his knuckles against the pulpit and called the church back to order. "A motion is on the floor. Is there a second?"

Shelly glared over her shoulder. Several "seconds" rang out.

"We've got a second. Discussion of the motion is now in order."

"Mayor, I want to say a word, please."

Stacy pointed to Bill Metcalf. "Go ahead, Bill."

Bill tugged himself up and hooked his thumbs under the straps of his faded overalls. "Mayor and friends, I don't know what happened last Friday night with Reverend Anderson and that girl. I admit it don't look too good for him to have been there, if we can even be sure he was. And I wholeheartedly agree with Mrs. Ricks' Bible verse there. But, it seems we might be rushing this if we vote to dismiss Reverend Anderson tonight. We ought to give him a chance to defend himself. I'm against the motion."

Margie snorted at Shelly as Bill eased himself down. "That wasn't much of a defense," she hissed. She raised herself and lifted her hand and sucked in her breath and pushed out her sentence. "Mayor, Bill has said it pretty well, it seems to me, and even he accepts that it doesn't 'look too good for Reverend Anderson to have been there' and those are his very words and the Bible tells us in I Thessalonians 5:22 to refrain from even the appearance of evil and Mr. Anderson failed in that admonition of God's Word even if in no other, so I support Mrs. Ricks' motion for that reason." She paused for only a half a beat, then skipped ahead. "We've got to let everyone know we expect our leaders to live up to the Bible message because if we don't hold ourselves up to the godly standard, how can we expect the world to take our gospel seriously?"

A number of amens rang out. Burke knew the wind was blowing in Shelly's favor.

He waited for someone else to defend him. He suspected more than half the votes were undecided, still leaning, leaves with no source of strength and no connection to a branch of their own, ready to blow wherever the breeze pushed them. No one spoke.

Then, to Burke's surprise, Bill pushed himself up again.

"Mayor Stacy, could I try one more time?"

"No," rang out several voices, "He's already had his turn, let someone else talk."

Stacy nodded. "Anybody can speak up to two times in a congregational meeting."

"Folks," started Bill, "I know Reverend Anderson pretty well. I've fished with him early in the morning. Last fall I helped him skin the first deer he ever shot. He stood by me when my little grandson was born six weeks early in that emergency C-section over a year ago. He's a good preacher and a good man. I don't know what happened last weekend. Neither does anyone here. We need to wait. Don't the Bible tell us we ought to 'do unto others like we would have them do unto us'? If we were in Reverend Anderson's situation, we would want this church to wait to get the full picture for us. I say it again, I'm against this motion."

Bill's face flushed as he slouched back into his seat. Barbara reached over and grabbed his hand.

Burke, sitting above in the attic, saw Bill's courage and a lump the size of an egg welled up in his throat. He searched his eyes over the congregation and tried to understand them. He knew they weren't mean people, not most of them. Even Shelley Ricks and Margie Whitson, his two main detractors, had parts of the truth on their side. No, his people weren't so much mean as scared and confused. And, in their fear and confusion, Burke expected they would follow the most self-assured voices. And those belonged to Ricks and Whitson. He stared back down at Mayor Stacy.

Behind the pulpit, Stacy peered into the crowd.

Metcalf turned and craned his neck to look over the crowd too. Above both of them, Burke watched also. Scanning the congregation, he saw lots of people who didn't come much on Sunday. Some he had never seen in his time as pastor. He didn't see many sure votes on his side.

He heard Bill's voice call out, "Tom, what do you think?"

Folks gasped. No one called the Mayor "Tom".

"Bill, you know the moderator isn't supposed to express an opinion."

"I know that, Tom, but these aren't normal circumstances. I would rather be a little out of line with procedure than go away from here making the wrong decision. Everyone here respects your feelings. You're the head of our elders. We deserve to hear your thoughts before we decide anything as serious as this. Step away from that pulpit and tell us what you think we ought to do."

"Is that what you want me to do?" he asked.

Voices rang out, "Yes, Mayor. Yes, Mr. Stacy. Yes, Tom." Somebody else, emboldened by the drama, called him by his first name. "We need to know what you think."

Stacy moved around the pulpit and walked down from the rostrum to the aisle, level with the rest of the people.

"Folks, I've thought and, yes, I've prayed about this matter all day. Still can't get any peace about it. I'm not like some folks who claim God gives them an unmistakable sign. This is a real struggle for me. I want to give Reverend Anderson every chance to prove his innocence. That's what our law compels us to do."

Stacy paused and everyone leaned in closer as his voice dropped, like he was talking to himself. Burke leaned closer to the open vent.

Stacy continued. "We respect the law of the courts and certainly uphold it. But, and here it gets tougher for me, we have another law to uphold. That's the law of the Lord. God's law calls us to live so a sinful generation can see what's right. Mrs. Whitson is right. We're to refrain from even the 'appearance of evil.' Reverend Anderson broke that law. We need to stand for it."

Bill's shoulders slumped. Tears formed in the corners of Barbara's eyes and dripped, like water from a spigot, onto her blouse. She shrank inward, practically disappearing, no longer a person, a skeleton now, pale and limp.

"So, you ask me what I think. I think when the police find Burke Anderson we do everything in our power to defend him. We visit him, we pray for him, we love him, we give him his rights in court. But, until he's proven innocent, we cannot connect the name of this good church to his. We tell the media we're not deserting Reverend Anderson. We're just making sure we follow the Lord's will in these vital matters. That's what I think."

Stacy turned to climb back into the pulpit. Burke stared through the vent into his eyes but saw nothing in them. Stacy faced the congregation again. "Any other discussion?" he asked the church. No one spoke. "Then, let's vote. All those in favor of suspending Reverend Anderson as the pastor of the First Methodist Church of Cascade, Georgia, please raise your right hand."

Hands raised skyward across the sanctuary. Stacy's eyes counted them. "All opposed, by like sign."

Bill and Barbara thrust their hands into the air, defiant loners. No one else. Many didn't vote either way.

"The ayes have it," said Stacy. "Until the complete disposition of this case in the courts, we hereby recommend the suspension of the Reverend Burke Anderson from this pulpit. I will advise the bishop of our decision. I'm sure the conference will accept it. Now, before we go, I want us to pray again. Let's bow." Stacy led it himself.

"Lord, we ask you to comfort us tonight. We've tried to do the right thing. We want to support Reverend Anderson, but not at the expense of your church. You guide him tonight and give him the wisdom to act correctly and to do your will. Hold us together as a church through these trying days. In Jesus' name, amen."

With a wave of his hand, Stacy dismissed the congregation. Shelley and Margie strutted out ahead of the others. Everyone avoided Bill and Barbara as they trooped by them. From the church attic, Burke watched and listened. He saw Bill wrap his arms around Barbara. "Pharisees," Bill said, loudly enough for Burke and everyone else to hear.

Shelley clucked her tongue at Margie. "Would you listen to that?"

"Shameful, just shameful," Margie said.

Les Atkinson grinned at his production crew and flipped them a thumbs up sign.

CHAPTER

14

B urke and Cody waited for the church to empty before they left. "It didn't take long," Burke said. Obviously, they wanted to get to the phones. News like this will spread like poison ivy and they want to report it to somebody."

As he waited on the crowd to disperse, Burke grew more and more angry. By the time he climbed into Cody's truck to drive home, he couldn't hold his anger any longer. He exploded to Cody. "I never really thought they'd vote me out. At least not so quickly! They didn't give me a chance!" He pounded the side of the truck door.

Cody tried to sooth him. "It'll be O.K., Preacher. They don't know anything; they're afraid. People always listen to the most intimidating voices when they're scared. Don't worry about their decision. It can be reversed when we prove your innocence."

"At least Bill defended me."

"He always liked you," Cody said. "And Barbara too."

"I can't believe they listened to Shelley Ricks. Nobody likes her."

"Don't fret about Ricks," said Cody. "It's a compliment to you she was against you. Everyone else just got swept away."

"And Margie Whitson," mumbled Burke. "She's hated me ever since I refused to date her daughter."

"Isn't her daughter a lot older than you?"

"Yep, by twelve years. And she talks as much as Margie does. Maybe that's why she never married."

"Better to be in prison than have to date her," said Cody, smiling ruefully.

"The Mayor made the difference," Burke said. "No one else has the power he has. Ricks hasn't been there long enough and Whitson has been there too long. Without the Mayor's statement, it wouldn't have happened. The people follow his lead. Stacy let Ricks and Whitson get control. They got the crowd going in one direction and he clinched it for them. Man, I hate him for that!"

"No choice but to accept it, though," said Cody, waiting for Burke's anger to subside.

"You're right, Cody. I have no choice. And, I don't know, if I sat where the Mayor does, I might have made the same decision."

They rode in silence for a couple of miles. Finally Burke forced himself to shift his thoughts to the meeting with Debbi Meyer. He couldn't change the past. So, he had to concentrate on the future, had to figure a way to assure Meyer's assistance in finding Walt.

"Looks like we're here," said Cody, turning off the interstate and parking the truck behind a weathered barn and out of sight. Burke guessed they were about five hundred yards away from the chimney, the point of rendezvous.

Burke glanced at his watch—9:20. He glued his eyes to I-85 and watched for a car to pull off the highway.

"O.K., Burke," said Cody. "Let's run through this again. I meet Meyer at the chimney. After I make sure no one else but her editor is with her, I leave him at the car and bring her up here to you. If anything unexpected happens, you head back to my place and try to come up with plan B. Here's my driver's license, like we agreed. If Meyer has reneged on our deal and brings in the police, they won't figure out who I am for a few hours and that'll give you time to get your stuff and head out. Is that about it?"

"Right," said Burke. "Only I have no plan B."

"Hang in there, Preacher," he said, "Maybe this Meyer is what she seems. Maybe this can all work out for good, like I heard you say a few weeks ago."

Burke stared into the sun-cracked dashboard of Cody's truck and whispered, "Who sounds like a preacher now?"

Cody laughed, "Get that notion out of your mind. You're the only man of the cloth in this truck. Look, I gotta go. It's almost 9:30 and it'll take me a few minutes to get situated. I don't want Meyer to get there before I do. She might think you've stood her up."

Cody turned the door handle.

"Cody?"

"What, Preacher?"

"Thanks. You're all I've got, you know."

"Then you're in worse shape than I thought. See you in a few minutes."

Cody's form clothed itself in shadows, then dissolved into the pine trees which shuffled in the breeze. Watching him leave, Burke closed his eyes and uttered a silent prayer. As he prayed, the breeze bucked up and caught the prayer in its breath and lifted it up like a kite and the prayer climbed up and up and up toward the moon. From above, the breeze tickled Burke's ears and blew the words into them. He heard the words and understood. Cody wasn't the only one with him.

* * * * *

Debbi Meyer gripped the wheel of her 1988 chocolate-brown Volvo—and made a left turn on the Highway 29 exit. She was alone. She had decided not to tell Wraps about Burke. She didn't tell him for one simple reason—if she cornered the exclusive on the hottest story in Atlanta, she didn't want to share her by-line.

She parked the car a few yards from the chimney and killed the engine. She reached over and patted her purse. The comforting lump of a Beretta semi-automatic .25 caliber pistol bulged through her black bag and eased the tension knot she kept trying to swallow. Gratefully, she recalled the hours she had spent with her father, a former Marine sergeant, on the firing range. He had forced her to take shooting lessons before she moved to Atlanta. After five stints at the range, her dad patted her on the head and said, "You shoot like you were born with a pistol in your hand. Keep that gun with you, kid. And use it if you have to. I don't want my daughter's life ruined by some strung out punk."

Debbi pulled the weapon from her purse and appreciated again its light weight and 4 and 1/2 inch length. She checked the 8 round clip—all was in place. She dropped it back into her bag and paused for one final instant. She opened the car door and stepped out. In journalism school at the University of South Carolina, Debbi had listened to professors tell her about chances like this. "A journalist might live a lifetime," one professor said, "working for some hometown sheet and never know how it feels to cover an explosive story. Or, it might happen someday without warning. These things happen the same way a golfer scores a hole-in-one—it takes a little bit of skill and a whole lot of luck. What you need to remember," said the teacher, " is that only those who play the game ever get a chance to make the shot."

Debbie faced the choice now. Would she play the game? Would

she take the shot? No doubt about it. Cautiously, she walked toward the chimney.

Bracketed by two giant oaks, the chimney cropped up like an ancient shrine to a god of burned places. The oaks moved in rhythm with the soft wind, bending inward toward each other, slowly dancing in the breeze, whispering gentle words, secretly, of people missing and people yet to come. Meyer shuddered. Reaching the chimney, she stopped and searched around it. No one there. She waited, tossing her head back in the wind, pushing her thick hair out of her eyes, squinting to see.

A voice riding the wind startled her.

"Miss Meyer."

"Yes?" She searched the shadows, looking for the owner of the voice. She pushed her right hand into her purse and wrapped her index finger around the trigger of her pistol and felt the cold comfort of the black steel.

"It's all right, ma'am, I'm a friend of Burke's. He wanted me to meet you. He's not far. Are you alone?"

The disembodied voice had connected itself to Anderson. Debbi's neck muscles tightened. "Yes, I'm by myself," she said, wondering why she was foolish enough to come without Stan Wraps.

"I thought you were going to bring someone with you."

"I changed my mind."

"I don't guess it makes any difference. Probably better."

"Where's Mr. Anderson?"

"I'll take you to him." Cody materialized out of the dark and beckoned her to follow. She obeyed. They climbed up a gentle slope, into another grove of pine trees, and over a short fence.

* * * * *

Burke heard them coming before he saw them. Their feet rustled over the pine straw and snapped downed twigs. Then, the two forms evolved out of the darkness taking on a sharper and sharper focus until they etched themselves clearly in the backdrop of the sky.

He could see that Meyer wasn't tall, but she wore a blue jean skirt and red pullover sweater. Even in the dark, her beauty was evident.

"Miss Meyer. I'm Burke Anderson." He held out his hand.

"Well, you sound like a preacher anyway, Reverend Anderson," Debbi said, accepting his handshake.

"Have you listened to many preachers?"

"As a little girl I did. Most were chaplains. My dad's a Marine and we went to services on base when he was home. Haven't heard many in the last few years, though."

"I'm glad you came."

Meyer stared at him. Not too tall, but not short either. Thick, dark hair, cut stylishly. A chiseled face and dark eyes. Muscular forearms, but not bulky. Better looking than any preacher she'd known. Maybe his looks got him in trouble.

"I guess I'll have to wait and see how glad I am, Reverend Anderson." she said.

"Just call me Burke. I don't feel much like a Reverend tonight."

"O.K., Burke," she agreed. "And you call me Debbi."

Burke decided to get to the point. "Look, let's cut to the bottom line. I told you I'd trade you my story for some information. That's why we're here, isn't it?"

"That's right. You tell me what happened Friday night and I give you information in return."

"So, who goes first?"

"You called me, so why don't you start?" urged Debbi.

"O.K. Mind if we walk as we talk?"

"Not at all," she said, "but only if he follows." She tilted her head at Cody.

"A deal," agreed Burke, shoving his hands into his pockets as they moved away from the truck. With the swaying pines watching, he spilled it all out—the Friday night visit, the temptation, the flight, the blackout, the trip home, the return on Sunday, the body found—he told her everything he could remember. She showed no reaction as she listened.

Finished, he stopped walking and leaned his back against a pine. "Were you ever a poker player?" he asked.

"Why do you ask?"

"Because you don't show much emotion."

"No, not much, not when I'm thinking."

"So, at least I've got you thinking."

"Without question," she said.

"So what you thinking?"

"You want me to be honest?"

"I have been with you." Burke hoped she believed him.

"I'm thinking it doesn't matter much to me whether you're telling the truth or not. I want to get your story. And, if you're lying, I'll know soon enough anyway."

Her frankness startled him. "Is that all you're thinking?" he asked.

"No, not exactly all. At a gut level I think you've told me the truth. That's what I want to believe anyway. 'Cause if you're not, then I could be in big trouble right now."

"It is the truth," said Burke, defending himself. "I just ended up in the wrong place at the wrong time and heaven only knows how."

"Heaven only knows how you're going to prove that, though. You said you wanted me to get some information for you. Am I right in guessing you want me to help you track down your friend Walt?"

"Exactly. I think Walt can give me some answers. At least he can tell me about Carol Reese. He could tell me about her other friends and clients. Any one of them could be the killer. If I can find Walt, I have a chance."

Burke found the courage to ask. "Will you help me find Walt?"

"Let me ask you one question before I answer. Do you think you killed Reese in those missing minutes? Did you go back in, get into an argument, strike her? Kill her?"

Burke walked away from the pine and stopped with his back to Meyer. Then, he pivoted to her again.

"Debbi, I've asked myself that question a thousand times in the last two days. Like I told Cody, anything's possible. I'm no better than the next person. I'm capable of the lust that rapes, the greed that steals, the anger that kills. In God's eyes, they're all the same. We're all guilty. Yeah, in one sense I am the killer."

Debbi paused for a moment, then said, "Burke, I haven't been to church in about 15 years so I don't know God like I should. Like I want to sometimes. But, if God sees us all as guilty, then what hope do we have? You paint a pretty bleak picture."

"I can't argue with you," he said, wiping his palms on his thighs and stepping closer to her. "It is bleak. We are guilty. But, you see, that's precisely why we need God. We need God to give us a way out of our guilt. Even though we're guilty, God wants to forgive us, wants to make us clean, wants to declare us innocent."

"That's a bit crazy, don't you think?" asked Debbi.

"How so?"

"Think about it. Our justice system tells us we're innocent until proven guilty. Then a whole battery of prosecutors work like the devil to prove our guilt. But you tell me God says we're all guilty. Then, a man named Jesus dies on a cross and God offers to make us innocent?" She chuckled as she finished.

"When you put it that way, it does sound a little ironic," said Burke.

"Ironic? Yeah, to say the least." Debbi pushed her hair into her mouth and chewed on the edges. She exhaled sharply. "But it's noble too. And good. We're all guilty. But God wants to forgive us and make us innocent. I like that."

"So do I," said Burke. "That's why I became a minister. To lead other people to believe it."

"Makes me want to believe it," said Debbi.

"No reason you can't," said Burke. "It's a matter of faith."

"You trying to convert me, Reverend Anderson?"

Burke smiled. "Well, I have to admit it's not my original purpose in meeting you, but, like the Bible says, 'God works in mysterious ways His wonders to perform.' If you're open to conversion, I'll sure show you how."

Debbi stared at him for a long moment. She shuddered. "Maybe you'll get the chance, Reverend, but not tonight. Tonight, we'd better stick to business, see what we can do to get you out of this fix."

Burke nodded. "So, you'll help me find Walt?"

"Yeah, I think I will."

CHAPTER

15

B roadus and Mays stood by the water fountain outside the briefing room of the Peachtree Street Station. The starched navy skirt and white cotton blouse Broadus had slipped on that morning now looked like two pieces of soggy bread. Mays looked even worse, but he always looked bad so no one noticed. The white-faced clock on the wall read 9:15 P.M.

"Ready to give it up for today?" Jackie asked, bending over for a drink of water.

"I don't know. Are you? We've been up for almost 36 hours."

"Maybe," said Jackie. "Sunday seems like a year ago."

"So you're ready to call it quits then?"

Broadus thought of her empty bed at home and the four walls staring back at her. She said, "No, I'm O.K. for awhile. Think I'll visit that truck stop off the interstate near Cascade. Sometimes truckers warm up after a few beers and something valuable slips out. You heading home?"

Mays shook his head. "No, reckon not. Guess I'll tag along with you, in case a trucker takes your interest in him as something more than professional. You might need old Avery to protect your flanks."

Broadus laughed. "Let me stop by the ladies room for a second. I do want to look my best for the boys."

"I'll meet you at the car. I need to ask the chief how we're doing with the names in Reese's client book."

Conners looked up when Mays walked in, his gray hair sprigged out like thin wires, his eyes hard brown rocks. "Tough day, Avery?" he asked.

"Absolutely. But we did pick up a couple of items worth noting. One witness saw a black Mercedes come in and go out in the time frame we'd expect if Anderson is the killer. Another one told us the Reverend has quite a temper. Flies off the handle, she said, when he doesn't get his way."

"The Reverend drove a Mercedes?" Conners leaned back in his chair and pulled his pipe out of the top drawer.

"No, Chief. They don't pay that well at First Methodist. Our witness said one man drove it in and two men were in it when it went out."

"So, someone was with the Reverend?"

"It appears so. We're tracking all the black Mercedes in Georgia through the computer. But, it'll take a little time."

"I expect so. I know three people myself who drive one."

"Yeah, ain't credit a wonderful thing?"

"It's the American dream. Drive it today. Pay for it tomorrow."

Mays headed the conversation back to his reason for stopping by. "Chief, what've we found from the names in Reese's book? Any leads?"

Conners stirred his pipe tobacco. "Nothing yet. We've verified 38 iron-clad alibis. One of the men was dead. A heart attack killed him on the fourth of July this past year."

"I bet one night with Reese could give a man a heart attack."

"Mays, your humor gets a little morbid sometimes, you know that?"

"Yeah, Chief, but I need that in this business. What about the other names?"

"We're still checking. Two of the men are out of the country. We haven't located the other four. We've got blue shirts on it."

"Thanks, Frank. Keep us posted."

"I'll do that. By the way—" Conners put his pipe down. "You should know something else, Mays. One page of the book is missing."

"What?"

"One page is missing," repeated Conners. "The sequence goes from 24 to 31. Reese wrote six names on each sheet and the numbers jump from 24 to 31. Apparently, something happened to the fifth page of her list."

Mays scratched his unshaven chin. "What do you make of that, Chief?"

"I have no clue. Maybe those clients had stopped calling on her and she just tore out their names." Conners stared at Mays. "Could be your

Reverend Anderson pulled off the one with his name on it. It's hard to say what happened to it. We pay you to find out."

Mays shrugged. "We'll dig up what we can, Chief."

Relieved, Mays didn't press it any further, Conners shifted the subject. "You and Broadus headed back out to Cascade tonight?"

"Yep, soon as she gets out of the girl's room and I finish up here."

"Well, try to get some sleep before tomorrow. I'll need you on hand when we start the house to house search in the morning."

"You think he's still in the area?"

"Sure do. No one's picked up his car on the APB and I don't think he has enough street smarts to ditch it and steal another one. He's got to be holed up somewhere near Cascade."

"Well, if I'm going to get anything done, I'd better get out of here."

"'Spect so. Keep me posted."

"You, too, Chief."

* * * * *

Conners slumped into his chair and stuck his unlit pipe into his mouth, sucking on it like a child with a pacifer, seeking comfort. With his head propped in his left hand, he slipped open the middle drawer of his desk and pulled out a piece of paper. Though he had read the name a hundred times since last night, it still scared him every time he saw it. The name *Raymond Steele* stared back at him.

* * * * *

Outside, Mays slammed the car door as he hopped into the seat. "Craziest thing," he muttered.

"What are you groaning about, Avery?"

"Get moving and I'll tell you as we go."

Broadus eased the car out of the driveway, leaving her window open to catch the cool air.

"I can't figure it, Jackie."

"Can't figure what?"

"The book we turned into the chief. The one with the names in it."

"What about it?"

"Chief says a page is missing."

"So? A thousand things could have happened to it. What bothers you about that?"

"Jackie, I glanced through that book before we took it in."

"So did I. Not long enough to catch any names, just flipped through it for a second."

"Yeah, me too. But I know a page wasn't missing."

"How can you be so sure?"

"Because I saw the numbers on the top of the pages." Mays didn't want to boast about his memory, but those numbers stuck out in his mind.

"The numbers?"

"Yeah, the numbers," he repeated impatiently. "Jackie, what color ink did Reese use in her book?"

Broadus sat up straight in her seat like a school child unexpectedly asked a question. "Blue, I think," she said slowly, without certainty. "Or black. A dark color, I'm sure of that."

"Black, Jackie, black for the names. But, I'm not talking about the names. What other color did she use?"

Jackie stared glumly ahead. Caught again without her homework. "I have no clue, Avery. I didn't look at it that closely. Thought we would do that later."

Avery comforted her. "It's O.K. You usually see the big picture long before I do. That's why we're good partners. I notice numbers and colors. You figure out who did it. The numbers were written in red at the top of each page."

"And you remember them?"

"Yeah, the numbers. I remember them all," said Mays. "Reese wrote them in red ink. Like a testimony to her trade. Reese had 9 pages in that book. Fifty one names, six names to a page, except for the last one which had three. Chief told me the numbers between 24 and 31 were missing. That would make it page five. I'm sure page five was in the book when we turned it in."

"Avery, you know what you're saying, don't you?"

"Yeah, I think so. Someone at the station ripped a page out of Reese's book. *Someone's hiding someone.*"

"Who would do that, Avery?"

"That's the tough part, Jackie. It could be the Chief."

"Conners wouldn't remove evidence. Maybe the squad cops did it when I gave it to them."

"I doubt it. Too easy to trace. Besides, why would they want to tear out one page?"

Broadus tried again. "Maybe Anderson tore it out. If he killed her, he would certainly want to remove a piece of paper with his name, phone number and address on it."

"That's a thought. But—you forget. I saw the number after Anderson was long gone."

"That'll be hard to prove, Avery. If you accuse the Chief or someone else within the department, the I.D. guys will laugh you out of the precinct. It'll be your word against theirs."

Avery clammed up.

"Look, Avery, you know I believe you," she said, trying to make up. "I've seen your steel-trap mind work too often not to trust you. But, I just don't think it'll fly downtown."

"You're right, Jackie. But I know what I saw."

Suddenly Broadus hit upon a new twist. "Maybe they did pull the page, Avery. But, not necessarily to protect a murderer. Maybe it was to protect someone from publicity! I'm sure Reese connected with some prominent people. Maybe your missing page listed the name of a well-known person who frequented Reese's services, but didn't kill her."

"Could be," said Mays, unconvinced. "But he would have a motive for murder, wouldn't he?"

"Can't argue that. But until we find the missing page we still have one key suspect—Burke Anderson." With one thought on him and another on a missing page, she pushed the gas pedal to the floor.

CHAPTER
16

Burke and Cody picked up a sackful of onion-laden hamburgers at the truck stop on the way back from meeting Debbi, then drove cautiously back to Cody's place. They had stopped only for the food, worrying every second that a cop would suddenly appear in their rearview mirror. Safely back in the secluded apartment, Cody slouched in the only chair and propped his feet against the wall. With all they'd shared in the last twenty-four hours, the barriers were down.

"It's funny, Preacher. Folks have to go through something traumatic sometimes before they'll open up to each other. Why is that?"

"If I could answer that, I'd be a billionaire."

"Didn't all your schooling teach you why people act like they do?"

"Not really. No one really knows what motivates people to do what they do. Everyone has his own reason, I guess. Take you, for example. Why did you get involved with drugs?"

"That's hard to say."

"If it's hard for you, then imagine how hard it is for other people. Why do you think you did? Let's take a stab at it."

Cody scratched his neck, thinking. "The simplest answer is I liked the feeling the drugs gave me."

"What was that feeling?"

"I don't know—release, I guess."

"What kind of release?"

"You know—a sense of freedom from feeling unwanted."

"What made you feel unwanted?"

"That's personal."

"I can make a guess."

"I'm sure you can. Anyway, the drugs gave me an escape, a way out of the hurt."

"What happened when the drugs wore off?"

Cody snorted an ironic laugh. "You know what happened. The hurt waited for me to come down. The escape never lasted."

"You said you didn't feel wanted."

"That's right. My dad divorced my mom and disappeared when I was eleven. I've heard from him only once since. When I went to jail for the first time, he sent me a note. Said, 'Don't let the system get you down, son.' Some note, huh?"

"Maybe that was his way of saying he cared."

"Strange way to show it."

"So, you used drugs to run?"

"That makes me sound like a coward, but it's probably close to the truth."

Burke backed off as Cody hung his head, the pain tugging at him, like the undertow of a river grabbing at his ankles, threatening to take him under. As he watched the pain crawling around Cody's eyes, it grabbed onto his own hurt, a pain hiding in his own gut, a pain he couldn't share even with Cody. *A pain he shared with no one.* It stayed with him, crawling around inside, a snake hiding in the rocks, its fangs sliding in and out, striking at unexpected moments, drawing blood but not killing, seeming to take pleasure in leaving its victim injured but alive. The wound stayed open, even now, ten years later.

Burke felt the snake slither close and he ran from it. He edged himself from the sofa and walked to the window. Scores of moths were banging against the screen, fighting to reach the stark light bulb hanging on a black cord from the ceiling of the bare living area. He interlocked his knuckles behind his head.

Finally Burke pivoted and stared at Cody. The moths bounced off the screen as he spoke. "Thanks for helping me, Cody. No matter what happens, you've made yourself a lifelong friend. You don't know for sure I didn't kill Reese. But, you've tried to help and I won't forget it. And, Cody."

"Yeah?"

"Your dad was a fool."

Cody dropped his feet off the smudged wall and rocked out of his seat. He took two steps and flipped on the television. "I appreciate those words, Preacher. Now, let's see what's on the news."

He turned through the channels. "Here's a good show, Preacher, 'Murder, She Wrote.'"

Burke picked up a cushion and tossed it at Cody, laughing loudly. "So, now you're a comedian, huh?"

"I've got to pick this party up. You're getting a little serious on me. Can't afford to do that, not yet. Not until we get you out of this mess."

Burke agreed. They had said enough for now; enough to build a bridge out of the loneliness and fear that stranded them both. He glued his eyes on the T.V. as the news began.

Les Atkinson stared out at them and Metcalf's dusty gas station, decorated with the lazy dog, framed his manicured profile as he began. "Here in Cascade today, the home of Reverend Burke Anderson, chief suspect in the Carol Reese murder case, folks don't want to accept the likelihood that their preacher is guilty. Unlike the police investigating the crime, and against the facts as we now have them, most of these good and simple people want to believe the best about their missing Reverend."

Atkinson showed the interview with the angry Metcalf, emphasizing Bill's simplistic nature and hostile defense of Burke.

The screen flicked again and Atkinson's waxy face, standing beside a "Welcome to Cascade" sign, beamed at the viewers. Tall weeds obscured the bottom of the rusty sign, buckshot holes punctured it, and bird droppings gave it a speckled look. Atkinson concluded. "As you can see from this sign, Cascade has not exactly kept up with the times. This speck of a town is old-fashioned, worn out, and left over.

"No matter how old-fashioned Cascade is tonight, though, they are modern in this one way—scandal has hit them. Yes, tonight Cascade has caught up with Charlotte and Baton Rouge and Atlanta. It looks like their preacher has sinned and they're having to learn how to deal with it. This is Les Atkinson, reporting from the *modern* city of Cascade, Georgia."

Cody snapped off the television as Burke pulled up from the sweat-sticky seat and headed toward the bathroom.

"I think I'll get ready for bed," Burke said. "Nothing else I can do tonight."

"Sleep well, Preacher. See you in the morning."

Within the hour Burke stretched out on the green vinyl of the couch and dozed fitfully. Against his will, he dreamed. In his dreams faces stared at him, smiling, then frowning, then crying, then shouting. Faces of Shelley Ricks and Bill Metcalf; faces of his dad and mom—sad and hurting; faces of Mayor Stacy and Les Atkinson, one firm and the other smirking; faces of Carol Reese and Debbi Meyer—one dead, the other very much alive, both smiling at him, but both standing at a distance from him.

Then it came, the one face he hadn't seen for years, the one face he didn't want to see, the one he refused to look at in his waking hours, the one which haunted him in his sleep when he least expected it—the cherub face, smiling like Debbi smiled, looking at him with love, helpless and trusting. Then the face turned red with screaming, then blue, then ashen white—like snow touched by soot. He watched the face change and he wanted to stop it, to keep it smiling, but he couldn't. His hands were tied, his desire to help chained to a post he couldn't move. He screamed, the torment ripping his soul and scratching at his heart. He died with the face as it died.

The memory stared at him, then moved away, back into the shadows where all the faces that people fear go as the morning light shoos them away. Burke woke up, sweating and shaking. "God," he prayed, "forgive me. I know I'm a failure. I wish I wasn't, but I am. Please, Lord, forgive me for that. And, Lord, let this end soon."

Pushing the damp sheet off his legs, Burke fought off sleep. He vowed he wouldn't dream anymore tonight—the face might appear again.

CHAPTER

17

T he sun peeped in through the Roman shades of Debbi Meyer's bedroom. Debbi pried open her eyes, pushed off the covers, and sat upright. She checked the time—8:12. Her meeting with Stan was scheduled for ten. Her resolve to help Burke had hardened overnight, but she knew getting the information wouldn't come easily. She had no contacts with anyone at Peachtree. But, she worked for Stan Wraps and he was drowning in them. Stan had contacts with everybody. If she could get Stan's help, she had a chance. Though she hated to share her headlines with anybody, she didn't see any choice. Besides, she owed Stan something. Boy, would he be surprised when she told him she had met with Anderson.

Right at 9, Debbi picked up her gun-heavy purse and locked the door to her apartment. Forty-five minutes later, after negotiating the morning traffic, she parked her Volvo in the six-story parking garage and took the elevator to the *Independent*. Squaring her shoulders, she stepped off the elevator and headed to Stan's office. "Mr. Wraps is expecting me," she told the secretary.

"Have a seat in his office, Ms. Meyer. Mr. Wraps will arrive shortly." Debbi surveyed the study as she waited. The picture directly behind Wraps' cherry-leather chair showed the smiling face of a gray-headed woman with snake lines around her eyes and weak skin under her chin. Flanking the lady, obviously his wife, sat two girls on her left and one young man on her right.

Debbi didn't hear Stan's entry. His voice startled her, "Glad you could drop by. I hope the decor meets your approval."

Debbi fumbled with her words, "Uh, Mr. Wraps, uh, I didn't know you had a family."

"Didn't think an old goat like me could get a wife, huh?"

"No, not that at all. But I never heard you speak of them."

"I don't think my family has much relevance to what goes on in these offices. No reason for me to speak of them." Wraps motioned her to a chair opposite his desk. "You said you wanted to talk to me."

"Yes, I need to talk to you—in the utmost confidence."

Wraps slouched in his seat and picked up a cigarette off his desk, stuck it into his mouth, but didn't light it. "O.K. Tell me what's on your mind."

"I don't really know where to begin," she said, pushing strands of hair out of her eyes.

"Just take a deep breath and start at the beginning."

"Thanks, Mr. Wraps."

"Call me Stan."

"Yeah, O.K.—yesterday, at about 8 A.M. I was about to go home. Then a phone call came in—"

He urged her to continue. "Debbi, let's not make a guessing game out of this. Who was it?"

"Stan, it was Burke Anderson! He had read my column and he called to ask me to help him prove his innocence. He said my column made him think I would listen to him, that I would give him the benefit of the doubt. He wanted me to meet him."

Stan bit down on his unlit cigarette and tasted the tobacco spill into his mouth. His eyes widened. "Is that where you were last night?"

"Yeah. I couldn't keep myself from going. I know it was foolish, but I got so excited I lost all sense of caution. I started to tell you but was afraid you might talk me out of it. So, I went to meet him alone. I decided if I really meant what I wrote, I had no choice but to go."

Stan stared at her. "Did you go 'cause you believed what you wrote or because you wanted to get the story everyone else would die to have?"

Debbi stared back. "Maybe a little bit of both."

"Gutsy move," said Stan, "But don't you think it's risky for a single girl to meet an accused killer in the middle of the night? Even to get a story? Dead reporters don't write too many stories."

"I don't guess it was the smartest thing I ever did. But he didn't hurt me."

"What did happen?"

"He told me his story. He went to Reese's house with a friend, without any idea what he was getting into." Debbi shared Burke's story with Stan. He listened without comment until she finished, then laid his gnawed cigarette on the desk and stroked his brow. "Do you believe him?"

"I'm not sure yet," said Debbi. "But, I think I do. He seemed so helpless, so scared, so . . ." She searched for a word, found it, "Innocent. I don't think he would hurt anyone. But the thing is, I think I'd try to help him even if I didn't believe him."

"Is the story important enough to take that risk?"

"I think it is." said Debbi. "A reporter my age doesn't get this chance too often. I would regret it the rest of my life if I passed this up."

Stan loosened his tie and stood up. He hovered over Debbi, then bent down and took her by the hand. "You may die young, Meyer, but you'll be one fabulous reporter while you live."

"I can live with that," said Debbi, basking in Stan's approval.

Wraps dropped her hand and turned back to business. "You said he asked for your help. What's he want you to do?"

"He asked me to find out if a guy named Walt Litske had turned up anywhere in the investigation. Said Reese might have kept a list with his number on it. Burke believes Litske can help him. If nothing else, Litske could prove Anderson ended up at Reese's through no fault of his own."

"We don't even know if the cops found such a list, Debbi."

"I know that. So does Burke. But, he asked me to find out if they did."

"How do you propose doing that?"

"Well," Debbi said mischievously. "That's where I need your help. I don't know the system and I don't have the connections like you do. To help Burke, I need your help."

"You call him Burke?"

"Yeah, I guess I do."

Wraps picked his cigarette up again and searched his pockets for a match. No luck. He grinned boyishly. "You want me to tell you how to get this information?"

"Either that or get it for me."

"If we get caught helping a fugitive, we could both get fired."

Debbi countered, "But think about what happens if we prove his innocence and get the story from the ground up! You and I will be on top of the world!"

Debbi's eyes sparkled, lit with the fires of ambition and potential fame. "Will you work with me, Stan? To give him a chance and get this chance for ourselves?"

Stan opened his desk drawer and found a match. He lit his Camel and blew a blue puff of smoke through his nose. "Debbi," he said, "this paper is in trouble. Nelson Steadman told me we have about 3 months to pull out of the slide we're in or he'll either sell the paper or close her down. I don't like either option. If we help Anderson, we get a good story even if you and I end up in jail with him. Folks will read about the reporter who tried to help a killer and failed, as eagerly as they will about the reporter who got the information that helped a wrongly accused person go free. Financially, the paper can't lose. It may not be enough to save the *Independent* but it can't hurt us either. I'll do anything I can to help you get this story."

Debbi reached over and threw a hammerlock around Stan's neck. He let her hug him for a second, then he coughed and pulled away. She smoothed her skirt and wiped the smile off her wide cheekbones. It was her turn to get practical. "How do we get the information, Stan?"

Stan chuckled. "I hate to do this, young lady, but I have to initiate you into the adult world of reporting."

Debbi balanced on the edge of her seat.

Stan continued, "You get information in this business in one of five ways. First, you can buy it. Reporters have been paying off policeman and politicians for stories for years. If you don't have enough money to buy it or if someone isn't for sale, then you can steal it. A friend smuggles out a document; one reporter distracts a secretary while a second one picks up a file; a computer hack breaks the code to the data files of the cops downtown—lots of ways to get what you need."

Stan searched for an ashtray. No dice. He stubbed the butt against the bottom of his shoe and began his lecture again. "In today's market, a few use sex. A reporter makes a date with someone in the know. Teasing may get results. If not, both men and women have been known to produce what they've teased if that's what it took."

"Stan, what happens if none of these work?"

"Then we're down to our next to last option—we use a threat. Most people have a few skeletons in their closets and we often know where the bones are. It's amazing what folks will tell you when they think you're holding something over them. So, if we need information and can't get it, we look for a private indiscretion and threaten to reveal it unless the person plays ball with us."

"It sounds awfully cynical."

"It is."

"Do you get tired of it?"

"Every day I think I'll quit."

"But you don't."

"No, Debbi, I don't."

"Why not? If you've got integrity, doesn't all this degrade you and the profession?"

"Sure it does, but I don't quit because we're essential—to the public, to the nation, to democracy."

"That sounds the opposite of cynical."

"Yeah, it does, doesn't it? But that's the way it is. The media really does hold a public trust."

"So, it doesn't bother you when your profession uses unethical methods?"

"Sure it bothers me!" Stan grimaced.

"But you do it anyway?"

"Sometimes, yes, but not all the time. There's a fifth way and it's not unethical. At their best, journalists gather information through friendships developed over the years, through public officials who trust them, who believe the people have the right to know. We get the news with hard work, and worn shoes, and fast talk."

"But that's the ideal, isn't it?"

"Yep. Ideally, public officials tell us the truth and we report it and trust the people. But, when the people who should give us the news straight bend it to their own ends, or refuse to tell us the facts, we have no choice but to get it any way we can."

"It's not an ideal world, is it, Stan?" Debbi rolled out the question slowly.

Stan laughed and bounced backward in his chair. "Did you ever think it was?"

"No, but I hoped I was wrong."

The two sat staring at each other for a second, then Debbi blinked. "The question is, what method do we use to find out about Litske?"

"First we have to decide who to approach."

"The police should be our best bet," said Debbi.

"Yeah, that's obvious. But we need specifics. Which cop can help us? And which cop will help us?"

"You'll know that better than I do, Stan," said Debbi, turning her palms upward.

"I know by their reputation the two detectives assigned to the Reese case. I'm sure Mays won't help. He's a good cop but he's as tight as a cat in a room full of rocking chairs. Treats words like a social disease he doesn't want to catch."

"What about Broadus?"

"She's certainly competent, but seems a little aloof."

"Maybe a woman would talk to a woman."

"It's worth a try. Why don't you give her a call? Be careful, though. Remember, you know more than she does. Don't slip and let her know you're involved with Anderson."

"Who else can we contact? You must have plenty of connections as long as you've been around."

Stan grunted. "I could get offended at that, young lady. I'm not a fossil yet."

"Oh, I didn't mean that. Just that, well—you have been around a long time!"

"Can't argue with you there. But I don't have much confidence my sources will loosen up much on this one. Too much at stake. But, I'll see what I can do."

Debbi lurched out of her seat and skipped out of his office. Stan closed the door, walked back to his desk and picked up the phone. Time to call in the big gun.

CHAPTER

18

T he phone rang in the bedroom of the three-story antebellum mansion which housed Nelson Steadman and his three dogs—two German shepherds and one collie. The white stone house, draped in the back with spinach-green ivy, and surrounded in front with "more azaleas than any other 100-year-old yard in Atlanta," as Steadman put it, was surrounded by a six-foot-high fence and 26 pecan trees. The house looked like Steadman himself—stately but not foreboding. Like him it was old, but still functional.

He hustled over on his oak cane and answered the phone before his maid got to it. "Yeah, Steadman here."

"Nelson, this is Stan."

"What's up, Stan? You forgot something this morning?"

"No, Nelson, something new has come up. Something which will interest you, I think. Can I come out and talk to you about it?"

"How quick do you need to talk, Stan? I'm supposed to tee it up with the governor in about an hour."

"You back out playing golf?"

"Sure am. You didn't think that prostate surgery would keep me down forever, did you?"

"No, but I did think it would slow you down a little."

"It has slowed me but it hasn't killed me. And it hasn't caused me to lose my good sense. You didn't call me about my golf handicap. How urgent is this conversation?"

"Extremely urgent, Nelson. Can I come out?"

Nelson looked at his watch. It would take Stan nearly an hour to drive out. Even if they talked only 15 minutes, he would miss his game with the governor. Worse, he'd miss the chance to talk politics. He didn't want to miss that meeting. Too much at stake, with an election barely a year away.

"Stan, I need to see the governor," said Steadman. "Can we talk on the phone?"

Stan didn't like it, but he had no choice. "Sure, Nelson, but you'd better sit down."

"I'm a big boy, Stan. What you got?"

Stan launched into his speech. "Nelson, do you remember the editorial we ran yesterday on the Reese case?"

"Sure I do. Creative thought to do that—play our front page off against our editorial page. What about it?"

"Well, the girl who wrote it, Debbi Meyer, took a phone call yesterday morning from a man who claimed to be Burke Anderson."

Steadman pulled out a chair and propped his leg on the seat, resting his cane by his side. "Go on."

"Anderson claimed he was innocent. Said he wanted a chance to prove it. Figured everyone would assume his guilt, so he ran. The next morning when he read Debbi's article, he thought she might give him a fair hearing. So, he offered her a deal."

"What kind of deal?"

"His story for her help. He claims a guy named Walt Litske took him to Reese's. Said he never saw Reese before that night and he left hours before she died."

"What does he want Meyer to do?"

"He wants her to get an address on Litske. He believes if he can find him, he can prove his innocence."

"That's a long shot, isn't it?" Nelson asked.

"Yeah, but even if Litske can't tell the cops anything about the death, he can at least verify the Reverend's story."

"If he's telling the truth."

"Debbi thinks he is."

"Why?"

"Because she went out to meet him last night."

The phone went silent. "Nelson?"

"I'm still here. Brave girl."

"She is that. Maybe a bit foolish. She didn't tell anyone what she was doing."

"But Anderson didn't harm her?"

"No, he didn't. That's why she believes him."

"Do you believe him, Stan?"

"I believe her, Nelson. That's good enough for me. If she says this Reverend is innocent, I'm willing to wait and see."

"And get the newspaper a hot story either way."

"Exactly. We can't lose."

"As long as the girl stays safe."

"Obviously."

Steadman hadn't earned his millions through hesitancy in a crisis. He was a careful but decisive businessman who liked to gather all the facts, make a choice, and let it ride. Whether right or wrong, he bragged, he never lost any sleep over the decisions he reached. He picked up his forty-year-old cane and tapped it against his knee. He looked down both roads and picked one.

"What can I do to help, Stan? As I see it, we don't have any choice. If she's the kind of lady you've described, she'll try to get this information without us if she has to. We might as well lend a hand if we can."

"That's the way I see it too."

"What'cha need from me?"

"Two things."

"I'm listening."

"Money and influence."

"How much money and where do we use the influence?"

"I don't know how much money yet, Nelson. But I do know where we can use the influence. The police chief at Peachtree Station is Frank Conners. I know Frank—"

"So do I, from a long way back."

"And he can tell us if Litske's name has turned up," said Stan.

"And if so, how and where."

"Exactly."

"Money won't buy Frank, Stan. I've watched him work for over 35 years, ever since he started on the force in the '50s. He's a good cop, a throwback to the old days. He's fairly clean."

"If we can't buy him, then what's our leverage?"

"I said he was 'fairly' clean. Frank's got one problem and it's gotten worse since his wife died 16 years ago."

"He never remarried?"

"No."

"'Spect that got lonely."

"It did. Frank began to drink pretty heavily. With one of our guys in fact."

"With Fontly?" Stan guessed. The two men were about the same age; Fontly often picked up bits and pieces of information no one else knew. Like Burke Anderson's name.

"Sure, didn't you know?"

"I hate to admit it, but no. Randy and I work together, but don't do much socializing."

"You should know your people better, Stan."

"You never complained before, Nelson, not as long as I did my job."

"Take it easy; no offense intended. Just making a point."

"Point made. So Fontly and Conners are drinking buddies. How's that going to help us? Get Conners drunk and talk the information out of him?"

"Nothing so amateurish," said Nelson. "Conners knows better. He would never have made chief if booze loosened his tongue."

"What then? If he won't take money and if we can't prod him with booze?"

A low chuckle started in Nelson's stomach and crawled up through his chest and arms to his face. For the first time in far too many years, he joined in the battle for news.

"Stan, nine years ago you took a vacation. You remember?"

"Sure do. My wife claims it's the only one I've ever taken. What about it?"

"One night, while you were gone, I got a phone call here at the house about 2 A.M. It was Fontly. Seems he and Conners had swilled down a bit of Irish Red and had stirred the old blood up. So, they went to the Fairborne Hotel."

"Isn't that torn down now?"

"Yep, but nine years ago it stood smack dab in the middle of the hottest part of Atlanta."

"Yeah, if I remember correctly, the Fairborne stabled a good crop of painted ladies."

"That's one way of putting it. Anyway, Fontly and Conners ended up in a room with two of those hookers at about 1:30. Just as they were about to consummate the deal, a police raid nabbed both of them."

It was Stan's turn to laugh. "So, the police grabbed their chief in a hooker sweep?"

"Not their chief, Stan. These guys were from the Ninth Street Station. Frank wasn't their chief!"

"And they were ready to press charges?"

"At first they were. The rivalry between these different city precincts can get fierce."

"What kept them from following through?"

"Fontly called me."

"And?"

"And I called the Mayor."

"And the Mayor convinced the powers in the Ninth Street Station to drop the charges."

"You got it," said Steadman.

"So, where does that leave us?"

"That leaves me to make a phone call to Frank Conners."

"You think he'll cooperate?"

"He will unless he wants the public to know about a police chief nearing retirement who once failed to uphold the duties of his office."

"Would you do that to him now, after all these years? No one would prosecute."

"I know they wouldn't. But, it would embarrass Conners to no end."

"Would you do that?" Stan repeated his question.

"I don't know. I hope Conners won't force me to find out."

Stan stroked his bushy eyebrows, marveling again at the toughness of his boss and friend. "O.K., Nelson. I'll stay on it from this end."

"And I'll get on the horn to Conners about this mysterious friend of Anderson's. Did you say his name was Litske?"

"Yeah, Walt Litske."

"That name sounds familiar to me for some reason."

"It should. He played ball with the Falcons several years ago."

"Yeah, now I remember," said Nelson. "I knew his dad. He was fairly prominent in real estate here in Atlanta for awhile. Then his business hit the skids. He got too extended in real estate on the west side. Not enough capital to keep it all afloat. Last I heard he was in bankruptcy."

"Do you think you could locate him?"

"Why don't you try that? Let me contact Conners. If you don't have any luck with Litske, I'll give it a try later."

Stan hesitated, then said, "Nelson?"

"Yeah?"

"It feels good to work with you again."

"My sentiments exactly, friend. It has been too long."

CHAPTER

19

Steadman punched the intercom and called his maid.

"Yes, Mr. Steadman?"

"Get Frank Conners of the Peachtree Street Station on the line for me."

He stood up, steadied himself with his cane, and crossed the maroon and gold oriental rug covering his floor and opened the liquor cabinet. He grabbed the brandy decanter and poured himself a thin drink. Though he usually didn't imbibe so early in the day, Nelson needed a bracer before he talked to Conners. He hadn't been involved in the day to day grind of the newspaper business in over 20 years and he wasn't sure his heart was still up to it.

What's the difference, he thought, slugging down the drink. *I'd rather die doing something than sitting in a chair with a blanket over my knees, dribbling chicken soup down the front of my shirt.*

"Mr. Steadman." He twitched at the sound of the maid's voice.

"I'm here."

"Mr. Conners on the line."

"O.K., I've got it." He eased himself into a chair.

"Frank! This is Nelson Steadman." He started like they were old friends.

"Nelson, it's been a long time," said Conners, cautiously.

"Too long, friend. You getting along O.K.?"

"As well as an old mule like me can expect. What about you? I heard you had some surgery here awhile back."

"Yeah, I did. The doctors decided I needed prostate surgery. I can tell you that's a little ticklish. But, it didn't kill me and I don't have to run to the bathroom as often as before. Plus, it doesn't take so long to get started once I get there." Nelson chuckled along with Conners. As the short-lived laugh died on the line, Steadman moved to the point.

"Look, Frank, I haven't talked to you in ages and I know this is a busy time. These two murders must have you hoppin'. You getting close to anything yet?"

Conners stayed noncommittal. "Not anymore than we've reported in our press releases. We've got two good people—Broadus and Mays—heading up our investigation unit. I'm sure they'll keep your folks up to date."

Steadman ignored the canned response. "You turn up Reverend Anderson yet?"

"Nope, not unless it's happened in the last few minutes. But, we're starting a house to house search of Cascade later this morning. We'll get him soon."

"Good, Frank, good. Look, I wanted to touch base with you personally to see if there's anything on background you might tell an old friend like myself." Steadman hesitated, waiting for Conners. Nothing happened. Nelson continued. "Is Anderson still your major suspect?"

"Reverend Anderson is still being sought for questioning, yes. We can place him at the scene, at the approximate time, and we can assume several motives for the murder. That's enough to make him a key figure in this investigation."

Steadman sensed a deep caution in Conners' words.

"Any other suspects?" Nelson pressed.

"What'cha mean?"

"That's an obvious enough question, Frank. Don't try to slide around me. Do you have any other people under investigation? Any other names turn up in the Reese girl's apartment? In a client list, maybe?"

Conners kept hedging. "I can't give you any more information, Nelson. I wish I could. But, that would jeopardize the whole situation. I know you wouldn't want me to violate any confidentiality."

"Not at all, Frank," said Steadman, his voice smooth and easy. "But I need you to share one bit of information with me. I'll not print it—you have my word, unless you say I can. I need to know if a certain prominent Atlanta name has appeared anywhere in your investigation."

Though Steadman couldn't see it, Conners placed a hand over his stomach and began to pat it like a drum. Sweat gave birth to yellow globes under the armpits of his white shirt. *How did he find out about*

Steele? he wondered. That had to be the name he wanted. Why else would Steadman, a millionaire Republican, take such a personal interest in this case? Did Steadman want the information to protect Steele or to harm him? Conners stalled.

"Mr. Steadman, I might not know if any other names have turned up. Broadus and Mays keep up with the nitty gritty details and I haven't received the most up-to-date reports yet. Maybe I can check with them and get back to you."

Steadman refused the brush off. His voice went flat and rigid. "Look, Conners, you and I didn't get where we are today by blowing smoke down the other guy's windpipe. You're the chief, for heaven's sake. Don't try to shovel your trash at me. Your people peeled through that condominium last Sunday. Did you find a client list in it or not?"

"I can't divulge that information to you," said Conners. His mind whirled. Did Steadman know he was the one who had given Anderson's name to Fontly? If so, Steadman might make it tough on Fontly if he didn't cooperate. But, no way could he give him Steele's name. Steadman might get mad at him if he didn't help, but Steele might destroy him if he did. Gotta respect Steadman, but gotta fear Steele. Everyone with sense does. I can't fight Steele. He's retired more than one public figure who crossed him.

"That's a dodge, Frank, and you know it. You divulge information all the time when it fits your purposes. All I'm asking you to do is tell me if one name turned up in the investigation. I don't plan to print it unless you give the O.K."

"If you're not going to use it, then what's your interest?"

"Let's just say I have a personal reason for wanting what you know about this individual."

"That's not good enough, Mr. Steadman. I ask you to respect the investigation at this point."

Steadman saw the dead end and decided to blast through it. "Frank, I didn't want to do this, but you leave me no choice. Do you remember a night in August nine years ago at the Fairborne Hotel?"

"What night do you mean? Nine years was a long time ago."

"Let's just say it was a night filled with surprises for you."

Conners remembered the night, all right. Never would forget it. His career almost went down the toilet that night. If the Mayor hadn't intervened and stopped the arrest, the boys at Ninth Street Station would have roasted him with a solicitation charge. "Could you be more specific?" he hedged.

"If you insist. You were caught in a prostitution sweep with a girl young enough to wear pigtails. Ninth Street cops pulled you in and were about to make a public spectacle of you when the mayor stepped in and shut down the charges. Does that jog your memory?"

Conners cursed silently and stopped patting on his stomach. He tugged his shirt collar instead, trying to loosen the rough edges of a noose slipping around his neck. "Yeah, I think it does. How did you know about that? And what does it have to do with the Reese case?"

Steadman answered both questions. "I know about it because Randy Fontly called me at 2 A.M. and asked me to help you two clowns. So, I called the mayor and the mayor made a deal and the whole episode disappeared. Except for my files."

Conners recognized the threat but wanted Steadman to play out his hand. "So, what does a nine-year-old arrest have to do with anything happening today?"

"I hoped I wouldn't have to square dance with you, Frank, but you seem bound and determined to make this difficult. If you don't give me what I want, I'll feel obliged to publish a story about a police chief and his arrest for solicitation."

Conners refused to buckle. "Don't make me laugh, Steadman! Nobody in their right minds will pay any attention to a nine-year-old charge and the statute of limitations ran out a long time ago."

"You must think I'm senile, Conners. I wouldn't do this to get a conviction, just to embarrass you. Don't you have three grandchildren?"

"That's low, Steadman."

"Wise up, Conners," Steadman growled. "I don't want to hurt you or your family. I just want one name and I want it bad enough to run a useless story about a good cop with a skeleton in his closet. You get my drift? Either give me the name or get ready to answer a lot of questions. I promise you, it won't be pretty. A police chief investigating the death of a prostitute having to defend himself against charges he solicited an under-aged prostitute. It won't get you jail time, but it will get you headlines and it might even get you early retirement."

Conners patted his stomach again. He didn't know Steadman too well and he couldn't tell if he was bluffing or not. But he couldn't chance it. Either way, he was probably ruined. The only hope he had rested in Steadman's fairness. He had to trust him not to release the name.

"If I tell you what we've turned up, what happens to that file of yours?"

"I burn it today," said Steadman.

"Can I count on that?"

"Ask Fontly, Frank. He'll tell you I'm a man of my word."

Conners caved in. Already knowing how Steadman would reply, he asked, "What name do you want to check?"

"Tell me if the name 'Walt Litske' has turned up in the investigation," said Nelson, swallowing his excitement.

"Could you repeat that?" asked Conners. "I didn't get the last name."

"Litske, Walt Litske."

He didn't ask for Steele! Conners jumped up from his seat and grabbed his pipe and stuck it into his mouth. He might make retirement after all. "Just a minute, Mr. Steadman. Let me check."

He grabbed the blue book from his desk drawer and flipped through its pages, looking for 'Litske.' On the third page he found it. Cradling the phone under his chin and holding the book open with his hands, he spoke, "Yes, I have that name in the book, Mr. Steadman."

"Tell me if an address or phone number is listed beside it."

Conners smiled and his grin wrapped around the stem of his pipe. "Yeah, here it is. Two numbers are listed, but no address."

"Give me those numbers."

Conners didn't hesitate. "First one is 555-3217. Second is 555-8989."

"Anything else listed by the name?"

"No, Mr. Steadman. Nothing at all."

Both men paused for a moment, then Steadman closed the conversation. "Thanks, Frank. The file in my office no longer exists. I think that covers it."

"I think so too."

The phones clicked back into place. Conners slumped forward in his chair, a soggy rag, drenched with sweat. Worn out but thankful he had survived. Three more years until retirement. He hoped it would pass quickly.

CHAPTER

20

A little less than an hour after she left his office, Debbi walked back past Stan's secretary and through his door. She took her place on his leather sofa again, naturally this time, like she belonged there, sitting demurely with her trim legs placed close together, and her hands clasped in her lap.

Speaking as co-conspirators, he questioned her, "You make contact with Broadus yet?"

"No, not yet. The sarge at Peachtree tells me she's not in. Seems she stayed up most of the night and hasn't slept in about two days. He also said they've started a house to house search in Cascade. Broadus might go straight there and not check in at the station."

"Anything turn up on that search?"

"Nothing reported. They just got started a little while ago."

Stan leaned in closer as his voice dropped even lower. "I just got a report from Steadman. He contacted Frank Conners, chief at Peachtree, and Conners folded. He got two numbers on Litske."

Stan handed Debbi a piece of yellow paper and she read the scribbled numbers. "Stan," she said, suddenly crestfallen, "Burke has two numbers too. What if these are the same ones?"

"Nothing we can do if they are. We'll just have to try them and see."

"But I'm scared."

"Of what?"

"That no one will answer. Or that someone will answer. I don't know. I've just never done anything like this."

"Who has?"

"You haven't?"

"No," he smiled. "I've covered hundreds of stories but never one where I actually ended up working with an alleged murderer trying to prove his innocence. I'm a first timer just like you are in this."

Debbi reached to Stan's desk and uncradled the phone. "Nothing to lose," she said.

"Nothing at all."

She dialed. 555-3217. The metallic voice of a computerized operator dashed her hopes. She hung up quickly, shaking her head at Stan.

She punched out the second number. She waited nervously as it rang, absent-mindedly twirling her fingers through her silky hair. Once. Twice. Three times. Past the time when a computerized operator normally answered. Six times she listened to it jangle. Then she heard a click.

"Hello," said a cheery voice. "Senator Raymond Steele's office. May I help you?"

Confused, Debbi stammered, "Excuse me, I, uh, this is Debbi Meyer with the *Atlanta Independent*. I was trying to reach Mr. Walt Litske. I must have the wrong number."

Eagerly, the voice tried to help, "Who did you say you wanted to reach?"

"Never mind," countered Debbi lamely. "Whose office did you say this was?"

"This is the Atlanta office of Senator Raymond Steele. Anything else we can do to help you, Ms. Meyer?"

"No, don't think so, thank you." Debbi dropped the receiver into its beige cradle, tilted her head at Stan and ran her tongue over her lower lip.

Impatiently, he queried her, "Who was that?"

"They said it was the office of Raymond Steele."

"Senator Raymond Steele?" It was Stan's turn to show confusion. "I don't know anyone else by that name. Do you?"

"No, not that I can think of. Are you sure they said Senator Raymond Steele?"

"Positively sure. What do you think it means, Stan? Why would Steele's number turn up in Reese's apartment beside Walt Litske's name?"

Stan chuckled. "Apparently, the Senator enjoyed at least one vice. No other reason for it to be there."

Incredulous, Debbi turned devil's advocate. "That's hard to believe. Steele has built his entire career on the back of old-fashioned morality. That's his platform—put prayer back in the schools, imprison homosexuals, stop pornography, ban books which contain curse words, outlaw R-rated films and put a ratings system on records. He's the darling of the religious right."

"I know all that, Debbi. Rumors say he plans to run for president on just that platform. He attends church faithfully, even teaches a Sunday school class. And he's a regular on the National Prayer Breakfast circuit."

"He sure has plenty of loyalists."

"Sure, he does. Why not? Lots of folks want crime controlled, a strong national defense, abortion on demand defunded by the government, and pornographers jailed."

"Lots of folks might want that, but Steele seems a little extreme in his methods, doesn't he? Life without parole for pornographers; the death penalty for drug dealers; prison sentences for women who have abortions."

"Methods may need to fit the situation," said Stan.

"You mean if it takes certain means to accomplish certain ends, then that makes the means O.K.?"

"I don't know if I'd go that far, but I would say Steele's methods often get results when no one else's does."

"So you think his number in Reese's book is a mistake? That he couldn't have been a client of hers?"

Stan doubled back on her. "Could be, but not necessarily. If a preacher or two can get caught with his pants down, I don't suppose it's too hard a stretch to think a senator might too. Seems to me we've turned up as many wayward senators in the last few years as we have fallen preachers."

"Then you think he might be one of Reese's customers?" Debbi narrowed her green eyes at Stan, exasperated at his equivocation.

"I'm not sure," he said, leaving her hanging.

"Then what should we do?" She almost stomped her foot at his fence-straddling, but decided against it as unladylike.

"I think we do what any good reporter does. We check it out." Stan picked up a pencil and pad. "We consider the options. Why would Steele's number show up in Reese's book?"

"Reese could have copied down the wrong number. It might be a simple writing error."

Stan wrote down her theory. "What else?"

"Steele might be a client."

"Keep going."

"Steele and Walt might be connected."

"How so?"

"Both are prominent members of Atlanta society. Walt a former football player. Steele a senator. It wouldn't be illogical to assume they met somewhere in the last few years."

"Anything else?"

Debbi twirled her hair again, first in one direction and then in the other, like she always did when she found herself under pressure. She pulled the strands into her mouth, sucking on them, making them wet with her spittle, shiny and matted.

"Maybe Walt and Steele were connected politically. Or perhaps Walt worked for him. Maybe Steele's a football fan and Walt knew him from his playing days."

"That should cover most of the possibilities." Stan pointed his pencil at her, halting her considerations. "Now we need to test these theories."

"How do we do that?"

"We set up a meeting with Steele."

"You mean we just make an appointment, tell him we found his number in a dead prostitute's client book and ask him how it got there?"

"Yeah, something like that."

"Won't he deny any knowledge of it?"

"Probably."

"What happens if he does?"

"We use the fourth method of investigative reporting," said Stan.

Debbi sorted through her mind, recalling the lessons Stan gave her that morning. "The first was money, the second theft, the third sex, and the fourth a threat, I think. How do we threaten Steele?"

"That's obvious, don't you think?"

"We tell him we'll print what we have unless he talks to us."

"You got it!"

Debbi pursed her lips. "But didn't you say Mr. Steadman instructed us not to divulge the information Conners gave us?"

"Nelson told us not to print Litske's name in the paper until Conners told us we could. As far as Conners knows, Litske has no connection to Steele. We won't be breaking any promise Nelson made about Litske. Besides that, we'll be bluffing at first anyway."

"Bluffing? You mean you might not use the information on Steele?"

"Maybe not."

Debbi shook her head in confusion. "Why wouldn't we use it?" Stan didn't answer her for several beats. She watched him as his face turned white and hard, a concrete slab face—chalky. The smell of fear suddenly drenched the room, seeped into her clothes, clogged her nostrils and shoved itself down her throat.

Stan dropped his pencil onto his desk and wearily pushed himself from his seat. He picked up the picture of his family and launched into a speech, as if talking to his wife. "Nobody prints negative information about Raymond Steele unless they know for sure they have the goods on him. He's got as much power in Georgia as God and he's a lot meaner in how he uses it. If we print some non-verifiable story about Steele, he'll put our paper out of business in a week."

He gingerly placed the picture back into its spot and stuffed his hands into his pockets.

"Are you scared of Steele?" Debbi asked softly.

Stan nodded. "You could say that. I'm scared for the paper and for the people who make their living from it. Plus," and here Stan searched for the right flavor for his words, "I'm scared for some reason I can't pinpoint, like I think Steele is dangerous, but don't know why. When I think of Steele I get a funny image in my mind."

"What image is that?"

"You're going to think I'm crazy."

"No, I won't," said Debbi. "You didn't think I was crazy when I told you I wanted to help Anderson."

Stan's voice shifted into a whisper. "Steele reminds me of a stray dog that turned up at my house when I was about 8 years old." Stan stopped, not wanting to go on.

"I'm listening," encouraged Debbi.

"That dog was starving. His ribs bulged out from his sides like he hadn't eaten for weeks. Red streaks shot through his eyes and most of his teeth had fallen out. He staggered into my yard and fell down. He had gashes across his back where someone had beaten him. When I rubbed my hands across his back, dried blood peeled off under my fingers."

Stan's memory slid back to the day when he first realized what evil meant. Hating the memory, he shoved the picture back into the closet, closing off the frames clicking through his mind.

Debbi asked gently, "How does that dog remind you of Steele?"

"It doesn't directly. But it reminds me of the victims of Nazi concentration camps I saw as a young man after World War II. That starving dog and those starving people wore the same marks of abuse and pain. Whenever I remember one, I always recall the other."

"Forgive me for not understanding, Stan, but I still don't see the connection to Steele."

Stan nodded. "It's easy, really. That stray reminds me of the Holocaust victims. And those victims cause me to remember the Nazis. That's what I think of when I think of Steele. Nazis—power driven by anger."

"That *is* a little crazy, Stan. Steele's a paragon of virtue to millions of people. They want him to be the next president. Many think that he's the only man with enough courage to clean up the streets and establish law and order again in this country. Lots of people would die for him."

Stan sadly agreed, "Lots of people died for Hitler too."

The phone jangled. Annoyed, Stan snapped it off the hooks.

"I told you no calls," he insisted.

"Sorry, sir, but the caller said it was urgent for him to reach Miss Meyer."

"Who's calling?"

"He refused to give his name to anyone but Miss Meyer. You want me to get a number?"

Stan turned to Debbi. "A man on the other end says he needs to talk to you. Says it's urgent and won't give his name to anyone but you. You want to take it?"

"Burke!" said Debbi, looking at her watch. It wasn't noon yet, the time they'd agreed on last night for him to call, but it had to be him. Who else would insist on talking to her and not give his name?

Taking the phone, she wondered what had happened. Had he changed his mind? Had he contacted Walt somehow?

"Hello," she said, "This is Debbi Meyer."

"Ms. Meyer, are you alone?"

It wasn't Burke. She racked her brain, trying to recognize the voice. "No, I'm not alone, but it's O.K. What can I do for you?"

The caller helped her remember. "Look, this is Cody Stimson, Burke Anderson's friend. I met you last night, didn't give you my name then. No reason."

Debbi pulled a strand of hair into her mouth and her eyes widened as Cody spurted out a jet of words. "You need to listen to me if you want to help Burke. I'm at the police station. They found my name in Burke's files at the church. I'm not under arrest or anything, but they are going to question me in a few minutes. They intercepted me up at a roadblock this morning as I drove to work. I haven't told them a thing, not even where I live. And I don't have an address listed anywhere. They're trying to track down my boss since I was in his truck, but so far they've had no luck. I don't have a phone at my place so I can't get to Burke myself. You've got to warn him. I'll have to cooperate sooner or later, I've got a drug record. Or they'll find my boss and he'll tell them where I live, or they'll find the place on their house to house search. You've got to warn him!"

The jet of words landed and Cody stopped, breathless.

His urgency infected Debbi. "I'll warn him," she soothed. "I promise. But you'll have to tell me where you live. I'll drive out there."

As Cody gave her the directions, Debbi checked the time. It was already 11:20. "Cody," she asked, "how's Burke planning on getting to a phone?"

"He's going to run from my place to the interstate."

"How far is that?"

"About seven miles."

"Can he do that?"

"Sure, he runs all the time. Has done some marathons."

"Is the road safe?"

"It's safer running than driving. It's a rural road, with plenty of trees for cover. He can run practically the whole way and never have to come out where any cars are."

Debbi made a quick calculation. "Well, Cody, if your place is 7 miles from the phone, and if he plans to call me by noon, then he's already left the apartment. I can't reach him before he calls."

"You wait on him to call, then," Cody pleaded. "And tell him he can't go back to my place. I'll have to cooperate or end up in worse trouble than I am."

"I'll wait on him to call," said Debbi, "and we'll figure out what to do next."

"Thanks," said Cody. The phone clicked dead.

* * * * *

Fourteen miles away, the diminutive Sonny Flake, chief of staff for Senator Raymond Steele, held a computer printout in one hand and an eighteenth-century Crown Darby coffee cup in the other. Irish coffee filled the cup and Flake primly sipped it. Between the gentle taste of his favorite coffee and the stark truth of the figures on the printout, he had a real warm feeling inside.

Senator Steele led his Democratic challenger by almost 35 points in the latest poll and the election was almost here. Better yet, in a

hypothetical, three-way contest between the likely Republican nomi-
nees for president, Steele topped the field by 8 points. Though it was
two years before the presidential election, it wasn't too early to get
strategy, people and money in place. Flake had already started the
process. He imagined himself waking up every morning in the White
House, the power behind the throne. He inhaled the aroma of the coffee
and leaned back.

The buzz of the phone destroyed his concentration. He answered
it. "Look, Sylvia, I told you not to interrupt me."

"Sorry, Sonny, but I thought it was important."

"It better be."

"I just got a call from a Debbi Meyer, a reporter with the *Independent.* She asked for Walt Litske and seemed real surprised when I
told her this was Senator Steele's office."

Sonny leaned up and put his coffee cup down. "What did you tell
her?"

"Absolutely nothing. I know how you feel about reporters."

"Good. The less the reporters know, the better. If she calls back,
switch her to me."

Sonny picked up his cup again and poured a drink of coffee
through his mouse-like lips. He pecked at the keyboard on the computer
on his desk, logging into a personnel file. He pulled up the name of
Randy Fontly and dialed the number listed on the screen.

"*Atlanta Independent.*"

"Get me Randy Fontly."

"Hold on, please."

"Fontly here."

"Randy, Sonny Flake. "How ya doin'?"

"Not bad, guy, but this is a surprise. What's up?"

"Who's Debbi Meyer?"

"A kid reporter who convinced Wraps to let her write an editorial
on the Anderson-Reese murder case. She's bright and beautiful and I
think I'm going to hate her."

"Anything else?"

"Yeah, one more thing. Word is she's tough. Digs in on something
and doesn't give up."

"Sounds like bad news."

"Yeah, but cute as a button."

"Your mind is always on the bottom line, isn't it, Randy?"

"Yeah, and I hope it never leaves it."

"Talk to you later, Fontly."

Sonny wrapped his short fingers around his favorite cup and leaned back again. Debbi Meyer. He'd have to deal with her. He knew he would.

PART

III

A DOUBTFUL FRIEND IS WORSE THAN A

CERTAIN ENEMY.

LET A MAN BE ONE OR THE OTHER

AND WE THEN KNOW HOW TO MEET HIM.

Aesop

GREATER LOVE HATH NO MAN

THAN THIS,

THAT A MAN LAY DOWN HIS LIFE

FOR HIS FRIENDS.

Jesus

CHAPTER

21

An hour and twenty minutes before Broadus and Mays pulled their car under the pecan tree in Cody's yard, Burke and Biscuit jogged away from it. Wearing gray sweats with gym shorts under them, a lightweight T-shirt, and a waist pouch filled with dog food, a water bottle and $78, Burke eased himself into a steady pace. Out of habit, he punched the clock on his digital watch.

Few cars used the weather-beaten road between Cody's place and the interstate and Burke ducked off the side of the black asphalt into the cathedral pines when he heard one approach. The biggest problem he had was getting Biscuit to keep up. He couldn't leave his best friend behind, but the inquisitive retriever caused delays when he lagged back. So, Burke had to stop more than once and urge his wayward buddy to stay beside him.

Almost 75 minutes after starting, Burke stopped the timer on his watch and paused to slow his breathing. He was at the store. He grabbed Biscuit's collar and tugged him cautiously toward the phone booth. Pulling a quarter and Meyer's phone number from his pocket, he dialed the number. While it rang he tugged his clammy sweatband off his forehead.

The switchboard operater connected him to Meyer.

"Hello," she said. He recognized her voice.

"Debbi Meyer?" Just to make sure.

"Yes, is this Burke?"

"Yeah, it is." Not sure what to say next, he paused.

She rescued him. "Are you O.K.?"

"Yeah, other than the fact I just ran seven miles. I'm a little tired, but not too bad. You find out anything about Litske?"

"Not much yet," she said, hurriedly, "but I've got something else to tell you."

"What's up?" he asked, hearing fear in her voice.

"They picked Cody up a little while ago. They found his name in your church files. He hasn't told them anything, not even where he lives. But, they'll find out soon enough so you can't go back to his place. The police may already be there."

Burke slumped backward against the housing which cradled the phone. Defeated. A sparrow flying into the teeth of a hurricane.

"Burke, you still there?"

"Yeah, still here. Nowhere else to be. Can't go back to Cody's, can't go back to Cascade. Can't go anywhere, except to the police maybe, to give myself up."

For several moments, silence fell over him. Debbi didn't say anything either. Burke wondered what she was thinking when she finally spoke, she sounded insistent, panicky almost.

"You can't give yourself up, Burke!" She said it as a command.

"What else can I do? I don't have anywhere to go, nowhere to hide."

"Do you want to give up? To face a trial, to be a public spectacle?"

"Of course not," he said, "but I don't know where to turn."

Debbi twisted her hair. "I know where you can go. You can come to my place."

"I can't ask you to do that."

"You're not asking. I'm offering. Fact is, I'm insisting."

"Why would you do this?"

"'Cause I want your story and I'm not going to let you foul it up for me."

"I'll give you the story anyway."

"There's more to it now, Burke. More than just you and Walt. I've connected Walt to Raymond Steele. If we can find Walt, we might also find how Steele fits into it. I've got politics, religion, sex, sports, and murder in one story. It doesn't get any better than this."

"You're doing it for the story then?"

"Yeah."

"That's all?"

Debbi knew what Burke wanted to hear. She said it.

"No, that's not all."

"Why else?"

"'Cause I think you're innocent."

He exhaled deeply and squeezed his eyes shut. Those were the words he needed to hear. They reminded him of others who believed in him, too, of Cody and Bill and Barbara, of his mom and dad and brother. Yeah, some assumed him guilty, but not all.

Without somebody believing in him, he couldn't go on. But with Debbi Meyer and the others believing in him, he could go on forever.

"Then I won't give up," he said.

"That's the spirit. Now, tell me where you are and I'll pick you up."

"You can't pick me up," he said. "They're searching every car that comes in and out of Cascade."

"How will you get here then? Can you hitchhike?"

"No, same problem," he said, making a quick calculation of the distance in his mind. "I'll have to run."

"Run? How? It's over 35 miles from where you are. You can't do that. It'll take all day and all night."

"I've got nothing else on my calendar today," said Burke. Hope welled up in him. "Besides, I don't have a choice, do I? Except to give up."

"Anything but that," she said.

"Then give me your address," said Burke. "If it's under forty miles and if I don't get caught, I should get there sometime early tomorrow morning."

Debbi nodded, "O.K.—the address is 1517 Buckhead Square. It's about three miles out on 285 toward the stadium. Take the Marriott Street exit, turn left and go two blocks. You can't miss the complex."

Burke repeated the directions for her, visualizing them as he talked, notching them in his memory. He knew the area, not far from Wesley Seminary.

"O.K.," he said, "I've got it. Here's what I'll try to do. I think I can make another 15 miles or so today, if I keep an easy pace. The hardest part will be the constant stopping and starting I'll have to do to hide from cars. But, by staying on the back roads, I should get to the outskirts of Atlanta by early evening. I'll stop at a cheap motel—one where they don't ask for an I.D., and rest for a few hours. Then, I'll try to run the rest of the way after dark. I don't know how long it'll take—with stops to rest and about a ten-minute-mile pace, I'll count on 10-15 hours—if I can make it at all. I'll do the best I can to make it by early morning. If I'm not there by daylight . . ." Burke's voice trailed off.

"You'll be here."

"We'll see." He paused. "Debbi?"

"Yeah?"

"Thanks."

"Just doing my job," she said. "No thanks required."

Burke eased the phone into its hook and bent over and took Biscuit's head with both hands. He looked into the placid eyes of his five-year-old friend. "Biscuit, this is serious and I'm going to need your help. I need you to stay up with me. No chasing women today or tonight. Can you do it?"

Biscuit whined soulfully.

"O.K., big guy. We gotta go." Burke lifted his head and looked toward Atlanta, capital of Georgia—more than that, capital of the New South, city of Olympian dreams, city of steel and concrete, city of blood and violence, city of hope for him, city of destiny. He began to run, settling into the slog of the marathoner. All afternoon long he ran—over blacktop country roads, with bucket-sized chuckholes in the middle of them, and dead possums on the sides. He ran mechanically, through Millwood and Pigeon Foot, and Cordoba and Pineville—towns without redlights, towns where local grocers were weathermen and druggists, too, towns where white-framed post offices were the biggest buildings. Towns where chewing tobacco was the national sport and Dixie the national anthem, towns where fried chicken was king and Dolly Parton queen, towns where no one was a stranger and strangers were visitors, towns where babies cried in church—towns where God meant wrath and liquor meant sin.

As he ran, his mind took on a life of its own, separate from his body, freed from it, soaring above it—higher and higher it went, climbing, climbing into heights the body couldn't imagine. Into celestial realms, godly realms. Realms where faith was born and doubts went to die.

He crashed back to earth. His doubts weren't dead. No, they were alive, mixed in with his faith—given birth by too many deaths. Deaths of good people who died too young, deaths with no explanation and no purpose. Carol Reese dead. Why? No answer as he ran. No answer period. For her or for anyone else. God why? No answer. If no answer then doubt. Death and doubt. Faith and doubt. Burke knew them all well, up close and personal. He ran faster, trying to leave the doubts behind.

He stopped only to relieve himself in the trees beside the snaking roads, to duck away from approaching cars, to hold a tiring golden retriever to his side and pat him gently, and to buy a drink at a gas station every hour or so. Burke ran through the four hours which Mays and Broadus spent in Cascade discovering his clothes and car at Cody's; he ran through the three hours they spent unsuccessfully interrogating Cody back at Peachtree Station. He ran through the time Debbi spent talking to Stan and trying to contact Broadus and visiting by phone with his parents and friends, putting together a profile of him for the Wednesday morning paper. Through the dancing shadows of the dying day, he ran the shadows right out of life, ran them right into the darkness and beyond.

He ran, right to the outskirts of Atlanta, on the fuel of fear and hope. He ran past that fuel into nothing, going on through muscle memory, the memory that told one foot to plod ahead of another. He ran to a boxcar motel where they asked for cash up front, a motel where they rented rooms by the hour. Burke splashed down the $19.95 requested by the filthy attendant, took the key to room 21 and, fifteen minutes later, after a cold, weak shower, collapsed into bed. Biscuit lay exhausted at his feet, breathing raggedly.

Four hours later Burke sat up, instantly awake. The metallic sheen of a full moon struck his face through the opened blinds and lighted his watch as he checked the time—almost 11. His stomach growled insistently, reminding him he hadn't eaten anything since morning. He placed his feet over the side of the bed, rubbed the sleep out of his eyes and rocked forward to a standing position. Though wobbly, he slipped into his stiff sweatpants and T-shirt and pulled a phone book from the top of the lamp table. Flipping through the book, Burke spotted the number of a pizza house and ordered a delivery.

He fed Biscuit the dogfood from his belly bag and watered him from the bathtub. An hour later, Burke swallowed the last slice of pepperoni and the last drop of a giant Coke. He washed his hands and shoved his red headband back over his head. Though he dreaded the thought of it, he knew he had to move. Debbi was waiting and time was running out. Slipping his shoes onto his sore feet, he winced as he touched a blister on his left heel.

Time to run again. Somewhere between fifteen to twenty more miles to Meyer's. If nothing happened, he could get there before daylight. Outside, under the flashing lights of the motel neon, he put his right foot in front of his left one and began again—his body groaning in protest, but his mind and heart pushing him forward.

He coaxed a reluctant Biscuit along. "Got no choice, boy. Got to keep going." He moved slowly toward Debbi's and his golden retriever limped with him. Nothing else to do, but run. Run from the police. Run from the pain. Run from yesterday, away from his own personal agony, from his guilt. Run. He ran through the outskirts of Atlanta, then into the black rim of the semi-sleeping city. Two hours flowed into four and Burke passed the point of thought; he moved into the between world—

between reality and dreams. Couldn't tell the difference between the two. Just one foot in front of the other. Not more than five miles left to run. Just keep pounding, pounding, running. That's all he had to do. Ignore everything else. The surroundings. The distance come. The distance yet to go. Ignore it all. The voices in his mind calling to him. Calling him to stop. Calling to him. . . .

"Hey, man, what'cha doin' down here? This is our turf. No white boy runs through our turf without paying the toll."

Burke snapped to attention. The voices weren't in his dreams. They were real and they were close to him. Wildly, he looked to his left, the source of the voices. "What'cha doin', man? This ain't your turf. You're in the wrong place at the wrong time."

Burke searched for Biscuit, then heard him growl. The voices drowned out the comforting sound.

"Where'd you get those shoes, man?"

The voices were closer to him, threatening, chasing him as he slogged ahead. "Hold it, man. Listen to me, man. I want those shoes. Pay the toll, man. Yeah, you cross our turf, you got to pay the toll."

A hand reached out at him, then hands grabbed him, six or seven hands jerked him to a stop. He lifted his arms to fight back but his strength was gone and his blows landed like BB's lobbed against an aircraft carrier. He saw a hand evolve into a fist and he watched it crunch into his face. The blood tasted warm as it spurted inside his mouth and he fell, knocked off his unsteady feet. A foot clubbed him in the ribs as his face kissed the pavement.

He heard Biscuit growl again and he tried to help as the great dog hurled its 60 pounds of limping fur into the legs of one of their tormentors. Burke screamed with terror as the tallest boy—the one with a gold glove on his left hand—held a knife up and shoved it down at Biscuit. The knife slithered in and bit Biscuit in the lung and the brave dog's growl collapsed into a gurgle and flecks of blood popped out on his nostrils. Biscuit shook his thick head and his teeth latched onto the boy's leg and gouged the flesh but the golden glove plunged downward again and again and Biscuit let go of his grip. He shuddered, whined, then lay still.

The boy with the golden glove turned back to Burke and laughed. "You go through my turf, you got to pay the toll."

Then they were all on him, pounding his body, their hands like clubs hitting a piece of meat, jerking at his feet, ripping his shoes away and his sweatpants and shirt and stomach pouch—leaving him in his gym shorts and socks, another statistic in Atlanta's crime file. Satisfied, the pack scattered away from him.

Through one torn ear he heard a voice complaining, "Man, can you believe it, these shoes got blood all in them."

"The blisters," thought Burke, as he drifted in and out of consciousness. Funny, as long as he stayed still, he didn't feel any pain, not really, just deadness in his flesh, like someone had chopped off the hurt spots and thrown them away. He curled up into a fetal position, cold and wet from sweat, and wondered where Biscuit was. Burke lay on the side of the road and faded in and out.

Then he saw faces. Faces? Who were those faces? Those two men? A big man, a wide body, a mobile home man. And the second one, nondescript, hidden behind the big man. The second one was any man, except for the bangs in his eyes. Bangs too long. A girl's bangs. Why did he wear them that way? Faces. Who were those two?

Then the third face appeared. A girl's. The girl from his dream. A grinning face that turned grim. Burke recognized it immediately. He watched the life fade out of her face. Seeing her hurt him more than his own swollen mouth. Seeing her face made him glad when he blacked out for good.

CHAPTER

22

Avery, his face covered with the black pepper dots of a morning without shaving, greeted Jackie at the coffee pot at 6 A.M. He didn't look too happy to see her and the feeling was mutual. Only 4 hours of sleep separated them from their second straight midnight visit to the truck stop outside of Cascade. After several hours of interrogation with Cody and a thorough search of the woods around the ex-con's rundown home, they had tried the truck stop one more time.

"Man, you look awful," moaned Jackie as they clunked their heels down the white-tiled hallway, headed for Conner's morning briefing.

"Thanks for the encouragement, friend," Mays shot back. "You don't look too great yourself. I see you've put your hair in a bun. Does that mean you didn't get to wash it last night?"

"It means I haven't washed it in four nights. Getting in at 1 A.M. didn't give me much time to pamper myself with clean hair. If I didn't know better I would swear an oil tanker had crashed in it."

"That's a disgusting thought."

"If you think the thought is disgusting, try combing through the stuff."

They stopped talking and stepped into the Chief's office. Conners stood behind his paper-littered desk, his back turned away from them. He stared out the window and puffed on his pipe.

"Smoking early today, aren't you, Chief?"

"You don't miss much do you, Avery?" Conners said, twisting around and motioning them to sit.

"You don't pay me to miss much, Chief." Avery noted Conners' gruff tone. Conners knows something he's not telling us.

Conners stayed serious, picking a manila folder off his desk and scanning the pages inside it. "Looks like you guys made some progress at the truck stop last night," he said.

"So you've read the morning report?" Jackie said.

"Yep. Says here you found a teenager who picked up a hitchhiker last Friday night near the condos where Reese lived."

Avery jumped in, "Yeah, a nineteen-year-old kid. Said he was driving home sometime around midnight last Friday when a man meeting Anderson's description flagged him down."

"Can he identify Anderson if he saw him?"

"Said he wasn't sure. But he said the guy had dark hair, was a medium build, and he let him off at the Cascade exit."

"That connects him pretty closely to Anderson, doesn't it?"

"Sure does, Chief."

"Anything else from this kid?"

Jackie picked up the ball from Avery. "Yeah, Chief. Two things. First, he said he noticed a ripped knuckle on the right hand, the one next to the passenger door."

"Interesting."

"There's more," said Jackie. "And this is the strange one. The kid said the hitchhiker seemed dazed, almost like a 'zombie,' he put it. He said his eyes were glassy. Said it scared him at first but the guy was so quiet, he figured he was just stoned. He let him out at Cascade and forgot about him."

"He didn't think we would want to know this?"

"I don't know about that. The kid said he'd been hunting all weekend and didn't hear the news about the girl's death until late last night. Then, he didn't know if his information was important or not. He said he stops at the truck stop two or three times a week, in and out of Atlanta."

"Well, his testimony tightens the noose around Anderson a bit more. He was at that condo. Can't question that." The Chief flipped through the report in his hand, as if he hoped to find something he had missed. He lifted his eyes.

"Anything from the Stimson guy?"

"Not a thing," said Mays. "He's clammed up pretty good. We'll hold him on abetting charges but that doesn't help us know where Anderson is now."

"Offer him a deal," said Conners. "He walks if he tells us where

Anderson headed when he left his place. Someone has to be helping him. He couldn't stay out this long on his own."

Conners puffed his pipe and turned to the window again."Do we have any other leads?" he asked.

"What do you mean, Chief?" Mays answered a question with a question.

"Is Anderson still the major suspect?"

Avery glanced at Jackie and arched his eyebrows. "Sure, as far as we know. He's the only one we can place at the scene near the time of the death. The fingerprints we took from his house in Cascade matched those found on Reese's locket and on the glass in her condominium. He had motive and opportunity."

Jackie added. "Plus we picked up a couple of hair follicles from Reese's sofa that coincide with those pulled from a comb in his bathroom."

"Add that to the Bible, the driver of a pickup who can probably identify him, and his flight from his church and you can build a pretty good case," said Mays.

"So, we don't think anyone else was connected?"

Jackie asked, "What'cha getting at, Chief?"

"Are there any more suspects?" Conners puffed harder on his pipe.

"None we know of. Should there be?"

Conners, still by the window, tapped his fingers on his stomach, deciding how far to go. Mays and Broadus deserved to know the full story.

"Have you come across the name of Walt Litske anywhere in your investigation?"

Jackie and Avery locked eyes, surprise registering in both. Mays took the lead. "No, should we have?"

"I don't know."

"Then why ask?"

"First, because Nelson Steadman called me yesterday and wanted to know if we had turned up that name."

"The Nelson Steadman who owns the *Independent*?"

"None other."

"Why would he do that?"

"That's the question I've been asking myself for the past 24 hours. Said it was something personal."

"That could mean almost anything."

"I know."

Jackie, listening to the two men and sensing an undercurrent she couldn't explain, zeroed a question at Conners. "What's the second reason you want to know about Litske?"

"Because his name turned up in Reese's client book."

"Interesting," offered Mays. "Steadman calls and asks you what you know about a man whose name turned up in the dead girl's address file."

"Exactly. The question is 'why.'"

Jackie stayed with her intuition. "How has the *Independent* covered this story? Any different from the other papers?"

"I'm not sure. Haven't paid much attention to it really. Figured one paper would do what they all did."

Mays interjected. "I've noticed one difference. The *Independent* carried an editorial Monday with a warning about jumping to conclusions about someone's guilt. The writer, a young woman named Meyer, suggested we remember the constitutional right of 'innocent until proven guilty.'"

"Sounds rather quaint, doesn't it?" said Conners.

"Yep, but she sounded sincere."

Jackie pulled up from the straight-back chair—her back aching—and started pacing. "So, we've got the owner of a newspaper which runs an editorial suggesting Anderson might be innocent, calling you and asking if we've run across the name of Walt Litske. Sounds like the paper might have something we don't. Sounds like we should add the name of Walt Litske to our investigation."

Conners threw the manila folder onto his desk and wiped his mouth with the back of his hand, "I put the computer guys to work on that early this morning. They should have a license number and a car make for you by now. Find out as you leave."

"One question before we go, Chief."

"What's that?"

"What if they have something important? Do you want us to go back to Cascade or start work on the Litske angle?"

"Make your own judgment," snapped Conners. "I've got other worries right now."

"We'll do just that," Avery said as he and Jackie shot for the door. Conners was already on the telephone, returning the governor's call. And the Mayor had set up a lunch appointment for 11:45. Conners unbuttoned the top of his shirt and tugged down his tie. Three years stretched out like an eternity.

Jackie and Avery poked their heads into the glassed-in room which housed the station's computer data base. Jackie teased Avery. "A computer would be the perfect match for you, Avery. You could match details with each other and see which one noticed the most innocuous facts."

"Those 'innocuous facts,' as you call them, keep us in business," he snorted.

They stood in front of a metal desk and stared down at a pair of glasses wearing a man. "Anything on a Walt Litske yet?" Jackie asked him.

"That the guy the Chief wanted checked out?"

"One and the same."

"Here's the printout." The technician handed them identical copies of a white sheet of paper. The stats lined up on it.

Name: Walter Ivan Litske, Jr.

Age: 27.

Address: Unknown at present.

Phone number: 555-3217.

Occupation: Real Estate Developer

Previous Record: None

License Plate: DOGS 66.

Car Make and Model: 1988 Mercedes. Color: Black.

Avery whistled. "A black Mercedes!"

"Like Metcalf said he saw driving in and out of Cascade on Friday."

"The same. We've turned up something we didn't count on."

"Maybe Anderson didn't do it."

"Maybe not, but don't jump to conclusions. Just because Litske was with him on Friday doesn't mean anything."

"But the two are connected," said Jackie.

"Apparently so."

"I wonder how."

"That's what we're paid to find out. Let's start by checking to see where these two intersect. What do we know about them before last Friday night?"

"We know Anderson's a native of Alabama. He moved to Georgia to attend college at the University. He went from there to Wesley Seminary and he's served as the pastor of the First Methodist Church of Cascade for the last two years or so. That's about it."

"O.K., what do we know about Litske?"

"Nothing more than what's on this sheet. No connection there."

Mays cracked a smile like a man with a secret. "We know a little more than that, Jackie."

Not wanting to appear ignorant, but unable to match Avery's cheeky grin, Jackie simply waited. His smile widened.

Finally, Jackie wilted. "What's behind that smirk, Mays? You've been one step ahead of me this whole case. What do you know?"

"Something I wouldn't expect you to know, Jackie. You're not enslaved to the Georgia Bulldogs like most Georgia males are. Men in Georgia know the names of the players on the Bulldog roster better than they know their own kids. Unless one of those children plays for the Bulldogs. Litske played ball at Georgia. Starred as a linebacker there. Even spent a few years with the Falcons."

"God punished him, huh?" Jackie kidded.

"Yeah, with an injury that ended his career. But, that's not the point."

Jackie summed up. "No, the point is, Litske and Anderson graduated from Georgia the same year. Maybe they knew each other there."

"It's highly possible. But what would a pre-seminary psychology major have in common with a football jock?"

"That's what we're paid to find out."

"Precisely. Jackie, what say we get out to the campus and see what we can uncover?"

"You think that's more important than the house to house?"

"Absolutely. The blue shirts can take care of the search. If anything turns up they'll call us. You ready?"

"Just let me run by the restroom a second. I ran out this morning without a bit of makeup."

"Tell me something I don't know. Makes me ashamed to ride with you. I'm liable to lose my reputation as a ladies' man."

Jackie smiled at Avery's suddenly talkative mood. "You're getting a little mouthy this morning aren't you, Avery? You feeling O.K.?

"Yeah, I'm feeling great. This case is finally taking on some personality."

"A dead prostitute with a preacher as the main suspect wasn't enough personality for you?"

"Not really. Too cut and dried, as you like to say."

"You change your mind about his guilt?"

"Not necessarily. Just glad to get a turn or so in it. Makes it something to chew."

"Well, chew on it in the car. I'll be there in a minute."

Jackie stopped at her desk for her purse, then pirouetted left, back down the hallway toward the women's room. As she walked past

Conners' office she glanced in. He was still at the window, slouching on the ledge, peering out, his pipe cradled in his right hand.

He didn't hear her go by. His mind reeled off in another direction. He felt like he was sliding toward a cliff and his brakes were failing and he was almost off the precipice. Raymond Steele had called him. Dreading the moment he would have to return that call, he waited and hoped it would never come.

CHAPTER

23

D ebbi had finished her family story on Burke and left the *Independent* about 1 in the morning. She had told Stan about her plans to let Burke stay at her place, at least for a day or so. Stan insisted she call him as soon as Anderson arrived and she promised she would. Now, she lay sleeping, her blond hair resting like corn silk on her pillows.

The clanging of the phone shook her awake. Licking her dry lips, she answered hoarsely, "Hello."

"Debbi, this is Stan. Are you alone?"

"Seems like everyone is asking me that lately," she said, rubbing her eyes. "Of course I'm not alone. I've got Mel Gibson here in bed with me."

"It's no time to joke, Debbi. Have you heard the news?"

Debbi reared up in bed and tucked her pillow behind the small of her back. "No, I've been asleep. What's happened? Did they catch Burke?"

"No, worse than that. They found another dead girl. About an hour ago. In a complex less than two miles from yours. Same M.O. as the first two. Beaten, her skull fractured. Cops think she's a prostitute like the others. They're still checking that."

The hair on Debbi's neck raised up; she hugged herself. "Burke's not here yet, Stan."

"I was about to ask you that. When do you expect him?"

"I have no idea. It's hard to know when he'll get here—if he makes it at all."

Stan gave her an order. "Don't let him in if he gets there before I do."

"Why not?" asked Debbi. "There's no way he could have done this. He's had no time."

"No time? Think about it. The one night he's alone since he skipped Cascade and another girl turns up dead. And, get this—she was holding a gold cross in one hand and an American flag in the other. Promise me you won't let him in until I get there. It'll take me at least an hour, but don't let him in. We've gone about as far as we can with this."

Debbi pushed the ends of her hair into her mouth and considered Stan's warning, but she stopped short of making a promise. "Get here as fast as you can," she said. "I'll take care of it if he gets here before you do. If he gets here at all." She dropped the phone before he could object and swung her legs over the side of the canopied bed and hopped up. Hurriedly, she squeezed into a pair of jeans and a pullover blouse, and turned on the coffeepot in the kitchen. Flipping on the television, she plopped down, looking through the channels for updates on the third murder.

Within fifteen minutes, the doorbell rang. At first it startled her that Stan would be so early. She eased herself out of her stuffed chair, walked to the door, reared up on her tiptoes and peeped through the eyeglass. No one was there. Confused, she waited for a second. The bell rang again, pushed twice this time. Debbie pressed her eye to the tiny hole a second time. Again, she saw no one. She crept to her bedroom, picked up her purse and grasped the stock of the Beretta semi-automatic pistol. Quickly, she checked the gun—it was loaded. The bell rang again, insistently, over and over. She held the gun in her trembling right hand and reached for the door knob with her left. Turning the knob, she flung open the door and jumped out of the line of sight. Nothing happened.

Waiting behind the door and still inside the apartment, she yelled, "Stan, is that you?"

A half-groan answered, like a weak cough—a hollow rattle.

Debbi stepped from behind the door, gun poised in front, both hands squeezing it, and peeked around the corner. A mound of flesh leaned against the wall to her left. A mound of discolored flesh, blue and black and red all squeezed in a lump together. Beside the human flesh lay a second hump, a mound of blood and fur.

She dropped the gun to her side and grabbed Burke under his armpits, steadying him against the wall, keeping him from falling.

He mumbled and she pushed her ear up to his lips. "What, Burke? Speak a little louder."

"Who were those men?" he whispered.

"What men?" Debbie looked around but saw no one else.

"Those men," he said, half lifting his arms and pointing down the hallway to the exit.

"There aren't any men, Burke. It's just you and me."

He pointed his arm at the mound of fur and blood. "Under him," he said.

"What?"

"Under my dog. Look under Biscuit!"

Debbi squatted beside the still form. She shoved her hands under the animal's back and and felt warm blood stick to her fingers. She gently lifted him, then pulled him away from the wall.

She couldn't believe her eyes. Four red roses centered in a crystal vase. Confused, Debbi looked up at Burke just in time to see him collapse to the floor.

* * * * *

A little less than an hour later Burke stirred and opened his eyes. He was lying on a cloth sofa and Debbi sat in a rocking chair beside it staring at him. He grimaced, and pushed the ziploc bag full of ice away from his left cheek. "That's freezing," he mumbled.

Relieved he was alive enough to complain, Debbi pulled the compress away. "Sorry, but I'm trying to help. Your face is swollen."

Burke struggled to sit upright. "I know, and I'm not complaining."

"You'd better not. It's me or nothing right now."

"I know," said Burke, "And I'm grateful." He closed his eyes again. "I didn't think I'd get here. Everything went O.K. for awhile, but a couple of hours ago a gang grabbed me, beat me, took my clothes, my shoes. Knocked me out and stabbed Biscuit. They left us for dead. I don't know how I got here."

"But you did," said Debbi. "And I'm going to take care of you. I don't know about your dog. He's lost a lot of blood. We'll need to get him to a vet soon. But, you've got to get some rest first." She rocked forward to stand up but Burke grabbed her by the arm and tried to pull himself up.

"Where's Biscuit?"

Debbi pushed his hand away. "You can't get up, you're beat up too badly."

"Debbi, I appreciate what you're doing, but if my dog's dying, I don't want him dying by himself. Now will you tell me where he is or do I search this place myself until I find him?"

"O.K.," she agreed. "But let me help you." She raised him up and steered him to the laundry room where Biscuit lay on an old towel on the floor. Debbi stepped back and Burke eased himself down by the dog. Biscuit struggled to lift his head, but failed and a thin whine escaped his lips. Burke cupped Biscuit's jaw with his hands and lifted his head for him and placed it in his lap. The dog's tongue rolled out like a thick string and stuck in the corner of his gaping mouth. Slowly Burke rubbed him behind the ears and Bicuit's eyes sparkled for a short second, then glazed over again.

* * * * *

For a long while, no one said anything. Debbi sat still and watched Burke hold his companion. Out of nowhere it seemed, Burke began to sing softly and Debbi listened to the tenderness in his soulful voice. *I am a poor, wayfarin' stranger, wanderin' through this world of woe. But there's no sickness, no toil or danger, in that bright land to which I go.*

Burke sang the words gently and the big dog heard them as they guided him to a land where fire hydrants are plentiful and no dog ever gets hit by a car and all dogs have masters who scratch them behind the ears. Biscuit took a big breath, his chest shook twice and his breath stopped. Burke leaned over and hugged him for the last time.

Debbi continued to watch Burke pull his red headband off and lay it on the floor. Then he placed Biscuit's head ever so carefully onto the cloth headrest. For several minutes he sat still by his friend, his eyes washed by tears. Debbi thought she saw his lips move, and she wondered if Burke was praying, but she didn't dare ask. Then, he opened his eyes and pushed himself up off the floor. He didn't say anything, just staggered back to the sofa and stretched back out and closed his eyes again.

"Just rest," Debbi said. "I'll get some water to wash you. Then some food."

He nodded.

She ran to the bathroom and pulled a plastic bucket from beneath the sink and filled it with warm water. A fresh washcloth and a bar of soap, a tube of ointment for cuts and bruises and a hairbrush completed her kit. Leaving it beside Burke, she hustled to the kitchen, pulled a bottle of Gatorade from the refrigerator, and crushed two bananas in a bowl. Back with Burke, she perched on the edge of the sofa as she lifted his head and pushed the drink to his lips. He gulped it down, almost a third of the bottle, before he paused for breath. He refused the bananas. "I don't think I can eat yet," he said.

"Just rest some more," Debbi encouraged, "I'm going to clean you up."

He didn't argue. She rubbed over his face first, noting again his sharply etched chin and round cheek bones. She cleaned dried blood and dirt off his lips and placed the ice pack back on his cheek. She wasn't sure, but nothing on his face seemed broken. A gash over his right eye and a busted lip were the worst of his injuries.

Next, she washed his arms with soap, wiping away flaky sweat and sand from his elbows and forearms. She noticed the firm tone of his chest as she sponged him off. Both his sides were swollen. "You might have broken ribs."

He winced and moaned softly as she picked up his feet. Her fingers traced over the thin lacerations which marked them, red map lines cut through the bottoms where he'd run the last few miles without shoes. His legs were muscled, defined with taut calves and stout thighs.

Finished, Debbi stopped to appraise him. Stamina. Discipline. Strong will. Courage. How else could he have made it? The doorbell rang. Burke didn't budge. He was asleep.

Stan! She'd forgotten he was coming. She jumped up and hustled to the door and opened it. Stan pushed her aside and charged into the room. "Is he here?"

Debbi put her finger to her lips. "Shush." She pointed to the sofa.

Seeing Burke, Stan whispered angrily, "I told you not to let him in until I got here!"

"Stan, look at him. He's not exactly a threat. He could barely walk when he got here. He's run over 40 miles in the last 24 hours and a gang mugged him just a few hours ago. I couldn't leave him outside the door anyway. Someone would've seen him and called the police."

Stan walked to the sofa and leaned over Burke. "What's the plan now?" he asked Debbi.

"I give him a couple of hours to recover. Then I wake him and see if he knows anything about Steele and Litske. That's my plan anyway. You got a better idea?"

"Can't say I have," said Stan. "But, I can't stay long. I'm supposed to meet Nelson for breakfast and I need to go by the paper before I do. Are you sure you're O.K.?"

Debbi pointed to Burke. "Do you think he's dangerous?"

Stan shook his head. "No."

"O.K., so we give him some time to rest. Want a cup of coffee?"

"No, already had three."

Stan pulled a manila folder from his coat and tossed it to Debbi. "You might want to look at this while you wait."

"What's this?"

"Don't ask questions. Just read it."

Debbi obeyed him, taking a seat beside the window, letting the fresh sunlight illuminate the pages of the police report Stan had given her. Stan sat down and waited for her to finish. Within minutes, she lowered the report. "Where'd you get this?"

"I do have my sources, remember?"

"I'm sure you do. But it doesn't tell us much more than we already know, does it?"

"Well, maybe a little more. Not only did Reese have contusions on her face, but she had a gash in her head where she crashed into a table. That's what actually killed her. Forensics found bits of hair and flesh on the edge of a table in the living area. They also found hair and skin under her nails."

"Nothing here to prove or disprove who killed her though," said Debbi.

"No, nothing concrete."

Debbi pulled a strand of hair into her mouth and sucked on it as she reread a section of the report. "Stan, what do you make of this?"

"What?" he asked.

"This American flag business."

"I don't know. Kinda quirky if you ask me."

"Did the first girl have one?"

"Don't know. I haven't seen the report."

"What about the death last night?"

"Yep, according to the story."

"And we know Reese did."

"That's what the report says. Why so much interest in a flag?"

Debbi stepped into her bedroom and then back out. She held the bud vase with the four roses in it in her hand. Shoved into the vase behind them stood an American flag. Three dead girls. She could make four.

* * * * *

Debbi shook Burke awake two hours after Stan left. The flag had baffled both of them. It was obviously a warning, they agreed, but they had no idea who sent it. Stan ordered her to keep her door locked and stay put until he returned.

Debbi nudged Burke.

He opened his eyes and squinted as the sun hit his face. "Yeah, I'm awake."

"How you feeling?"

"Like I'm alive but wished I was dead," he tried to joke but failed as a sharp pain sliced through his head. "You got any aspirin?"

"Yeah, just a minute," said Debbi.

Burke studied the room as Debbi gave him the pain reliever.

"You feel like talking yet?"

"I think so," he said. "If I can get something to drink, a bite to eat and a bath I might get some strength back. I'm banged up, but don't believe anything is broken."

"Good," she said. "You'll want to read this." She tossed him the file and he read it carefully.

"It's more complicated than we thought at first," she said. "Walt's phone number was in Reese's address book. In fact, two numbers were listed there."

"I'm not surprised," countered Burke. "He probably owns more than one place anyway. He works in real estate."

"The first number we tried was disconnected."

"Probably the same one I had."

"Probably so. Anyway, when we tried the second number the whole situation got more complicated."

"How so?" he asked.

"The second number connected us to the campaign headquarters of Raymond Steele."

"The Senator?"

"None other."

"What'cha think it means?"

"I don't know yet. I was hoping you could shed some light on it. Do you know of any connection between Steele and Litske?"

Burke ran his fingers through his hair, searching his memory. "None I can remember. In college, Walt didn't pay much attention to politics. He never mentioned Steele as far as I can remember."

"What about after college?"

"I don't know, Debbi. I lost track of him, so I'd have no way of knowing. I can see how Walt and Steele might have connected after college. Walt's dad owns a construction company and a chunk of real estate in Atlanta. Any politician worth his salt probably tries to tap into their money."

"If so, we'd have a plausible reason for finding Steele's number in Reese's book."

"You think Walt knew Steele and introduced him to Reese," said Burke.

"Or Steele introduced Walt to her."

"Yeah, that's possible. But knowing Walt, I wouldn't expect it to go that way."

She frowned. "Or Steele might not know the girl at all, and his number showed up because Walt gave it to her as a place to reach him."

"Which would indicate a pretty close relationship between Steele and Litske," Burke concluded.

Debbi stood up and paced the floor. Burke watched her move. She was stunning in the morning light. Her teeth especially struck him—milky white in contrast to her dark skin—and straight like a picket fence, surrounded by the curve of full lips. He warned himself, *Don't even think it.*

Oblivious to his appraisal, Debbi asked, "So, what do we do now?"

"We talk to Steele," he said. "But I doubt he'll tell us anything."

Debbi grinned, "If he doesn't we use method number four."

Confused, Burke asked, "What's method number four?"

"Method number four is 'threat.'" Debbie explained.

"Could you elaborate?" said Burke.

"Sure. To get information in the news business, you either pay for it, steal it, seduce for it, or threaten for it."

Still ignorant, Burke asked another question. "And the threat is?"

"We tell him we'll print what we already have—his phone number in a dead prostitute's book, beside the name of a man who has fallen out of sight."

"That should shake him up."

"And that can be dangerous," Debbi warned.

"What do you mean? What can he do?" asked Burke.

"He can sue for libel. He can put the paper out of business. He can end a young reporter's career—or a young preacher's. He can do pretty much what he pleases. If he's connected to these homicides, it looks like he can kill too."

Burke pulled himself off the sofa and limped to the phone. He picked it up and handed it to Debbi. "Let's see what we can find out about Steele's connection to Litske. Maybe we can tie him to Reese. If we can, maybe we can keep him from hurting anybody else."

"It's dangerous," said Debbi.

"I know."

"You still want me to call him?"

"Absolutely. Don't you?"

"Absolutely."

Debbi dialed. As before, the voice of a sweet-sounding secretary answered, "Senator Steele's office. How may I help you?"

This time Debbi was prepared. "I'd like to speak to Senator Steele, please."

"Hold on a second, I'll connect you with the Senator's secretary."

Debbi lifted her eyes and locked them with Burke's. They were in this together.

"This is Senator Steele's executive assistant. May I help you?"

"Yes, ma'am, this is Debbi Meyer, reporter with the *Atlanta Independent*. Could I speak to the Senator please?"

"I'm sorry, Ms. Meyer, but the Senator is not available today. He's in conference with his campaign advisers. Could I get his chief of staff to call you back?"

Debbi hardened her jaw line. "No, I need to talk with the Senator. My call is urgent."

"I'm sure it is, ma'am, but you must understand. The Senator receives scores of calls every day from news people and they all believe their calls are urgent. I'll be glad to get Mr. Flake to contact you when he's finished with his meeting."

"Could you hold on a minute, please?" Debbi turned toward Burke. He nodded to her, urging her ahead.

"Ma'am," she said, "I need to speak to the Senator within the next thirty minutes. Just tell the Senator I've got reason to believe he's connected to Carol Reese, the young woman who died this past weekend. Tell him if I don't hear from him within the next thirty minutes, I will go to press with what I have and allow him to disclaim it later. Tell him that and see if he'll talk with me."

"Give me a number, ma'am, and I'll relay your message to the Senator," said the secretary, cooly efficient.

Burke noticed the rocks in Debbi's voice. No more sugar and spice.

"Call me at 555-2212. I'll be here for 30 minutes."

"I'll tell the Senator."

"Thank you, ma'am."

Hanging up the phone, Debbi glanced at Burke. Awkwardly, Burke offered her his hand but she ignored it and wrapped her arm around his waist instead. They hugged each other standing there, a couple in the center of the room, washed by an early sun bathing the apartment.

"I'm going to have some kind of article to write when this is over," she said.

"Article nothing," argued Burke. "You're going to have a book."

"Until then," said Debbi. "How about I fix some breakfast?"

CHAPTER
24

The ornate figure of Raymond Steele leaned back in his chair—all the way back, his two hundred dollar shoes resting on the desk in front of him, his fingers interlocked behind his head, a vise grip around his silver mane. He had headphones in his ears and his right foot tapped in time to the sounds of Lee Greenwood. "I'm proud to be an American, where at least I know I'm free, . . ." The Senator loved country music and he played it constantly in his office, car and home. It helped him concentrate on matters of state. Like now. He pulled the earphones out and laid them on the table. Automatically, the volume switched to the speakers in the ceiling.

Steele spoke over the background music and his voice made the leather on the chairs around the table crinkle. "Only a few days before the election, Sonny," he boomed. "You think we're O.K.?" He sounded like Darth Vader and when Raymond Steele spoke, people listened.

"I think so," said Sonny Flake, standing across the table from him, sipping coffee. Even with Steele sitting, Sonny could barely look his angular boss in the eye. Sonny was barely five-four and weighed no more than 130 pounds. To most people he looked sickly. Far from being a liability though, Flake used his slight frame as a weapon. Enemies who mistakenly assumed his physical weakness made him a pushover always suffered for their ignorance. He more than made up for his lack of size with a spinning top of energy and a computer for a brain.

"The polls give us a 65 to 35 percent majority," he said, pleased with his work as campaign manager.

"Can't always trust those polls," cautioned the Senator.

"I don't ever trust them," agreed Sonny, pushing his sandy hair off his forehead. "That's why we spent almost five million dollars on advertising—so we don't have to trust the polls."

Steele's chuckle sounded like thunder rolling. "It does cost to lead the people." He stood up, circled the desk and perched himself on the edge of it, facing a retinue of political troops gathered in his office.

"If we can win by 70 percent it'll send a resounding message to the people of Georgia and the whole South. It'll make the suits in Washington sit up and take notice too. I'll be the number one contender for the nomination for president two years from now."

"Contender nothing," said Sonny. "No party can win the presidency without the South and you are the South. They'll have to give the nomination to you."

A chorus of amen's rang out from the conclave of pollsters, advance men, and advisers seated around the conference table. The loudest agreement bellowed from the corner where Hock stood.

Steele lifted himself from the desk top and walked toward his monstrous bodyguard. Like a grizzled football coach energizing his team for a game against a hapless opponent, Steele pushed himself to his tiptoes and stared into the cupcake-sized eyes of his six-feet, eight-inch-tall protector. His breath mixed with that of the dullard and a slender smile creased Steele's ruddy face. Time to get Hock's blood up.

"Let me hold your hands, Hock," commanded Steele.

The 300-pound man obeyed, pushing his cushion-sized hands out for Steele to grasp.

"These hands are strong," preached Steele. "That's why I picked you off the street when you were 16 years old, Hock, when you were digging through my trash cans. You were already a man then, Hock. But you needed me to take care of you. That's why I made you my bodyguard. That's why I trust you—'cause you need me and you're strong. I can count on you to tell me the truth, can't I, Hock?"

"Yzzzzz, Sa," said the childlike Hock, the voice slurred from his mental deficiency.

"You wouldn't tell me no lie."

"No, Sa," said Hock, grieved the Senator would even ask the question.

"We gonna win this election, Hock?" yelled Steele.

"Yzz, Sa, Missa Steele." Hock's voice got louder too, matching Steele's.

"By over 70 percent?" Steele bellowed.

"Yzz, Sa, Missa Steele," screamed the warrior.

"Am I going to be the next President of the United States?"

"Yzz, again, Sa."

"Will we clean up this country?"

"Yzz, Sa." Hock's voice notched higher.

"Will we throw the communists and the homosexuals in jail?"

"Yzz, Sa." The veins in Hock's neck rose up, alive—blood-filled snakes crawling around looking for a way out. Steele watched Hock's heart thump through his veins.

"Will we execute the terrorists?"

"Yzz, Sa. We'll hang 'em."

"Will we make this country safe for decent, God-fearing folks again?"

"Yzz, Sa, that's what we'll dooo." Hock slushed the words out and the drool sloshed over his biscuit-like lips. He raised his mammoth right hand and wiped the spittle off before it fell on Steele.

The slobber stuck to the back of his hand as the phone buzzed and interrupted Steele's agitation of his protective giant.

Flake put his cup down and leaned over the table to take the unwanted call. "What's the problem?" he asked.

"I'm not sure," said the secretary. "But Debbi Meyer of the *Independent* just called and—"

Flake cut her off. "I told you we're not taking any reporter's calls. You know that."

"Yes, I know that, Sonny, but this wasn't just any call. Meyer said she had connected the Senator's name to the prostitute who was killed this past weekend."

"How could she do that?"

"I don't know, Sonny. I'm just relaying a message."

Sonny rubbed his forehead. No time for emotion to overrun reason. They could deny any connection. Could stonewall any investigation way past the election. If they wanted, they could shut the *Independent* down and bury its reporters.

Steele turned from Hock to Flake. "What's up, Sonny?"

"Nothing, Senator, just a reporter hounding you."

"A reporter? Sylvia broke into our meeting to tell us a reporter called?"

Flake knew he couldn't lie to Steele. He motioned for Steele to bend over. He whispered to him. "It's a woman named Meyer from the *Independent*. Says she's connected your name to the Reese woman the cops found last Friday."

Steele's eyes narrowed, then returned to normal—brown and clear. "What does Meyer want?"

"She wants you to call her back."

"Then let's give her what she wants. Get the girl on the phone. And put in my new Randy Travis tape."

Steele snuggled himself back down into his chair. Hock smelled his boss's concern and clumped over and took his position behind him—a guard protecting his emperor. Steele waved his hand at the entourage gathered around the conference table. "Clear the room, guys. Everyone leave but Sonny and Hock." The cabal trooped out, obedient automatons.

"Senator Steele?" The secretary's tinny voice filtered through the speaker as the advisers shut the door behind them.

"I'm here."

"Meyer's on line 1."

As Steele picked up the phone, Sonny dropped a copy of the morning paper on the table where he could see it and opened it to a picture of Debbi Meyer beneath the by-line of her second editorial. Steele looked at the article and said, "Raymond Steele here, Ms. Meyer. What can I do for you today?"

Debbi pulled her hair out of her mouth and glanced at Burke. He nodded encouragement. Go ahead.

"Senator, it's come to my attention that you were an acquaintance of Carol Reese, the young woman found murdered last weekend here in Atlanta. Would you like to explain your connection to Reese?"

Steele stalled. "I'm afraid you have me at a disadvantage, ma'am. I don't know what you're talking about. Could you tell me where you learned of this so-called connection?"

"I'm not free to divulge that information."

"Then how can I be sure you actually have it? I don't know anything about you and I sure don't know anything about a dead woman. Unless you give me cause to believe you, I have no reason to make any explanation."

Debbi covered the phone with her hand and whispered to Burke, "He says he won't comment unless I can give some proof I really have something."

Burke advised her. "Tell him again you have him connected and you're confident enough to print what you have whether he comments or not. You'll let him deny it to the press after you run the story."

Debbi relayed the message to Steele. "Hold on a minute," he said. Steele turned to Flake.

Sonny and Hock were the only people privy to his monthly visits with Reese. He had been giving himself this reward for the last two years, 12 times each year, on the 30th of each month. It was his only vice. Just this one. This one kept him sane. Almost 60 now, he needed a young woman to soothe his ego. Reese performed that task for him—at least for the last eight months she had. Others had preceded Reese and someone would surely follow her. *How could she have connected me with Reese?*

Flake tried to answer Steele's question. "Did you leave anything with your name on it with her?"

"I'm not stupid, Sonny."

Steele turned back to Meyer. "Listen, little lady—I don't know what you think you have on me, but let me assure you, you're making a major league mistake. I don't know anything about Reese and if you print a word indicating I do, I assure you of two things—one, people will be using the paper from the *Independent* to line hamster cages and two, you'll be the one cleaning those cages out. If you follow my reasoning."

Debbi's voice stiffened to match Steele's. "Yes, Senator, this little lady gets your drift. Now, let me assure you of this. Tomorrow morning you'll find your name in our headlines. It'll say something like, 'Senator A Suspect.' We'll connect you to Reese. You can read how we connect you while you eat your Cheerios. Then you can face the press and explain it to everybody all at once. Then you can get back on the campaign trail and explain how you got mixed up in all this. I'm sure you'll still win your election. But a little sex and murder scandal should put a damper on your percentage and it might slow down that Presidential Express you want to catch a couple of years from now. *If you follow my reasoning.*"

Steele didn't fold. "Simple enough, Ms. Meyer," he said. "It's your call."

They simultaneously slammed down the phones. Debbi lifted her hand and held it out to Burke. It was shaking. Burke took it in his and gently cradled it. "Do you think your paper will print the story?"

"If they don't maybe we can get a cell beside each other." They both laughed, but nervously.

* * * * *

Raymond Steele laid his glasses down and rubbed his tired eyes. Flake stood by him and slurped at his cold coffee, smart enough not to speak. Hock stayed put behind his boss.

"How'd she do it, Sonny? How'd she tie me to Reese? I told Carol over and over how important secrecy was. She wouldn't deliberately implicate me, would she? Sure, she threatened me a time or two—but that was to drive her price up. That was business—blackmail. I understood that. That's why I sent Walt to see her. To shake her confidence, to get her to back off and stop pressing for more money every time I went to see her. But, it still makes no sense. How'd she connect me?"

Sonny was asking himself the same question and then, suddenly, he knew. Walt Litske. Meyer had called yesterday asking for Walt Litske. She thought she was dialing a number for Walt and she had reached the Senator. Litske had left this number with Reese. Someone had given Meyer Litske's number. That number led to the Senator.

Sonny told the Senator, "It was Litske, Senator."

"I don't know that I believe that."

"I don't mean deliberately—but Meyer called yesterday asking for him, not knowing he worked for you. She wanted Litske and through him, she got you."

Steele rotated his neck in a circular motion like a toy dog in the back window of a car as he pondered the situation. After a couple of seconds, he grabbed Sonny by his shirt collar and pulled him down to lip level. "We've got to take care of Litske," he said. Noticing Hock's undisguised interest, Steele dropped his voice into a whisper. "Pay him off and send him to Mexico or somewhere. We can't let them find him. Not now. Not ever."

Sonny stood up, straightened his tie and nodded—he understood. He gathered his papers off the desk and stuffed them into his briefcase. He emptied his coffee with one gulp and put his cup in the case too. Efficient as ever, he talked as he headed to the door. "It may take a day or so to handle Litske. Can you deal with the press in the morning?"

Steele was looking at Meyer's picture in the paper. He raised his silver mane and peered over the edge of his glasses. "Don't worry about me, Sonny. I was playing with the press when you were still an infant. Even if Meyer proves I adulterated a little, it won't kill me. I'll just admit my sins and make a tearful apology. Forgiving me will make my constitutents feel real righteous. If I handle this right, I might actually gain a few points in the polls. The rednecks will be glad to know their good Senator can still rattle a mattress every now and again. Yeah, I'll come out O.K.; don't you worry none. Turn up the music as you leave."

* * * * *

Flake smiled broadly and obeyed. He had confidence in the Senator. He also had confidence he could find Walt. Walt would go where he always went when he required a little "R and R." Walt was probably on the island right now snoozing off a drunk. Sonny would pick up a change of clothes and head toward St. Simons. Walt would be there. He knew he would.

* * * * *

Hock followed Sonny out of the room. He was excited and he blinked his eyes over and over and clucked his tongue in time with his eyes. The Senator's words rattled around in Hock's clouded brain. He didn't know exactly what he planned to do when he found Walt, but he would find a way to fulfill the Senator's wish. "We've got to take care of Litske," said the Senator. Hock had grabbed those words and crunched them in his hands, like he would grab Litske and crunch him when he found him. Sonny would take him to Litske. Then he would take care of the rest.

CHAPTER
25

A very tugged his socks up as Broadus settled into the brown-cushioned seats in Conner's office and waited on him to show. Mays smelled the smoke hanging in the room and pointed at the ash trays full of limp soot from the cigarette smokers.

"This place stinks," he said, twisting his mouth into a look of disgust.

"Give it a break," said Jackie. "A police station is about the only place you can smoke these days. The environmental crazies have made us smokers the last endangered species." She pulled out a "California Lady," lit it and leaned back, dragging deeply.

"I wish you'd give that up."

"I have," Jackie said. "Six times."

On her second draw, the Chief slammed the door and stormed in. He tugged at his shirt collar as he headed across the room. *Not a happy man*, Avery decided.

"Have you read the report on this third murder?"

"Sure," shrugged Mays. "We looked it over a few minutes ago, first thing after we got here. Not much in it. Same M.O. as the first two. Head crushed. No fingerprints this time though. Nothing else turned up but the cross and the flag."

"What do you make of the flag business?"

"Hard to say, Chief. First girl had a flag, but no religious artifact. Second two have a flag and a religious symbol."

Jackie expounded a theory. "Is the killer adding a new wrinkle every time? Like country, then God and country?"

Avery shot it down. "If so, then what's added with the third death?"

"Maybe somebody missed something with the third girl. Who did the report, Chief?"

"Stith and Gaskone. They do a good job."

"Yeah, but maybe we ought to go by and make sure they didn't miss anything," suggested Avery.

"I agree," said Conners. "I want you to compare notes with them as soon as possible." Conners took a bite off a danish, sloshed down a mouthful of coffee, then changed the subject. "What did you find out about Litske yesterday?"

Mays pulled out a blue notebook, but he really didn't need it. He kept the facts in his head. "He's 6'2", 260 or so pounds, played linebacker for the Bulldogs, made All-American, maintained a 3.1 GPA, stirred up a little harmless trouble, and made everyone proud of him." Mays stopped.

Conners' eyes bore holes through him. "Don't tease me today, Mays. This has gotten too serious and those stats don't tell us a thing. When you mix sex, death and religion in Georgia, you've got a powderkeg. So wipe that smirk off your face and give me what you've got."

Mays grinned. "Here's where it gets interesting, Chief. Anderson and Litske roomed together at Georgia."

Conners' eyes widened. Mays continued. "Seems Anderson started as Litske's tutor, then became his best friend. They got an apartment together after their first semester. Folks called them Neon and Freon."

"Any particular reason?"

"Yeah, Litske was flashy, reckless, a woman chaser. Anderson, on the other hand, was cool, much less emotional."

"Could they be connected in the murder?"

"It's possible. A man named Metcalf identified a black Mercedes like Litske's in Cascade on Friday and said two men left in the same time frame. So, we can assume they were together the night Reese was killed."

Frank held up his hand. "You should know a guard at Foxfire also I.D.'d the car and said two men passed through between ten and eleven."

Jackie stubbed out her cigarette. "How many left?"

"Guard said one."

"Did the Mercedes reenter the complex that night?"

"Guard didn't think so. But he said he had to leave the guardhouse a couple of times to take care of some business."

"So, Litske could have returned and killed her without the guard seeing him," concluded Jackie.

"Yep."

Mays chimed in, "Or, Litske could have returned to pick Anderson up later."

"That's possible," agreed Conners. "The two could have been working together."

Jackie asked the obvious. "But for what motive?"

Conners opened up a manila folder. "Maybe I can suggest a motive. You're not the only ones who've been busy. While you were scouting around the University, I went digging myself."

Jackie and Avery leaned forward.

"As you know, Litske played for two years for the Falcons. In his third year he got clobbered from the blind side and the knee went out. He never played again."

"That's not unusual," offered Avery. "Lots of football careers end because of knee injuries."

"Sure they do. And, like many others, Litske went through a severe depression after it happened. Spent a bundle on therapy trying to work through it all. And, you won't be surprised to hear this, he started using drugs. Went from amphetamines and downers to cocaine and heroin."

Frank looked up from his file. Mays nodded his head. Not the first time a player faced this kind of downfall. Won't be the last.

"Is he still on drugs?" asked Jackie.

"We're not sure. He cleaned up after about a year of heavy use and stayed straight—apparently for another year afterward. Got involved with his dad's business."

"How'd he do there?" Avery asked.

"O.K. for awhile. Then the bottom fell out of the market and the Litskes lost their underwear. My reports say his father filed Chapter 11 bankruptcy about two years ago."

Jackie rubbed her eyes. "That's enough to drive anybody to drink."

"Or to some other drug," said Frank.

"The question we've got," said Mays, "is whether or not Jr. went back to the smack after his father's business fell apart."

"We have another question."

"What's that, Jackie?"

"Did he start selling to make some money for himself and for his dad?"

Avery whistled. "And, if so, did Reese know and try to blackmail a former football star with her knowledge of his business?"

Broadus turned to Frank. "Any evidence Reese was a user?"

Frank smiled slightly. "Pathology shows us she liked a little coke every so often. Not an expensive habit really, just recreational drugs."

"But enough to need a supplier."

"Precisely," answered Frank.

"Which could have been Litske," said Avery.

"Or Anderson," said Jackie.

"Or both," Conners suggested.

"So we have another suspect to go with our preacher," concluded Jackie. "Litske could have killed her—to shut her up."

Their thinking ground to a halt. The cut and dried now took on the form of the soft and formless. What had seemed so simple, with its clean edges now shifted and evolved—into an ooze of "what ifs," and "it could bes," and "it's possible."

Frank stood up from his desk and drummed his fingers on his stomach as he leaned toward them. "We need to add Walt Litske to our pick-up list."

"It would appear so, " said Avery, slapping his hands to his knees and rocking forward, signalling Jackie he was ready to leave. Conners held up his hand—a stop sign.

"Before you go I need to tell you one more thing." His tone forced them to sit up straighter. Avery stared at his soft face—mashed potatoes, he thought—lumpy and off-whitish.

The white face spoke and he listened intently.

"I've not told you everything."

Avery and Jackie exchanged glances.

"Another prominent name turned up in Reese's book."

Frank watched their reaction, wondering if they would ever trust him again. He couldn't tell, but no matter. He couldn't keep his secret any longer. "Raymond Steele's name was in Reese's book."

"The plot thickens," mused Avery.

"Why didn't you tell us this from the beginning?" Jackie snapped.

Frank pulled his pipe out of his desk drawer, stuffed it with tobacco, and torched it with a cigarette lighter. The smoke curled toward the ceiling. His yellow fingers cupped the pipe as he stared at Jackie. When he spoke, his voice softened. Only one was really true.

"Steele scares me. I'm three years away from retirement. He's the most popular man in Georgia and I've heard horror stories about what happens to people who oppose him. I figured we had the goods on this preacher boy, so why rock the boat."

"So, why tell us now?" she asked.

"'Cause this whole mess is getting more complicated by the moment and I don't want to put the wrong guy behind bars. Plus, I don't want you two operating in the dark. You deserve better. Besides, I'm not accustomed to lying to protect anybody, not even a U.S. Senator."

"Even if telling the truth means you retire a little early?"

"Exactly."

Mays pulled himself up from the sofa and walked toward Frank. He stuck out his hand and indicated to Frank he should shake it. "I don't blame you, Frank," he said. "You did what you thought right. I'm just glad you told us. I already figured out the missing page, anyway. Just a matter of time before Steele's name turned up."

Sheepishly, Frank nodded. "Thought maybe you had picked up on it. That's another reason to tell you—so you won't turn me in for withholding evidence."

"I wouldn't do that, Chief. As long as we've been at this, you deserve the benefit of the doubt."

"We do go back a ways, don't we, Avery?"

Feeling like a school girl who has mistakenly walked into the boys' locker room, Jackie turned her head to the side and coughed. "Chief, I think it's time we bailed out of here, don't you?"

Frank shifted his attention to her. "Can't argue with that," he agreed. "Do the check on the third murder and then see if you can find Litske."

"Any idea where to start?" she asked.

"Yeah. Check out his dad's old place. Here's the address. According to the report, Sr. was keeping a skeleton crew out there."

Avery and Jackie stood to leave. Avery asked, "What about Steele, Frank?"

"I'll check him out myself. Is that O.K. with you?"

"Whatever you say. If we can help, just call and we'll get there."

As Avery and Jackie left the station house, Avery nodded his head up and down. "Makes me glad to be a cop," he said.

Jackie countered with less charity. "He should have told us at the beginning."

"I know," said Avery. "But, he was scared. I can understand that. Can't you?"

"I don't know."

"Haven't you ever been scared?"

"Sure, but it's been a long time."

"How long?"

"Six years."

"What scared you, Jackie?"

"Loneliness. Six years ago my marriage broke up."

"Are you scared now?"

"Yep, but I don't like to talk about it."

"Neither does the chief."

CHAPTER

26

urke slept through the morning. After the phone call to Steele, Debbi had helped him stagger to her bed where he collapsed, still exhausted. She passed the morning reading the paper and watching the news, hoping for more information on the most recent death. None was forthcoming. Not even Les Atkinson offered any additional details.

The whistle of a teakettle woke Burke right after noon. He held up his arms in an "x" formation to block off the sun driving into his swollen eyes. "Debbi?" he called, raising into a sitting position.

"I'm here," she said. "In the kitchen, making some tea. What do you need?"

"Just wondered where you were."

"Well, I'm here. You hungry?"

Burke paused to check, rubbing his hand over his stomach. "Yeah, come to think of it, I'm starved. Couldn't remember for a moment when I ate last. Over 12 hours ago, I guess."

"No wonder you're so weak. Rest a few more minutes and I'll throw something together."

Burke slumped back into the cushioned pillows.

Thirty minutes later Debbi padded into the room and handed him a platter loaded with baked chicken, potato salad, rolls, a slice of peach cobbler and a glass of iced tea.

"How'd you fix this so fast?"

"The miracle of the microwave," she said, taking a seat on the edge of the bed. "Eat it and don't ask questions."

She didn't have to ask him twice. He gobbled the first bite like a starving wolf, but his busted lips wouldn't allow that kind of haste. He groaned in pain and took the second bite more gingerly, nibbling it. That was better and he went to work on the meal.

"Does it hurt?" Debbi asked.

"Only when I chew," he grinned. "Aagh—and when I laugh."

"I'll leave you alone while you eat. If you need anything, holler."

"Don't go. Stay with me," he said. She nodded and sat down and watched him eat.

He ate the meal in silence, washing down the last bite of cobbler with the cold tea. "I think I'll live now," he said as he wiped his fingers with a napkin and fought back a burp.

"Good, 'cause we've got work to do. We've got to find Walt before the police connect you to me and throw us both into jail."

"I don't know where to begin. Walt could be anywhere by now."

"Let's start at the beginning. When you were in college with Walt. Where did he like to go then?"

Burke laughed. "Walt spent most of his spare time in college at any one of a number of bars."

"Any one in particular?"

"Not one I can recall. I didn't go with him to those places."

"Not ever?"

"Well, not often."

"Sometimes then?"

"Well, yes, once or twice."

"Where did you go when you went?"

"I think I'd better plead the fifth amendment."

"You think your answer will tend to incriminate you?"

"No doubt about it. You'll think I'm a hypocrite—a student planning for the ministry going to a local joint."

Debbi clucked her tongue and shook her head. "You've been serious way too long, Burke Anderson. I'm not going to condemn you because you went to a bar. I'm not Mother Teresa here. Now, tell me—where did you and Walt go?"

"To the Silver Slipper," he said.

"The Silver Slipper?"

"Yeah." Burke turned cardinal red, like a fourteen-year-old caught kissing in the den.

Debbi had heard of the place. An upper crust saloon only one step away from a strip club. She couldn't resist teasing him. "Isn't the Slipper a bit out of the way for a gentleman preacher?"

"Yeah, it is, that's why I didn't want to tell you."

"You said you went once or twice. Did Walt go there more often?"

"Sure—almost every weekend during his junior and senior years. By then he was an All-American. Guys lined up to buy him drinks and girls flocked to him like flies to a jelly jar. He loved the place."

Debbi pushed up from the bed and paced—twirling her hair as she walked, pulling it into her mouth, chewing on it. Burke followed her with his eyes.

She asked him, "Do you think he kept going there after college?"

"Don't know why he wouldn't."

"Do you think he kept going there in the last few years?"

"I suppose so." Burke suddenly saw the direction of her inquisition. "You think we might find someone at the Slipper who can help us find Walt!"

"It's possible someone can at least tell us where to start looking. I can go there this evening, ask a few questions, try to get a lead on Walt."

"You're not going without me," Burke said sternly.

"Don't you think it's risky for you to go out?"

"Well, sure, I suppose, but the Slipper is pretty dark inside. Chances are good nobody will notice me."

"It's dangerous."

"Doesn't matter. I'm going. I saw the flag in those roses and read the report on Reese's death. Whoever killed those girls was warning you. You're in danger and I won't let you go out alone. Case closed."

Debbi could see arguing wouldn't help. "So you think we should go to the Slipper?"

"I don't know of too many other options," he said.

"I guess not."

She glanced at her watch. "What time do they open?"

"Around five or six," said Burke. "Since it's Halloween I'm sure they'll crank up pretty early tonight."

"It's nearly two," noted Debbi, stopping her pacing. "We've got close to three hours to kill before we go."

"I know how to kill at least a couple of those hours," said Burke.

"How's that?"

"We can go buy me some clothes. I can't walk into the Slipper like this." He lifted the bedclothes draped over him and looked at the filthy gym shorts he still wore.

"You're right," laughed Debbi. "Those definitely won't do. Let me change and then we'll see what we can do about some clothes for you."

Watching her grab a skirt and blouse out of the closet and bounce out of the room, Burke wanted to tell her how grateful he felt. But he didn't. He didn't because he felt something else too. Something he'd never felt for any girl before Debbi. An attraction. Part of it was physical, like with Carol Reese. But with Debbi it was more. It was, well, he didn't know what to call it. But he felt it and that warmed him. He lay back in the bed and waited for her to get ready.

Fifteen minutes later Debbi strode back from the bathroom dressed in a black jacket draped over a purple silk blouse. Her skirt matched her jacket and the combination set off her blonde hair and green eyes. With her lips touched by the outline of fresh lipstick, Debbi stole his breath.

She noticed his limp-jawed stare and appreciated it. But, she had no time for that. Not now. "Time for you to get dressed," she said, matter of factly, tossing him a pair of navy sweat pants and a shirt to match. "Fortunately, sweats will fit just about any figure. Take a shower, shave and put these on. They'll get you by until we can get to a men's store."

"I'll hurry," Burke said lamely as he crawled out of bed and tottered to the bathroom.

Forty minutes later Burke reappeared from the bathroom, clean-shaven, showered, and wearing Debbi's sweats. He wore Band-Aids over the cuts on his right eye and lower lip. He'd found an Ace bandage in the towel drawer and had wrapped it around his ribs. In spite of everything, he felt reasonably sound.

"You look better," said Debbi.

"Not too bad," Burke agreed.

Fifty-five minutes after they left the condo, Debbi walked out of Reimer's Men's Store with a full set of clothes—tan slacks, a navy blazer, a blue cotton shirt, a belt, jockey shorts, and socks and shoes. She tossed the bag into the car where Burke waited. Five minutes later, he grabbed the clothes and furtively sneaked into the restroom of a gas station across the street from the mall. Within minutes he emerged fully dressed and hopped into the car.

"You look like a million bucks," exuded Debbi.

"I feel like a dollar ninety-eight."

"Ready to go?"

"As ready as I'm going to get."

"To the Slipper then," she chirped, eager to get started. "It'll take an hour to get there—even with normal traffic."

As he settled into the car, Burke's short surge of energy deserted him. He thought of Biscuit and felt a golf ball swell up in his throat. He listened to the rat-tat-tat of a rain beginning to fall and sensed he was getting close to his last chance. He leaned his head against the door and stared out through the raindrops sliding down the window. If he couldn't get a line on Walt at the Slipper, he was at a dead end.

He asked Debbi, "Do you believe in prayer?"

"I'm not sure," she said, changing lanes to pass a slower car.

"Do you ever pray?"

"Not much anymore. Used to when I was a little girl."

"What did you pray for?"

"Oh, you know, different things, little girl things."

"Anything in particular?"

"Yeah, one thing anyway."

"What was that?"

"I prayed for God to keep my mom and dad together."

"What happened?"

"Six months later they got a divorce."

"What did you do?"

"I stopped praying. Haven't really prayed since." Debbi swerved to miss a dog crossing the lane in front of her.

"So, now you don't believe in prayer?" Burke asked gently.

"I'm not sure I don't believe in it. I'm just not sure what it is anymore." They stopped talking for an instant and listened to the swish-swump, swish-swump of the windshield wipers. Then, Debbi started up again. "Why the concern for my views on prayer?"

"I don't know. Well, yes I do. It's because I feel like I need to pray now."

"I can understand why you would."

"If we don't find Walt soon, I'll have to turn myself in. You can't hide me indefinitely."

"I don't mind. It's actually been fun."

"It won't be fun if you get arrested for harboring a suspected murderer."

"No, when you put it that way, it gets more serious," agreed Debbi, slowing down behind a line of heavy traffic. She stopped talking and concentrated on her driving in the suddenly heavy rain—afraid of an accident that would expose them both. She threaded the car through the gridlock, right through the dusk, into the slick dark—a dark broken by headlights and billboards and red lights on turnoffs. She threaded the car through the six o'clock hour, right to 6:20, right to the Silver Slipper, to the parking lot outside.

The blue and white lights of the Silver Slipper strobed into Debbi's Volvo and she and Burke heard raucous music seeping through the walls. Burke remembered his previous visits to the Slipper. It had shocked him then—the lifestyle the Slipper symbolized. The lifestyle marked by late afternoon cocktails and brown tinted bottles of beer; the quick pickup of a nameless body to hold close for an evening in a pretended intimacy; the meaningless chatter of nothing words—foreplay with the voice and no substance to follow; the togetherness of lipstick smeared on sheets and bad breath in the morning and quick dressing when the sun arose, and hurried goodbyes and I'll call-yous. That kind of lifestyle. Not the kind anyone wanted, but the kind some people settled for.

Debbi reached for the door handle to the car, but Burke grabbed her arm. "Just a minute Debbi. Would it be O.K. if we prayed?"

Debbi tried to laugh it off. "Afraid of the temptations inside, huh?"

"Yeah, but more than that." Burke stayed serious. "I want to pray for Walt, wherever he is. For the people inside this place who're looking for something they're not finding. For God to guide us to someone who'll know where we can find Walt."

"If there is a God," said Debbi matter-of-factly.

"Do you disbelieve so completely, Debbi?"

She breathed deeply. "No, I don't really disbelieve. But I don't know how to do anything else. I don't know how to believe, don't know what it means to believe, to trust God, to practice faith. No one ever taught me."

"You can learn," urged Burke. "I'll teach you."

"Are you so sure of it, Burke? So sure of the God you say loves you? Can you prove your God beyond a shadow of a doubt?"

Burke took a second to think. The rain splattered harder on the roof of the car. "I'd be lying if I said I could do that, Debbi. And I'll admit I've struggled with doubts in my life, especially in the last two days. Most Christians do at one time or another. Especially when the dark times fall on us. But that's when faith makes its presence felt the most. Faith doesn't mean the absence of doubts, but the presence of trust in the midst of them."

"Don't, Burke. No sermon, please."

"You asked me a question. I'm just trying to answer it the best way I can. No, I can't prove God beyond a shadow of a doubt, but I believe I can prove God beyond a reasonable doubt. And that's all we can expect. Think about it. What makes more sense of what you see every day? We live by total chance or by divine—?"

"But what about all the suffering?" she interrupted. "What about your own suffering?"

Burke shrugged. "I can't answer those questions easily. No one can.

But I can say this. Sin causes most of our suffering, so it's primarily our fault, not God's. And second, our suffering pales in comparison to what Jesus suffered on our behalf."

"So you've kept your faith in spite of all that's happened to you in the last 48 hours?"

Burke stared deeply into her eyes. "Yes, Debbi, I've kept my faith."

The rain splattered harder on the car. Obviously confused, Debbi twisted a strand of hair and then pushed it into the corner of her mouth. Finally, after several moments, she seemed to come to a decision. "O.K., Burke," she said. "When this ends, I'm willing to listen, willing to give you a chance to prove God to me beyond a reasonable doubt."

"Then you'll pray with me now?"

She smiled. "I don't see how I can refuse."

"O.K. Great," he said, a wide smile crossing his face. He bowed his head. She did too. His words were simple and short. "Oh, God, though we don't understand what's happening to us we ask for your divine help to see us through it. Extend your mercy to Walt, your protection to us, and your wisdom to our steps. By faith we pray. Amen."

"Let's go," Burke said. "I'm ready." They climbed out.

Walking over the concrete, slick with the water from the rain, Debbi reached over and took Burke's arm. "First time I've ever prayed with a man before. Felt kind of good. Scary, but good."

"First time I've ever gone into a nightclub with a girl before," responded Burke. "Feels kind of good. Scary, but good."

Laughing almost deliriously, they walked through the door into the smoke and smell of one of Atlanta's most infamous night spots.

CHAPTER

27

The metal sign dangled sideways from its post, like a tooth hanging by a root from a gum. The words "Litske Building and Construction," written in a tired blue and red ink, stared out at Broadus and Mays as their car crunched to a halt on the empty lot. Someone had shot the sign full of nickel-sized holes and rust chewed at the edges. Green weeds tugging at the bottom and broken glass at its feet added the final touches to the picture of neglect.

"Looks like we've wasted the whole day," growled Mays, noting the shrinking rays of the sun.

"Apparently," agreed Jackie, "But we had to check with Gaskone and Stith to make sure nothing was missed and see if our M.O.s matched up."

"I just hate it took all day to do it," said Mays. "We've given Litske and Anderson another day to slip through our fingers. A few more like this and they could be anywhere."

"The wheels of justice do grind slowly, sometimes, don't they?" Jackie opened the car door and stepped onto the glass covered concrete. "I thought our reports said a skeleton crew might still be in place."

"Skeleton crew about covers it," Mays said, a wry grin breaking his face as he crunched over the pavement. "'Bout the only thing we'll find here will be dead."

"Suppose you're right. But we'd better look it over anyway."

"Yeah, just to be thorough."

With trained eyes both of them scanned the deserted construction yard.

"I feel like I'm in a ghost town," said Jackie.

"I wouldn't know how that feels."

"You know what I mean."

"No, I'm not sure I do. What *do* you mean?" Avery teased Jackie as they walked over the grounds of what had been a thriving business.

"It feels like no one's here, but that someone's still watching us."

They reached the front door of a sagging warehouse. Jackie peered into one of its broken windows. Avery, slipping quietly away from her, picked up a rock and tossed it over his head. He watched with glee as Jackie stumbled back in alarm and grabbed for her gun as the stone smashed through a window.

"What the —"

Avery broke up. "Whoa, girl, you're a little spooked, aren't you?"

"You jerk," she blasted him. "I ought to use this gun on you."

"Hey, lighten up a little. You're making me nervous with all your ghost town talk."

Jackie turned serious. "Don't you believe in spirits, Avery?" The two of them continued their walk, inspecting the area as they talked.

"We've had this conversation before, Jackie. You know I don't believe in anything I can't see, touch, taste or smell."

"But that's all so dry and scientific. What about these out-of-body, after death stories of white lights and gardens?"

"It's all a bunch of hokum, if you ask me. If I'm going to believe in anything it's going to be what I learned as a little boy."

"And what's that, Avery?" Jackie had never gotten him to go this far in their philosophical debates.

"I believe in myself. In my own abilities. In my capacity to figure things out and muddle through my problems. So far, that's been enough."

"Are you happy with that?"

"Happiness has nothing to do with it. I survive with that. That's about all we can ask for. Survival. Making it, day by day, doing the best we can."

"Survival's fine, Avery," Jackie slowed to a stop, "until you die. But, what's after survival?"

Avery stopped, too, and turned to look at his partner. "Mercy, Jackie, if I knew that, do you think I'd still be a cop? Let's just take care of now and not worry about what's going to happen then. Besides," he waved his hand over the empty lot, "I don't think we're going to answer those questions in this dump. Let's get out of here. Your train of thought gives me the willies."

Jackie nodded assent and pivoted toward the car. A flashing sign across the street attracted her eyes. It beckoned to her "Bu_gers and __ies." She hadn't eaten since breakfast and the thought of an onion-laden hamburger suddenly appealed to her.

"Avery, wait a minute," she said.

He followed her glance. "You hungry?"

"As a bear, and a little curious too. Wonder how long that place has been there?"

"By its spic-and-span appearance, I would say it's probably brand new."

"Sarcasm does become you, Avery. If it's as old as it looks, it's been here since the Litskes were. And it sold tons of food to construction workers and real estate people from Litske's over the years."

"Yeah, and the waitresses probably warded off tons of clumsy passes too."

"Wouldn't be surprised. If that's the case, they might know something about the whereabouts of the Litske family."

"That's possible."

"Want to check it out?"

"I'm right behind you," he said. "If it's a dead end on Litske at least we get a bite to eat."

Crossing the road and opening the door of the ragged cafe, they paused and let their eyes adjust to the dim light. On the table nearest the door a half-eaten hamburger greeted them as they passed. A juke box spewed out a Hank Williams, Jr. number. Jackie groaned, then bent over to look at her shoe—a wad of pink gum pasted itself to the bottom. Doing her best to scrape it off against the leg of a yellow chair, she whispered to Avery, "This is disgusting."

"Yeah, but didn't that hamburger make you want one real bad?"

Jackie groaned again, then called out, "Anyone home?" No answer. Avery tried, "Anybody in here?"

"Quit your hollerin'. And give a body a chance to finish up her business. I'll be right out."

The voice came from behind the door marked "Ladies."

Avery bowed his head toward Jackie. "100 to 1 that whatever comes from behind that door ain't no lady."

"Shhh," Jackie cautioned. "We need her help, even if she isn't a debutante."

They waited, then heard the unmistakable flush of a job completed. A second later the shiny knob of the door turned and a rumpled woman emerged from the bathroom. "What you yellin' about out here? Need a burger and some fries?"

"Not exactly," Jackie offered, her hunger stopped in its tracks by the underarm appearance of the little restaurant.

"Then what you doin' here?" The gray woman blew her breath at a strand of lead-colored hair which had fallen into her left eye.

"We'll take a Coke, ma'am." Suddenly Avery was all smiles and courtesy.

"That be one each or one between the two?"

"One apiece, please."

Avery motioned for Jackie to sit down on one of the stools at the bar as the Cokes were plopped down in front of them.

"How long you been runnin' this place, ma'am?" Avery took a sip.

"What's it to you?" Suspicion.

"Nothin', just curious."

"Just curious don't drive no cop car and spend twenty minutes looking over the Litske place before it walks over here." Direct.

"You're right, ma'am. We're more than curious. We're cops."

"Tell me something I don't know." Amused.

Avery laughed along with her. "I 'spect that might be kinda hard to do. You impress me as a lady who knows a whole lot about most things."

"I thought you didn't figure on me being a lady." Resentful.

"You heard me?"

"This tile and plastic carries sound a long way. 'Specially if you're accustomed to listening and not talking." Honest.

Avery scanned the old woman standing in front of him. Eyes blue and deep set, with red puffs around them, like she'd looked at small things from a long distance for many years. Wrinkles spread out on her pinched cheeks like cracked glass on a windshield. Hair refusing to be blown back in place, sharp lips.

Time to level with this lady. "Ma'am, we're trying to find Walt Litske."

"That don't surprise me. Lots of folks been asking me about him."

Mays glanced at Jackie. Someone else looking for Walt.

"Do you know where I could find him?"

"Which one you want? Jr. or Sr.?"

"We'd prefer to find Jr. But, if you don't know where he is, then Sr. would be fine."

"Name's Tess, Mister," the lady said, extending a thin hand to him. "And I ain't been called ma'am for a long time. Don't use it if you don't mean it."

Avery cringed, "Sorry, Tess, sometimes I get sassy. Don't mean nothin' by it."

"I know. Just don't do it with me." She turned to Jackie. "You a cop too?"

"Yes."

"Do you like it?"

"Yeah, I do."

"Why should I help you find Litske?" She directed the question to Avery.

"'Cause it's the right thing to do."

"Who decides that?"

"I guess we all do."

"What's he done?"

"We don't know that he's done anything. But we need to talk to him."

"About what?"

"About a murder."

"'Bout those dead prostitutes?"

"Yeah, how'd you know that?"

"Don't take no genius to figure Jr. might be messed up in that. He did have a way with the ladies. Kept my waitresses busy when he came by, I can tell you that. Until his dad shut down two years ago."

"Do you know where we could find either of them?" Jackie broke into the conversation. "They've moved out of Atlanta and left no forwarding address."

"I don't know nothin' about Jr.'s whereabouts. But I know where his family used to live. The place is for sale from what I hear. You go to Raintree Court out past Twin Forks Mall. I don't know the exact number of the house. It's a three-story yellow brick with a gate as tall as I am around it. Walt took a couple of waitresses there a time or two. They told me about it. That's the best I can do."

Avery reached out to shake her hand again while Jackie pawed around in her purse for change to pay for the Cokes. Tess waved them both off.

"Get on out of here. Time to close up. Don't 'spect we'll get much more business today."

Laying a five dollar bill on the counter, Jackie trailed Avery toward the door. Tess called out to them as they closed it, "Hope you find them girls' killer. It ain't right for someone to do that and get away with it."

"You're right, ma'am," Avery called back. "And I mean that 'ma'am' part."

It took them 40 minutes to reach Raintree. Another three brought them to the corner between Raintree and New Castle Lane. They saw the three-story brick on the corner between the two streets. The house was imposing.

A "For Sale" sign split the front yard, keeping the twin magnolias on each side of it company. The concrete drive which snaked its way in a semicircle through the front of the lawn was empty of cars. The shutters were pulled shut over the windows and bits and pieces of broken tree limbs dotted the scraggly lawn. A stringless gray tennis shoe sat on the walk leading from the driveway to the front door.

"Another ghost town," started Jackie as they turned the car into the driveway.

"You are morbid tonight, aren't you?"

"I've got a right to be. Everywhere we've been today we've found empty places, dead places. Wonder how long ago the Litskes moved out?"

"Hard to tell," said Avery.

Jackie pulled her belted sweater tighter to her chest, protecting against the first fall chill which had crept up on them since the sun went down. A light rain began to spatter her head and shoulders.

"It gets depressing, doesn't it, Avery?"

"Are you going tears on me, Broadus? What's gotten into you? You've never been this way before."

Jackie paused, looking for a response. She stumbled with her words. "I guess I'm thinking of these three girls. All of them in their twenties. All of them beautiful. All of them with life just beginning. Now, all of them dead. For no apparent reason. It makes me wonder what life's all about."

Avery studied Jackie's sagging face—he felt the cold too. Not just in the weather, but in the world. A cold seeping into the heart and causing it to scale over like skin left exposed in icy weather. A cold whistling through the ears and whispering, "No one cares." A cold laughing in the face of laughter because it knew the laughter would end far sooner than the cold would. Avery pulled his jacket tighter, shivering with Jackie. He'd forgotten how to cry, so he shivered instead.

"I can't tell you what 'life's all about' as you put it, Jackie. All I know is we've got a job to do—find those who did the killing and drove you to ask the questions you're now asking. For me, that's what life's all about—revealing the guilty and making them pay for their crimes."

"Is that enough for you, Avery? Don't you ever want more?"

"Sure, I want more. I guess we all do. But I don't know where to find more. Do you?"

"Not now, I don't. But, I think I'll start looking." Jackie bowed her head, staring at her hands, giving the pool of tears congregated in the corners of her eyes a minute to dry.

"If you find it, Jackie, will you show it to me?"

"Sure, partner. If I find it, I don't think I'll want to keep it from those I care about. You'll be the first to know."

A smile emerged on her face, a smile born of a friendship she could trust. She sniffled her nose and said, "You ready to go or you want to scout the place for a second?"

Avery had already grabbed the door knob. "Let's poke around a bit. You never know what you might find in a man's backyard."

Glad to do something now that her grief had passed, Jackie followed him across the sidewalk to the back of the mansion.

"Would you look at this!" he whispered as they turned the corner into the rear yard. "The whole back is made of glass."

"Not quite," corrected Jackie. "Just the bottom two floors."

"Now who's quibbling over details?" he teased her. "I've never seen so much glass, have you?"

The entire back span of the house was encased in a shining window, glinting in the silver of a waxing October moon. Jackie peered inside and counted 11 mummified lumps scattered across the floor of what looked like a huge entertainment room.

"Covered furniture?" she inquired.

"That or a bunch of old Volkswagens shrouded with sheets."

Jackie ignored his humor. "Looks more like ghosts who dropped out of Weight Watchers Anonymous to me."

Avery ignored hers. "Back on ghosts again, huh?"

They continued to stare through the windows, sliding to the right as they scanned the interior of the impressive home. Avery stopped his movement, threw up his hand to silence Jackie, and pressed his eyes tighter to the pane.

"What is it?"

"I'm not sure, but I thought I saw a light flicker upstairs." Both tensed, straining to identify the movement. "There. Did you see that?"

"Yeah, looked like a candle moving."

"Or a flashlight."

"Maybe," agreed Jackie. "What next?"

"We knock and see if anyone will answer."

"Now why didn't I think of that?"

"Why didn't we do that at the beginning?"

"'Cause it seemed so dead, that's why," she said.

"Appearances can be deceiving."

Moving to the door, Avery rapped sharply on its frame and waited. Nothing. He pounded again, more insistently this time. Nothing. For a third time, he struck the back door, this time shaking the whole rear of the home.

"Easy, Avery. You don't want all this glass coming down on you."

"No, I just want whoever is upstairs to know we're here."

"If they don't know you're here after that knock, they're either dead or deaf."

"Well, if they're dead, we can be fairly certain they're deaf, don't you think?"

"You are funny tonight, aren't you?"

As Jackie asked her last question, a dim shadow shuffled its way down the open stairwell from the third floor into the great room below. The shadow carried a flashlight in its hand and stopped to tie a knot in the belt of its bathrobe as it dismounted the stairs. A feeble voice rang out, "Hold on a minute. I am not deaf. I am slow, but I am not deaf."

Avery and Jackie obliged the request. The shadow glided toward them and gradually took on a shape and a face. Opening the door, the shadow became an old man with skinny fingers and thin hair, a nose which hooked at the end like a coat hanger, and an age spot the size of a buffalo nickel on his chin.

The shadow spoke, "May I help you with something?"

Avery stepped forward. "Sir, I'm Avery Mays and this is my partner, Jackie Broadus. We're from the Peachtree Street Station of the Atlanta Police Department." Avery presented his badge as he spoke. The shadow nodded in recognition. Avery moved ahead.

"We're here searching for Walt Litske, Jr. or for someone from his family. We have a few questions we need to ask him. Do you know where he or his family might be?"

"Sir," started the aged gentleman, "I appreciate your position as an officer of the law, but I'm not sure why I should divulge any information, even if it is within my possession, which I am not, of course, saying that it is." The shadow's words were clipped.

Jackie jumped into the exchange. "Out of curiosity, sir, what is your connection to this house?"

"I don't suppose answering that can do any harm. I'm the former butler of this estate. Now, I watch over it for the family until a sale can be consummated."

"Then you do know the Litskes?"

"Yes, I do."

Avery chimed in again, "We need your help Mr.—"

"Smucks, sir. Mr. James Smucks."

"We need your help, Mr. Smucks. I suppose you've heard about the murder of three young women in Atlanta in the last few weeks?" Avery stated it as a question, but Smucks refused to bite.

"We've connected Walt Litske, Jr. to at least one of them," said Jackie, "And we want to ask him a few questions about it."

Smucks held up his hand to stop the two-pronged interrogation. "I heard a young clergyman had committed that bit of mayhem. How's Junior connected to it?"

"The young clergyman remains our chief suspect. But, Walt has a connection to him also. The two roomed together in college."

Smucks almost gagged. "That's right! Walt did room with a religiously oriented young man in college. That had completely slipped my mind. Getting a bit older, you know."

"Aren't we all." Jackie helped the gentleman out. "We have no evidence to make Walt a suspect. But, we do need to question him."

Avery tried again. "Do you know where he might be?"

Smucks stood in the doorway with the flashlight lowered in his hand, lighting the ground at their feet. Lifting the light, he scanned their eyes. Avery noticed his hand shaking, whether from the cold or from age, he couldn't tell.

Smucks' voice quaked as he answered. "I raised him, you know. Since he was in diapers. He was always big, and into everything. His dad didn't give him much time, too busy making money to give him anything else. I remember his first bicycle—he ran crying to me when he crashed it into his mom's car and scratched his elbows. He wrecked his first car, too, a Corvette Mr. Litske bought him after high school graduation. He seemed to wreck everything he touched."

Smucks talked to himself, staring through Avery and Jackie, into the door of the past, into memories. "That football injury nearly killed him. Turned him into an addict, into a whimpering child, into a nothing—a man with no pride and no hope of getting any. He's still fighting his addiction, but most of the fight went out of him when his injury killed his career."

Spent from the effort of digging up old graves, Smucks shook and ceased.

Jackie reached out and touched his arm. "We want to help him, Mr. Smucks, not hurt him. Do you know where he is?"

"I'm not sure, but I can make a guess." Smucks gathered himself and stood straighter. "The Litskes own a house at St. Simon's Island. They're trying to sell it, but so far it's still on the market. I saw Walt on Saturday of last week. He looked terrible and he told me he planned to get away from everything for awhile. That's where he always goes when he wants rest."

Jackie pulled out her notebook and jotted down some notes. "Do you know an address?"

"Sure, 8118 Grace View Drive. On the ocean. A paradise."

Avery offered his hand to Smucks. "Sir, we want to thank you for your cooperation."

Smucks took it, gingerly, his toothpick fingers brittle in Avery's grasp. "You're welcome, Mr. Mays. I see no reason not to give you my assistance. If Walt's guilty, he needs help. If not, he needs exoneration. I will be anxious to discover which it is."

With a nod of the head he turned and trundled off, flashlight in hand, back toward the stair. Avery and Jackie watched him go, then directed themselves back to their car.

"That's a nice man," offered Avery.

"Reminds me of my grandfather," conceded Jackie as they crawled inside.

"You never mentioned your grandfather to me."

"No reason to. He's dead."

She turned the car toward the Peachtree Street Precinct. They would check in with Conners, then head to St. Simon's.

PART

IV

HE'S ARMED WITHOUT

THAT'S INNOCENT WITHIN

Alexander Pope

FOR WE MUST ALL APPEAR BEFORE THE JUDG-

MENT SEAT OF CHRIST

THAT EVERYONE MAY RECEIVE THE THINGS

DONE IN THE BODY;

WHETHER IT BE GOOD OR BAD

St. Paul

CHAPTER

28

T hat'll be a $20.00 cover charge for each of you." A tall, heavily muscled security guard dressed in a navy suit held out his hand for the money as Burke escorted Debbi into the Silver Slipper. Debbi pulled out her wallet, peeled off the money and handed it to the bouncer.

"Here . . . you'll need a mask," said the guard, gesturing at the costumed crowd and holding up a box of extra rubber faces for Burke's inspection. "It's Halloween and the only people who get in without masks are the waitresses. Pick one."

"What's your pleasure, Debbi?" Burke asked.

"Doesn't matter, whatever you think," Debbi said, her eyes darting over the crush of bodies squeezed into the glitzy room.

"How about a Leona Helmsley?"

"Perfect." She took the mask from him and slid it over her face. "And here's one for you." She handed him a Ronald Reagan model and he pulled it on and steered her forward into the cloud of smoke.

Three steps into the door, a waitress dressed in a skimpy black bikini yelled over the music, "What can I get you from the bar?"

Burke looked at Debbi through his mask. "How about a Club Soda?"

"Sounds good."

Burke held up two fingers to the waitress. "Give me two Club Sodas."

With a twist and a turn, the waitress left them. Burke's eyes swept the room—it was just like he remembered. Not a low-rent dive, but a bar for the upper crust, a bar where the men wore starched shirts and

204 BEYOND A REASONABLE DOUBT

suspenders and the women paraded their sequined dresses and dia-
mond necklaces.

People were everywhere and women obviously outnumbered the
men. Many of the women were like the waitress who stopped them as
they entered—attractive and scantily clad. Others were dates or wives—
dancing in rhythm to the loud music with their escorts. A wrap-around
bar surrounded the dance floor on all four sides of the room and men
and women alike stood at the bar and watched the dancing.

Burke and Debbi pressed against the bar, surveying the scene.
"Quite a place isn't it?" yelled Burke over the music.

"Incredible," nodded Debbi, shaking her head.

"It seems so unnatural to me," he said, "like a dream."

The waitress interrupted his thoughts. "That'll be $6.50," she said,
handing them their drinks. She grabbed the $8.00 Debbi handed her and
pranced off.

"Want a seat?" Debbi asked.

"Sure, you see one?"

"Over by the wall on the left."

Burke led Debbi through the crowd. Seated, he tilted his head at
the mob scene. "Why do they come here?"

"Not sure I can answer that," she said. "Maybe it's an escape from
work."

"Or from wives or husbands."

"Or from loneliness." Debbi paused for a second, then continued.
"I've always thought places like this were like a bunch of guys going
hunting or a group of women meeting every Tuesday morning to play
bridge and drink coffee."

"What'cha mean?"

"You know, where people get together and bond. A bar provides
a setting for people to drink and laugh and pretend they have intimacy."

"A person can bond in other places."

"I suppose so, but apparently many don't."

"So, they come here for companionship?"

"Could be."

The waitress loomed beside the table inspecting their glasses.
"Need another drink?" she asked.

The taped music stopped as she spoke and the couples on the dance
floor pushed their way off it and steered themselves back to their tables.
A man in a black tuxedo stepped to a microphone sitting on a small stage
in the center of the dance floor and addressed the crowd. "Friends," he
said, "as usual at the Slipper, we provide the finest nightly entertainment

in Atlanta. As part of that quality, I am pleased to introduce to you a regular on our stage. You've loved her before and you'll love her again tonight. So please welcome our live entertainment for this evening—Ms. Tricia Pauley."

The emcee clapped and the crowd joined in. A tall woman in a blue sequined dress glided onto the stage. She grasped the microphone in both hands and the band hit the beat and she belted out the words to a pounding song. Couples moved quickly onto the dance floor and the room jumped alive with their movements.

Burke waved the waitress away and turned his eyes to the woman on stage. Focusing on her face, he felt a jolt—he knew this woman!

He slammed down his drink and grabbed Debbi by the arm. "I recognize that girl!" he said.

"What?" Debbi cupped her ear toward him.

"I know that singer."

Incredulous, Debbi queried him, "How?"

"I met her in college. She dated Walt for about three months."

"Burke, are you sure you're not imagining things?"

"I'm positive. She gave us our nicknames."

"And what was that?"

"She called us Neon and Freon and the names stuck all through college. I'm absolutely certain I know her."

He stared at the woman with the microphone. Her black hair fell over her forehead, but Burke had no doubt—Tricia Pauley had spent hours at his apartment during her brief but torrid romance with Walt.

"When her set ends, I've got to talk to her," he said.

Debbi cautioned him. "What are you going to say—'haven't I met you somewhere before?'"

"Something like that."

"Don't you think that'll sound sort of lame?"

"I'm sure it will, but I don't know what else to do. You got any suggestions?"

Debbi fell silent as the singer moved to a slower number and the heavy beat slowed and the dancing couples edged closer to each other. "Not really, just wanted you to think about it before you go running up to a strange woman, using some ancient line on her. Besides, if she does recognize you, what's to keep her from yelling for the police?"

"I hadn't thought of that."

Burke took a swig from his glass. He shrugged his shoulders at Debbi, "Only one thing to do."

"I'm listening."

"Why don't you talk to her for me?"

"What?"

"You go to her, tell her you're a reporter and you're looking for Walt as a suspect in a murder case."

"Why would she talk to me?"

"For a couple of reasons. You could offer to pay her. Or, you can remind her how Walt walked out on her eight years ago for another co-ed. Love's grudges can last a long time."

"It might work," she said. "When she stops singing, I'll give it a try."

They leaned back in their chairs to wait, but their anxiety level increased as Tricia Pauley moved her way through her music. Burke sipped nervously at his Club Soda and stared at Pauley through the eyes of his mask. Debbi pulled on her hair and stared alternately at him and at Pauley on stage. The minutes passed slowly—the music ebbed and flowed as Pauley's rich voice surged soft and loud through her set. Finally, after what seemed like an eternity to them both, Pauley bowed to the applauding crowd. "Thank you," she glowed at them. "Thank you. I'm going to take a short break, so stick around. Thank you." She bowed once more and moved quickly off the platform.

Debbi moved hurriedly too, pushing back from the table and stepping toward her. Though Burke bent forward and cupped his ear in their direction, he couldn't hear their conversation.

"Excuse me, Miss, could I talk with you for a moment?" Debbi pulled off her mask.

Pauley looked confused, but nodded. "Sure," she said.

Debbi took a deep breath and began. "Ms. Pauley, my name is Debbi Meyer and I'm looking for a guy named Walt Litske. Do you know where I can find him?"

Pauley glanced around for a second, then answered. "Walt Litske. I dated him in college."

"Have you seen him lately?"

"Not in the last few months. He used to come in regularly, almost every night he wasn't out of town. But, he dropped out of sight some time back and hasn't shown up since."

Tricia wrapped her arms around her shoulders. "Why do you want to find Walt? You dating him or something?"

"No, nothing like that."

"It would be like Walt, to walk out on a girl and not tell her why. He's never been one to develop a real deep relationship."

"But that's not why I'm looking for him," Debbi repeated.

"Why then?"

Debbi turned her head and glanced back at Burke. Tricia followed her gaze toward him, then laughed at the mask. "Who's the guy?"

Debbi replied casually, "My boyfriend." To shift attention from Burke, she answered Pauley's first question directly.

"I'm searching for Walt because I'm a reporter from the *Atlanta Independent* and Walt's been connected with the death of the prostitute who was murdered in Atlanta this past Friday."

"Is he a suspect?" Tricia's surprise seemed genuine.

"Not yet, but he could be. I want to talk to him before the police catch up to him."

"That would be a big story, huh?"

"Sure it would, if I can find him."

Glancing in Burke's direction again, Tricia said, "I thought some preacher was the killer in that case."

Debbi bristled, then relaxed her shoulders, hoping Tricia hadn't noticed her reaction. "He's still the chief suspect I think, but Walt's name has come up also."

"But not as a suspect?"

"Not officially."

"Then why should I talk to you?"

"If Walt's not guilty, my story can help him."

"And if he is?"

"Then I probably won't find him before the police do."

Pauley rubbed her shoulders with her hands still crossed over her chest. "I don't know where Walt is now," she began, "but I do know where he used to go."

Debbi asked softly. "Where's that?"

"When we were dating, Walt's folks owned a place on St. Simon's Island. Walt loved it there. We went almost every weekend while we were seeing each other. It was so quiet and Walt didn't get much of that anywhere else. He always calmed down there on the beach—like a big turtle going into a shell, I used to tell him. We'd walk on the beach for hours, holding hands like two kids. I guess we were kids then, splashing water on each other and dreading the time we had to leave."

Debbi wanted to pat Tricia, to comfort her, but she held back. She stuck to business. "Does Walt still go there?"

"I think so, at least as far as I know. If he still owns it. He's faced some tough times in the last year or so."

"When did you talk to him last?"

"On July 4. I remember it distinctly. Walt was as drunk as I've ever seen him, making quite a racket. He gave me a $100.00 tip. Said it was for old time's sake."

Shaking her head at the memory, Pauley glanced around again. "Look," she said. "I care about Walt, always have. He's gone through a lot. If you find him, tell him to call me. Maybe I can help him. Heaven knows he needs it."

Debbi nodded and reached out and touched Tricia on the shoulder. "Thanks for your help."

Tricia nodded and turned away, walking into the elbowing crowd, past a group of smiling men, heading toward her dressing room through the light-streaked smoke of the club.

Debbi threaded through the crowd, back to Burke.

"Let's get outta here," she shouted, standing over him and picking up her purse.

"Did you find out anything?" he asked as he pulled off his mask and they pushed out the door.

"Yeah, she's Tricia Pauley, like you thought."

"Did she tell you anything?"

"Maybe."

"Don't make me beg, Debbi. What did she say?"

"Did you ever go to St. Simon's with Walt?"

Surprised, Burke snapped his fingers. "Yeah! Once, I did, on a weekend, right after Easter, during our first year as roommates."

"Did Walt go there often?"

"Yeah, a lot when football didn't keep him at school."

"Why didn't you go more than once if you two were best friends?"

"'Cause I never fit there."

"What'cha mean?"

"Walt usually took ten to twenty people at a time—guys and girls. Everybody started drinking on the way. By the time they got to the island, they were totally looped. And, they usually went in pairs."

"So you felt out of place."

"Completely. Like a long finger at a retired butcher's convention."

"And you never went back."

"Never. Walt tried to get me to go. Said it would do me some good—help me loosen up."

"But you never did."

"No, I never went back."

"I think we should try St. Simon's Island."

"So do I. If Walt's hiding from something, that's where he would go."

"Can you remember how to get to the house?"

"I'm not sure, but I do remember the name of the street. A house on Grace View Drive."

"A preacher wouldn't forget that."

"No, at least I didn't. With the street address we can ask directions, if we need them."

"You ready?"

"If you are."

"Here, you drive," Debbi tossed him the keys. "I want to catch a little rest if I can."

CHAPTER
29

Hock and Sonny were two hours ahead of Burke and Debbi and almost three ahead of Avery and Jackie on their way to St. Simon's Island. After scurrying out of Steele's office, Sonny picked up two packages before he left for the island.

The first package he plucked from the campaign safe, a brown manila folder stuffed with a thousand 100 dollar bills. As a marginal part of an election year war chest which had climbed above 5 million already, no one would miss this $100,000. Sonny also picked up a second package—this one from the top drawer of the desk at his apartment—a holster encasing a Glock 17L pistol. Though it slowed him by almost two hours to get it, he figured an ounce of prevention was worth a pound of cure. He placed both items in a tan briefcase and handed it to Hock. He never questioned Hock's presence. They always went together when the Senator needed a mess cleaned up.

As Sonny had told Hock more than once, "I'm the brains; you're the brawn." Hock liked that and smiled the same crooked smile whenever Sonny said it.

"Ready to go, Hock?" Sonny asked, leaving the apartment.

"Yeah, Sonny, I don't need to get nothin'."

"Let's go then."

On Highway 75, Hock noted, "Isss rainin', Sonny. I don't like it when it rains."

"No one much does, Hock, but we wouldn't like it if it didn't rain either."

"Rain gets in ma eyes, Sonny, so's I can't see so good."

"Don't worry about the rain, Hock; you don't drive anyway. You just sit back and rest."

"Can't res', Sonny, gotta find Walt. Senata say we gotta take care of Walt. I gotta do what da Senata says."

"Don't get yourself worked up now, Hock. We want to get Walt out of the country so no one can find him for a few weeks. That's all. With this money we can ship him away long enough for the cops to find the real killer or until the election is over and we can take care of whatever complications might arise."

Hock listened and nodded. Inside his helmet-sized head, though, he wasn't agreeing. Sonny was wrong. The Senator wanted Walt taken care of. Sonny wouldn't want to do that. But, Hock would. *Hock don't like Walt anyway. Walt makes fun of Hock and the Senator don't stop him. Walt is big, too, like Hock is, and Hock is afraid the Senator likes Walt better than he does him.*

Hock lolled his head back and pretended to sleep. The drive would take five hours or a little more. He snuggled Sonny's briefcase with the gun in it close to his chest, thinking of the slick feel of the shiny gun, remembering its smell when fired, and wondering what Walt would look like with several of the bullet holes puncturing his stomach. Hock didn't figure to use the gun on Walt, but he did like the thought of Walt's blood mixing with the sand on the beach. Yeah, he liked that thought. That one put him to sleep.

CHAPTER

30

A very and Jackie stopped at a pay phone outside a mini-mart to call Conners. They had missed him at the station when they went by after leaving Smucks. After waiting almost an hour for him to return, they had pulled out. Better to move on to St. Simon's and call him on the way.

Avery performed the honors of the call, standing uncovered in the increasingly heavy rain. Conners answered the phone. "Chief," said Avery, "we think we've got a line on Litske. His parents own a home on St. Simon's Island. An old butler told us Walt used to go there when he needed to get away from things. Jackie and I agree it's worth a shot to head down there. What'cha think?"

"Sounds like a possibility," agreed Conners, chewing on the end of his pipe. "I'll call ahead and see if I can get a search warrant ready for you to pick up when you get there."

"It'll be past midnight."

"I know. But, if I can get hold of a judge now, he can leave it at the police station in St. Simon's. You can drop by and get it."

"Sounds good, Frank. Anything else on the third murder? Or on Anderson?"

"Not really. We've talked to the folks around Cascade. But no one has seen anything. Anderson has dropped out of sight."

"Pretty elusive for a preacher, huh?"

"Yeah, maybe God's on his side."

"Not if he did it, Frank."

"No, I guess not. Maybe the devil then?"

"That'd be my guess."

"You'd better head to St. Simon's, Avery, before the trail gets cold."

"On the way, Chief."

The rain dripped off Avery's ears, two faucets of cold water pouring onto his shoulders, as he slammed the door of the squad car and slid under the wheel.

"It's turned messy out there," Jackie offered.

Avery's mood turned foul. "Brilliant observation."

"Don't jump me, fella, I'm just making conversation."

"Well, if it doesn't get any better than that, this will be one long drive."

"Maybe you'd like it if I didn't talk at all."

"Maybe I would."

Jackie shut up. Avery always groused this way when he sensed a break in a case. He admitted his nerves. "Sorry, Jackie. I'm a little brittle right now."

"Me too. This thing could be coming to a head."

"What makes you think so?" He wanted his hunch substantiated.

"We know Litske and Anderson are connected."

"Right."

"And we know Anderson was in Reese's apartment on the night of her death."

"Right again," he said.

"And Litske probably was too."

"Yep."

"So, if we can find Litske we might find Anderson also."

"And one of them probably killed her."

"Or both of them."

"Exactly."

"And, Avery, I think he's on this island."

"Why?"

"It just makes sense."

"A woman's intuition?"

"Same as a man's hunch, the way I see it."

"I suppose it is."

"Then you agree with me?"

"Absolutely, Jackie."

"Good."

"Good."

The warm air blowing from the heater caressed Jackie's feet and anesthetized her mind with its slight whirring. Closing her eyes, she wrapped her arms around herself. The night slickened up, the rain bathing the car with wet hands, washing it from top to bottom, slinging the chilly moisture off the tires as they whistled across the pavement.

"Someone said it might sleet some later tonight," Avery said.

"This far south?"

"That's what the man said."

"It's cold enough."

The wipers slished across the windshield, a rhythmic chatter to match the singing of the radials as they zinged across the wet pavement. The headlights glared off the highway, bouncing over the white and yellow stripes, searching for direction through the wet night. Mays and Broadus were alone and it was dark.

"Wake me if you need my help driving," Jackie said, dozing off.

Under his breath, where she couldn't hear, Avery replied, "Go to sleep, little girl, go to sleep."

She obeyed him without knowing it.

CHAPTER

31

Fifty miles ahead of them on Interstate 75, Debbi also slumbered, succumbing to the same combination of coziness on the inside of the car in contrast to the bleakness of the outside. Burke listened contentedly to her even breathing. He liked sitting in the same car with her, smelling the scent of her skin. He tried to breathe the smell into his mind so he would remember it forever.

They had covered almost 120 miles through the splashing rain. Burke had turned on the radio to keep him company. The low strains of country gospel swelled through the car. "Why me, Lord," the song lamented, "what have I ever done, to deserve even one, of the blessings I've known?"

Burke's spirit resonated with the words of the song and he sang softly along with them. They were sad to him, even though they spoke of blessings. Sad, because they evoked pain as well as pleasure; because they implied that blessings can be found in the midst of sorrows. The singer knew that and didn't skirt it. Burke celebrated that truth, wrapping his plaintive voice around it and making it his own.

A sense of blessedness overwhelmed Burke as he listened to Debbi sleep. A sense that in spite of the insanity of the last few days, all would be well. He and Debbi were not alone in the car sloshing toward St. Simon's. Another rode with them and wrapped them in a cocoon of protection. Peace rose up and pushed away his fears. He glanced over at Debbi and admitted to himself for the first time that he hoped this night wouldn't end his relationship with her. He wanted more than that. Much more.

She stirred, quickly, without warning, like she had been privy to his thoughts. She shuddered, then jumped to a dulled consciousness. "Where are we?"

"We just passed Macon."

"How much longer?"

"About three hours I think."

"That long?"

"I'm afraid so."

Debbi shivered.

"Are you cold?" Burke asked.

"Yeah, a little."

He turned up the heat. "You jumped a moment ago. A bad dream?"

"Something like that."

"Want to talk about it?"

"I don't know if I do or not."

"We've got a long drive ahead of us. Might help pass the time."

"Are you my counselor or something?"

Stung, Burke retreated, "No, just trying to be friendly."

"Sorry." Debbi said, apparently noting that she had been too curt. "It's just painful to talk about some things."

"I can identify with that."

He sensed their relationship was about to take a turn, toward a retreat into more loneliness or toward a movement into intimacy. He didn't want to take the first step. He didn't have to.

"I told you my parents were divorced."

"Yeah, you did. I'm sorry about that. It must have hurt."

"Yeah, it did. I always thought it was my fault. My folks argued about the way to raise me. My dad was always stricter than Mom, believed in strong discipline and few privileges. Mom seemed to trust me more, to give me more room to make my own mistakes and to learn my own lessons. So, when they divorced, I figured it was because they couldn't agree on how to raise me. Thought if they hadn't had me, they might still be married."

"Most kids of divorced parents think they're the cause of it."

"I know that now, Burke, but I didn't know it then. I figured if they loved me enough they would stay together. But, that didn't do it."

"Nothing we can do to fix some things." For a beat, only the sound of the windshield wipers broke the silence. Then, Burke circled back to his original concern. "What scared you a moment ago?"

"My dream."

"What was it?"

"I saw my dad and mom together again. They were older than they are now and they were holding hands, like they had made up."

"What's scary about that?"

"I wasn't with them."

Debbi didn't want to go any further. She turned toward Burke and touched his arm as he drove.

"Do you ever dream?"

"Often."

"Anything ever scare you?"

"Plenty."

"What?"

"I don't know if I can tell you."

"I just told you." Debbi said it gently, coaxing him.

"I know, but my dream is even worse than yours."

"How can it be any worse?"

Burke sighed deeply, as if he were drawing his last breath. He didn't want to think of the face that haunted his dreams. In fact, he expended tremendous energy every day to keep that face caged in its corner. He'd hoped to kill the face by imprisoning it, but he hadn't succeeded. The face lived and he confronted it far too often to suit him. He dreaded its appearance, but somehow he needed it, too, needed to see it smiling—before the smile turned to a scream.

He choked out the words, "I killed her, Debbi."

Stunned, Debbi's eyes expanded, dimes into silver dollars. "What?"

"I killed her."

Debbi went rigid in her seat. "Burke, don't! Don't talk nonsense!" Her voice rose three notches, barely below a panicked scream. "You told me you didn't kill her, you were there but you didn't kill her! Don't do this to me now, I'm in too deep, this is frightening me. What do you mean you killed her?"

Her words poured out in a torrent before Burke could interrupt. Now she stopped, breathless, her heart clipping in high gear, her chest heaving.

Burke edged the car to the side of the muddy road and turned to face her. "I didn't kill Carol Reese, Debbi," he said, "I killed . . . I killed . . . Sarah." Burke's voice sounded dead, without emotion, drained beyond speech.

Searching her mind to recall the names of the other dead prostitutes, Debbi failed to remember. She dared to ask. "Who is Sarah, Burke?" she asked in a tenative whisper.

He choked out the answer. "My little sister. She died when I was sixteen. My parents went bowling and left me to baby-sit. She was two years old. A blond-headed, blue-eyed baby sister—the family surprise we called her, a package of sunshine and blue sky, gift wrapped and given to all of us. My older brother Richard had already moved to college. Sarah loved me. Followed me around all the time. She'd just started talking, called me 'bid brudder.'"

Debbi noticed the tears creeping out of the bottoms of Burke's eyes. "What happened, Burke?"

"We were playing on the floor. Sarah said she was hungry. I went to the kitchen and cut a hot dog in half for her. Handed it to her on the floor. She took it and bit off a chunk. The next thing I knew she started choking, playing one moment, laughing, then choking and turning blue the next. I picked her up to help her, to pull it out of her throat with my hand, to squeeze her little chest, to get that hot dog that was choking her out. I knew I could save her. But, I couldn't, 'cause it suddenly hit me." Burke's voice broke into sobs, wracking cries of anguish, letting the face out of the closet, peering into her eyes again, watching them laugh, then scream, then glaze over. He never saw them die, only dead.

"You couldn't get it out?"

"I never had the chance."

Puzzled, Debbi pressed, "But you said you were there and that you tried."

"I wanted to try, but I couldn't."

"Why not?"

"It's so hard to say."

"Trust me."

"An epileptic attack hit me. The first one in over four years. I had stopped taking my medicine, even though the doctors said I shouldn't. I was a teenager who didn't want to admit he had a weakness, to let others know I needed medicine to keep a seizure from occuring. So, it struck. In my panic I couldn't stop it. The last thing I saw was Sarah's blue eyes, pleading with me to help her. I couldn't. The next time I saw those eyes they were empty, like a glass without water, fish eyes, no life in them. I can't forgive myself."

Burke slumped over the wheel, his head touching the top of it, still as death itself. His voice shifted lower, into a whisper, his tears spent, a man almost dead himself, a man who wanted to die.

"That's what I dream about, Debbi, my sister's eyes. I want to see them laughing, so I remember them. But they never keep laughing, they always end up pleading to me for help. And I never can."

"You couldn't help it, Burke," said Debbi, putting her hand on his back and rubbing it to soothe him. "It wasn't your fault."

"My mind tells me it wasn't my fault, but that doesn't help my heart."

"We have something in common then."

"What's that?"

"I thought I caused my parents' divorce, but you tell me I didn't. You think you caused your sister's death, but I'm telling you, you didn't. It's guilt—that's what we have in common."

"And it weighs a ton."

"I wish I knew how to get rid of it."

Burke shook his head and wiped his eyes. "It's even worse when you know how, but still can't do it."

CHAPTER

32

S onny nudged Hock awake.

"Where are we, Sonny?"

"We're at the Lighthouse Hotel."

"Is Walt here?"

"I think so. This is where we always stay when we're taking some time off. You've been here lots of times. Don't you remember?"

"Not toooo much. Seems like I've been here, but I'm not for sure."

"It's O.K., Hock. You have. All the Senator's friends come here from time to time. And Walt is one of the Senator's friends."

* * * * *

Hock unfolded his ponderous frame, pulled himself out of the car and followed Sonny. He squinted his eyes against the lights and hunched down in his jacket to keep the rain off his face. He bent over to avoid the door frame and walked into the lobby of the Lighthouse.

The desk attendant nodded affirmatively when Sonny asked for Walt Litske's room number.

"He's in 505."

Sonny thanked him and said to Hock, "We'll get the luggage out of the car, then go see Walt." They trudged back out. At the trunk of the car, Sonny opened the lid and leaned down the seat to get his briefcase.

The blow crumpled him instantly.

Powered by an anger created by loyalty and jealousy, Hock slammed his interlocked hands across the back of Sonny's head. The meat on his right hand split below the second knuckle. Hock needed only one lick. Sonny collapsed like a loaf of bread, soft and pliable in the middle.

The giant lifted his friend, laid him in the trunk and slammed the lid shut.

"505. 505. 505." Hock repeated the number to himself so he wouldn't forget as he walked through the lobby, and waited for the elevator. As he stepped off on the fifth floor and searched for the correct door, he kept repeating, "505. 505. 505." He found it.

His heavy hand pounded on the door. Again. A third time. No answer.

With a two-step start, Hock lunged into the door. It cracked in the center and Hock clumped into the room. He adjusted his near-sighted eyes to the dim light. Unable to see beyond a couple of feet in front of him, Hock searched over the room, confused that Walt didn't rush at him.

He found no one in the small entry to the suite. He heard flies buzzing and then saw them feasting on a plate of dried french fries sitting on a table by the door. A step further and Hock tripped on a stack of bottles and went to one knee to keep from falling headlong into the floor. He reached down and picked one up, vaguely making out the letters: "J-I-M B-E-A-M." Though unable to read very well, he recognized the label as liquor. Using his fingers, Hock counted eight such bottles under his feet. He stood and picked his way further into the cluttered room.

A cold breeze, courtesy of an open window to his left, billowed his red hair outward and covered his face and body with dampness, making him feel sticky.

He turned right and spotted the bed. A heavy form sagged down in its center. Hock froze and listened for the sound of breathing. A weak sigh rewarded his stillness, a sigh too small for such a large bulk, a sigh for a small girl maybe, but not for a hulking linebacker of a man.

Confused, Hock stepped across the carpet, to the edge of the bed. His shadow cast a black block over the figure lying there. Hock tried to stay quiet—he wanted it to go easily, like the breathing he now heard, without noise and shouting. Someone might hear and that would be bad.

The bulk on the bed moved quickly, arching upwards toward him with a suddenness totally unexpected in such a quiet room. Hock watched the fist aimed for his nose but couldn't move fast enough to avoid it. It crunched into him, breaking his nose instantly and opening a three-inch gash on his upper lip. Hock shook his head slightly at the impact and licked the warm blood off his lip into his mouth. Pain. Unusual, but not unbearable.

Though slowly, Hock moved now too. He grabbed Walt in a mass and tossed him out of the bed, onto the floor. He tried to pin him so he could smash his face as his had just been smashed.

Rolling like two redwoods in a river, side to side, over and over, Hock and Walt wrestled for control. Fists punched outward when the openings came, hitting air and body almost equally, popping holes in the night and opening bloody gashes over eyes, on cheeks and across knuckles.

Hock reached above his head to slash again and his hand bumped a brass lamp sitting on the nightstand beside the bed. Though angered at first because the lamp had interfered with his punch, Hock's mind suddenly experienced a flash of insight. He closed his fingers over the base of the lamp, and turned it upside down to put the weighted end out, like the barrel of an ax head. Liking the fit of the weapon, he let go of Walt's neck with his left hand and stood up. He pulled the brass lamp above his head and grasped it with both hands and slammed it downward, like a logger chopping wood. The sound of skin and bones tearing and cracking rewarded his effort. Again he lifted and slammed, the lamp brushing aside Walt's hand and arm as they raised upward, seeking to ward off the attack. A third time and Walt stopped moving and a grin splashed across Hock's face as blood splattered across his shoes. Walt wouldn't take his place now.

Happy, Hock stopped to look at his ax. Blood dripped off the edges. He touched it. It was wet and warm. He tasted it, lifting the base of the lamp to his lips and sticking out his tongue. Slightly bitter. But otherwise no taste at all. Satisfied, Hock struck one more time, clubbing Walt in the head. Then he placed the lamp back on the stand. He plugged it up, switched it on and inspected his work. Not bad, he decided. He had taken care of Walt, like the Senator wanted him to do. He knew the Senator would be pleased.

The flies stirred from the fries and circled around Walt's head for a second before deciding to land. Hock listened happily to them buzz as he walked out of the room and closed the door.

CHAPTER

33

A bloody hand raised itself to shoo away the flies. Walt wasn't quite ready for flies and worms, not yet. He moaned and gritted his teeth, but even with the pain, he pulled up by the bed and rested on one knee.

He touched the parts of his body which hurt the most. His head felt larger, like it had swelled to twice its normal size and the skin wasn't elastic enough to hold the skull anymore. He lifted his hand to wipe sweat out of his eyes, but saw that the wetness was blood instead. He didn't know how long he had been unconscious.

He knew, though, he couldn't stay where he was. The cops would come for him and if not the cops, then Hock might return. Though surprised at the violence of the Senator's attack it didn't surprise him that the Senator wanted him out of the picture. He'd hoped to get enough money to leave the country. But, the Senator had apparently decided to play it another way. Well, the rich and powerful made up the rules. Not much he could do about that. Except opt out of the game.

But not yet, not here. Walt wanted to go home. Not to Atlanta. That wasn't home. Not really. Just a place to go to school, play football, make money, have fun. No, home was his folks' place, here on St. Simon's, where he lived as a boy, down by the beach, where he could lose himself in the bigness of it, where he could build sand castles and touch the salt in the air, where he could disappear into the ocean, a dot bobbing up and down, alone and at peace.

Staggering, he pulled himself up and opened the dresser drawer beside the bed. A full bottle of Jim Beam greeted him and he picked it up enthusiastically, like he would take the hand of a friend to shake it.

He rummaged through the back of the drawer and found the gun he wished he'd had a few minutes ago.

Armed with his gun and his bottle, he inched his way down the stairwell of the hotel and ducked out the entrance by the soda machines. The cold air and heavy rain cleared his head and eyes as he fumbled for his car keys. At least he could see.

Fifteen minutes later he pulled himself out of the leather seats and dragged his body across the screened-in front porch of his old home place. A "For Sale" sign in the yard creaked in the ocean wind as he stumbled by it. He kicked at the sign in his anger, but missed it and kept walking. No longer owning a key, Walt punched his puffy hand through the front window by the door, unsnapped the latch, slid up the window and pulled himself through it.

His room faced the ocean on the left side of the house. Though fumbling through the blackness, he reached it and opened a window. The choppy breeze grabbed the drapes and held them up in his face as he stood by the window and took a deep breath, sucking in the cold, wet air. A deep pull from the booze helped the chill.

Gazing out at the ocean, Walt felt a flood of memories churn through him. The memories washed away the years and towed him out to his youth, to warm suns and relaxed afternoons picking up shells, running in the surf, flying kites. The memories tugged him back in now, toward recent years of belly-up plans, toward hopes crashing white-foamed and angry on rocks of injury and bad luck. The memories sucked him forward into the tormented whirlpool of the last six days, into the apartment of Carol Reese and the effort to get her to back off her plans to blackmail the Senator, into her stubborn refusal, and the feel of his hand slapping her, then hitting her, full and flush, hot and furious, out of control, like a hurricane punching ashore, crushing everything in its path.

His memories eddied him onward, out of her apartment, where he'd left her sprawled across the kitchen floor, toward the island, his lifetime place of refuge. Walt slumped down into the corner of his room and slugged down another long drink. Man, that tasted good.

CHAPTER

34

B urke pulled into the parking lot of the mini-mart and killed the engine. He looked at his watch—almost 1:00 A.M.! He and Debbi were bone tired, but the night wasn't over—not by a long shot.

He unsnapped his seatbelt, nudged Debbi on the shoulder and woke her. "We're on St. Simon's. In a few minutes, we'll know if Walt's here or not."

"I have a strong feeling that he is," said Debbi, rousing herself awake.

"I hope so. But I'm not sure what I'll say if we find him."

"You'll say you want him to tell the truth—you didn't go to Reese's house on your own; he took you there without telling you what Reese was."

"What if he killed her?"

"If he did, I don't guess he'll help you."

"Not unless he confesses and gives himself up."

"Do you think he'll do that?"

"Heaven only knows, Debbi. Walt was always so out of control. Never tied to one spot. Jail would kill him."

"If an executioner doesn't."

"And he might be innocent."

"If so, he can still help you," she argued.

"That's probably the only way he will help me."

Debbi's creeping fear registered in her voice. "If he did kill her, do you think he might hurt you? You're probably the only one who can definitely place him at Reese's apartment."

"I don't think he'd hurt me. We were best friends."

"But, you haven't seen him in five years. People change."

"Yeah, even best friends drift apart."

"Almost always best friends drift apart," she said.

"That's a cynical view."

"You saying it's not true?"

"No, it's probably very true. But it seems so sad to admit it."

"Yeah, it is sad. Sad, but true."

"So you think he could hurt me?"

"He might."

"But I don't have any choice but to try."

"I know."

"See you in a second," he said as he opened the door.

"Yeah, in a second," said Debbie.

Wet sand blew into his face as he walked into the bright glare of the store to ask directions.

"Do you know where Grace View Drive is?" He directed his question at a frail-looking woman who sat perched on a bar stool by the cash register.

"I'm not sure," she answered, pulling a cigarette from her pocket and sliding it between cracked lips. "Is that near the Lighthouse Hotel?"

"Could be. I think I remember a hotel near there."

Turning to a co-worker, the attendant yelled, "Any idea where Grace View is?"

"Yeah," the second worker said, smacking gum, "Go two red lights, turn left, then one red light and turn back right. It's the third street on the left, headed toward the ocean. My grandmother lives there."

"Thanks a lot," Burke said.

Burke trudged outside, pulled open the door to the Volvo and threw himself in out of the wet. He was almost settled under the wheel when it hit him—Debbi was gone.

CHAPTER
35

H ock knew he couldn't drive himself back to Atlanta. He'd never learned to drive. Never any need to learn. Sonny did all the driving for them.

Stopping by the rest room of the Lighthouse Hotel to wash his hands and face, he grabbed a handful of paper towels, wet them and headed back to the car. He would wake Sonny with the towels and explain what he'd done. Sonny would understand it wasn't personal. He'd just finished what the Senator wanted finished. That's all.

He needn't have bothered with the towels. Rhythmic thumpings pounding out of the trunk greeted him as he walked back. Sonny was conscious again.

* * * * *

Inside the trunk, Sonny decided to keep this quarrell between Hock and the Senator and not between himself and Hock. It wouldn't do to get either of the men mad at him. As Hock lifted the lid, Sonny lit into him, peppering him with questions, still sitting in the trunk, his face livid with rage.

"Hock, what have you done? You could've killed me. You better have a good explanation for this or the Senator is going to kick you out on your own."

"I tuk care of Walt Lisske for da Senata, like he said we should."

"What do you mean, Hock?" Sonny asked, ashen faced.

"I tuk care of him. I kilt him."

Frightened by the ominous figure looming above him, Sonny decided visible anger at Hock might be dangerous. So, he stayed calm.

"You killed him, Hock?"

"Yeah, I did." Hock pushed out his chest, like a proud child over a job well done.

"Where, Hock?"

"In da hotel. In izzz room." He slurred the words.

"Let me out, Hock, I've got to check to make sure. The Senator would want me to verify everything." Hock stepped backward and Sonny crawled out of the boot. He knew what to do. He would blame the death on Hock, directing the cops toward a deranged man with a jealousy over another of the Senator's bodyguards. That wouldn't be hard to sell, two mammoth men fighting for attention. They could pin the prostitute's death either on the preacher or on Walt. Didn't matter with him dead. A good deal all around.

First, though, he had to verify Hock's story. Not that he doubted it. Just needed to find out and report it.

They entered by the back stairs. Back to 505. The door stood slightly ajar for them and they stepped inside. Sonny gagged for a second at the smell of stale liquor, old cigarette butts, and unflushed urine.

Hock pointed him toward the bed.

"Ova here, Sonny. I left him here."

Sonny peered through the pale lamplight as he walked across the room and inspected the area by the far wall. Bending over, he stroked the carpet with his fingers—blood stains. Standing again, he picked up the lamp and touched the base. Yes, someone had suffered from it. But that someone was missing.

"Are you sure it was here, Hock? You didn't drag him anywhere?"

Confused, Hock glanced around the room.

"I left him here, Sonny. Dead. I hit him wid dat lamp. More dan once. I knows I kilt him." Tears jumped into Hock's eyes, a child's tears, a child who knows he has messed up and disappointed others.

Sonny touched Hock's arm. He'd watched him cry before and it was at a time like this, when Hock thought he had failed the Senator.

"It's O.K., Hock. We'll find him. If he's still alive, we'll take care of him. If not, we'll get away from him. You come on with me."

Hock sputtered through his choppy heaves, "Where? Where we goin', Sonny?"

"To the only other place Walt might be. To his home place."

With fatherly compassion Sonny took Hock's hand. "Come on, Hock, it's going to be okay."

"I hope so, Sonny, I don' want da Senata mad with me."

CHAPTER

36

Burke didn't panic. His emotions were too exhausted for panic. As if in a trance, he walked back into the mini-mart and searched for Debbi. Not there. He checked the women's bathroom. Not there. Leaving the building, he stepped cautiously around the back and looked by the garbage dumpsters. Not there.

Knowing of no other path to follow, he crawled back into the car and pounded the steering wheel in utter frustration. "Where are you, Debbi?" he shouted, his voice hoarse. His mind fogged. He tried to clear it. Had Debbi left him? Gone on to Walt's without him to get a story? No, someone had grabbed Debbi. But who? Senator Steele? or his men? Burke gritted his teeth. No way to know where she was. But she wasn't here. Someone had takeen her. But where? Where to start looking? Walt's place. He had to get to Walt's place. He had to find Walt, had to find Debbi. He'd go ahead with their original plan. His only clue to her whereabouts was the connection between Steele and Litske. He couldn't go to the police. They would simply arrest him for Reese's murder and for Debbi's disappearance too. Someone could kill her, dump her body and he'd never see her again and he might even get charged with her murder. He had to prove his innocence so he could stay free; so he could do whatever it took to find the girl he loved. Only one road open to him—the road to Grace View Drive.

Burke followed the directions given to him. It only took a few minutes to reach the street and spot Walt's house. When he saw the blue-framed cottage with the wrap-around porch, he stopped the car dead in the wet road and pulled off and parked. He sat for a moment and listened to the pounding of the rain against the windshield. He leaned his head back against the seat and closed his eyes and he'd never felt so alone. The Presence he'd sensed in the car earlier seemed to have deserted him. Jesus' question from the cross *My God, why have you forsaken me?* rose up in his mind and the agony of the phrase jolted him. But he had to go on. Like Jesus had to go on. To see what lay on the other side of what felt like death.

Quietly, he stepped out of the car, across the drenched yard and onto the porch. The door was locked. He saw an open window and crawled through it into the pitch black room. He held up his hands, but couldn't even see the dim outline of his fingers. A shutter slapped against the side of the porch and rain sprayed through the window he'd just entered. He eased through the house, holding his hands against the walls to guide him. He heard the wind blowing in a room ahead and he tiptoed into it. His foot kicked the bottle without warning and it ricocheted over the wood floor and cracked against the wall.

"Huh, who's there?" Burke heard the muffled voice over the wind. It rose up from the floor to his left.

He stopped moving, suddenly afraid.

"Who's in here?" Burke recognized the voice.

He called out, "I'm here, Walt. Burke Anderson."

"Don't come any closer, I've got a gun."

"It's me, Walt. Your old roomie. Are you O.K.?" Walt ignored the question. Or just didn't hear it.

"What'cha doin' here, Burke?" Walt tried to stand but his legs failed him.

"I've been looking for you, Walt. I'm looking for a friend too. For Debbi Meyer. Do you know anything about her? Who might have abducted her?"

"No," said Walt. "Don't know a Debbi Meyer. I'm alone."

The words slurred. But there was pain and confusion in Walt's voice.

"You didn't hurt Debbi, did you Walt?"

"I'm telling you, Burke. I'm alone. So what do you want with me?"

"We need to talk, Walt."

"'Bout what?"

"About Carol Reese."

"What about her?"

"She's dead, Walt. The police found her Sunday afternoon."

Walt didn't respond.

"Walt, you O.K.?"

"Yeah. Just thinking."

"She's dead, Walt, and they think I did it."

"Why would they think that?"

"'Cause I was there Friday with you. They found my Bible under her body, by the sofa. My fingerprints were all over the place. They have a warrant for my arrest."

Walt's broken ribs stuck a knife in him as he doubled over to laugh. "Man, if that don't beat all."

"What's so funny, Walt? You don't sound so good."

"You go to a hooker's house one time and she ends up dead. I've heard of preachers slaying them in the aisles, but in the sheets, never."

Burke wanted to enjoy Walt's familiar humor, but the night had a cloak on it and the rain was a cellophane bag covering the earth and the wind pulled at the sides of the house and three women were dead. Dear God, don't let it be four.

"Walt, I need you to tell them I didn't kill Carol Reese. That I didn't know her until you took me there. That's the only way I can clear myself."

"I don't know if I can do that, Burke." Walt said.

"Why not?"

"'Cause I killed her." Walt sounded dead himself, a hollow log lying on a forest floor, rotting from the inside out.

"How'd you do that, Walt?" Burke asked it gently, a brother concerned for a hurting brother.

"It was an accident. She called me right after you left. I told her to let me know what happened. I was at a bar right down the street. She said she wanted to get out of the profession, wanted to start over somewhere. She wanted money. Told me she wanted $500,000 to stay quiet. I couldn't give her the money and I couldn't let her reveal her clients."

"Why not? It wouldn't hurt you to be named as one."

"I wasn't worried about me. But one of her clients was Raymond Steele."

"The Senator." Burke said it matter-of-factly, not surprised by anything now.

"Exactly. I work for him."

"Why?"

Walt sucked in his breath and his voice grew quieter.

"'Cause he took me in after my career ended. I was about dead on drugs. The Senator gave me a job as his bodyguard. I did what he asked me to do."

"And he asked you to shut Reese up?"

"Yeah, something like that."

"Did he ask you to kill her?"

Walt's voice stiffened. "No, Burke, I didn't mean to kill her. That just happened. I was high, mixing booze and cocaine. She kept threatening me. Saying she would go to the media. I couldn't let her do that. Not before the campaign. I had to stop her. Anyway I could."

"So you hit her."

"Yeah."

"More than once."

"Yeah, three or four times. I don't know for sure." He paused as his voice faltered. "Knocked her against the refrigerator. Left her lying there in the kitchen. Dead, apparently. Didn't stop to see. Just left, headed here, to get away, to drown myself in booze and darkness."

Walt fell silent. The rain outside sounded like nails being driven into the roof.

"You've got to go back with me, Walt. Tell the police what you've told me. Since it wasn't intentional, they'll go easy on you, if you give them the Senator."

"I can't do that, Burke."

"Why not?"

"The Senator won't let me live. He's already sent one of his boys after me. Practically beat me to death. Left me for dead. I 'spect he'll be surprised when I turn up in a different place than he left me. But I wasn't going to die there, not in that hotel room. It doesn't matter much how a man dies, but it matters a lot where he dies. A man ought to die where he lived, so he doesn't drift around—lost in some place he doesn't recognize when he's gone. That's why I came back here. To die here."

"You don't have to die, Walt."

"Yeah, I do, Burke. I killed that girl. Even if Steele never reached me and even if some electrician never pulled the switch on me, I'm already dead. I deserve to die. I can't live with myself anymore. His words trailed, barely audible now like a pitiful moan. "That's the problem. Even if I got off scott-free, I'm still dead to myself. I deserve death. I still got the bruises on my hand where I hit her. No, I'm dead already, Burke. Didn't you always say, 'The wages of sin is death'?"

"I said that, Walt," agreed Burke, easing his way nearer to his friend, and dropping his voice a notch, "but that's not all I said. I also said, 'While we were yet sinners, Christ died for us.'"

"Yeah, I remember that. That's what I'm doing. For Carol. Like Jesus. I'm going to die for Carol. 'Cause I guess she was a sinner. And I killed her. Now, I got to die for her."

Burke took another step closer. The rain suddenly ceased and an eerie quiet wrapped around them. Walt filled the quiet with his words. "Don't come any closer, Freon. Like I said, I've got a gun."

Warmed by his old nickname, Burke spoke gently, "Walt, let me help you. We can go back. I'll take you back." He inched forward.

"One more step and I'll hurt you and I don't want to do that."

"You couldn't hurt me, Walt. We were best friends."

"You didn't think I could kill Carol either, but I did. Don't come any closer. I'll use this if you make me."

Burke took another step, catching the shadowed form of his friend, stuffed in the corner. The mass raised its arm and cocked the pistol.

"I'll kill you too, Burke."

"No, you can't."

"Yes, I can." Walt pointed the weapon and squeezed the trigger.

CHAPTER

37

Sonny spotted the brown Volvo in the glare of the headlights as he braked two houses up from Walt's cottage.

"So, Walt's got lots of company tonight," he said quietly. "That's good, we can kill two birds with one stone."

Sonny parked the car and the two men climbed out, closing their car doors softly, not wanting to disturb anyone in the cottage. Sonny opened the back door and dragged Debbi out of the seat. Her hands were tied; her mouth was taped shut and she wore a blindfold. He held a gun to her head and whispered, "If you don't do exactly what I say, I will kill you and your boyfriend without hesitation. Do you understand?" She nodded.

They picked their way carefully to the house and tiptoed onto the front porch. Through the broken window, they heard voices. Sonny bent low so he could hear the words.

"I'll kill you too, Burke," said one man.

"No, you can't," said another.

"Yes I can."

The shot from inside rang out and Sonny yanked Debbi down to her knees. The three squatted on the porch and listened to the sounds spilling out of the house.

* * * * *

In the bedroom, Burke threw himself to the floor, out of the line of Walt's voice, away from the bullet he feared Walt had fired at him.

But the bullet wasn't aimed at Burke. The spark from the gun pointed downward, toward the lump sitting in the blackened corner. Feeling no impact, Burke raced toward Walt, confused. Had Walt tried to kill him and missed? No. Walt had turned the gun on himself, firing into his chest cavity at point blank range. Burke heard the gun thump to the floor, rolling out of Walt's hand. He kneeled beside his friend, picked up his limp hand and searched frantically for a pulse. He felt one pumping erratically—he felt it getting weaker and dying in his hand—the life fleeing, a scared child released from its fears.

Burke wanted to call the life back, but he knew he couldn't. He wanted to stay and mourn the death of a friend, but he knew he couldn't do that either. He couldn't because he had scores of people looking for him and a Senator who wanted to be President needed to be stopped. He needed to call the police. So, he stood up, pulled off his jacket and draped it over Walt's bloody remains.

"Thank you for your help, Reverend Anderson." The calm voice rose up from the darkened door behind him, a ghostly, unnamed voice. He turned, unable to see the speaker. It moved toward him and he saw its shadow, plus a much larger, silent bulk behind it.

The voice said, "Don't move. I have a gun and a rather large and angry friend here who will do precisely what I tell him to do. Plus, I have a friend of yours with me." The man pulled a silhouette from behind the second man. Burke took a deep breath and knew it was Debbi. The man ripped the tape off her mouth.

Burke forced himself to focus—to keep his breathing regular and his mind working. "Who are you?" he asked.

"Maybe you would like to answer that," the voice directed its attention at Debbi.

"Burke, this is Sonny Flake, Senator Steele's chief of staff."

"Isn't she the smart one, Reverend Anderson? Even with a blind-fold, she recognizes me. And so pretty too. We might have some fun with her before the night is over."

"What do you want with us?"

"I think you can figure it out, Reverend. With a bit of arranging I can make this look every bit like a double murder and suicide tragedy. Walt Litske, a drug-tormented ex-athlete kills a prostitute. His former best friend, also present at the scene of the crime, tracks him down to get him to admit his crime. An enterprising female reporter tags along to get a good story for a failing newspaper and to build a promising career. Only the old friend won't cooperate. He kills Reverend and the reporter and then, in a fit of deep remorse, turns the weapon on himself. Fairly tidy, if you ask me."

It struck Burke like a kick in the groin. "So, Walt didn't kill Reese?"

Flake chuckled. "No, not at all. And the police would have figured it out sooner or later."

"Walt said he left Reese by the refrigerator."

"But they found her in the living room, by the sofa," noted Sonny.

Shocked, Burke said, "Yes, the police report said she actually died from hitting her head on a table. Reese didn't have a table near her refrigerator. Plus, my Bible was in her hand when they found her."

"And if our friend Walt left her dead or dying she wouldn't have taken the time nor had the energy to pull out a Bible and read from it. You're getting it now, Reverend."

Burke remembered one other fact. "The police reports said they found several strands of hair under Reese's fingernails."

"Wonderful," laughed Sonny.

"And Walt was bald."

"As a baby's backside," agreed their tormentor. "Has been since his first year in the pros."

Burke groaned out his grief. "I was so disoriented when I read the police report this morning I didn't figure it out."

"Guilt killed him," said Debbi. "Guilt over Reese's death. He couldn't live with the vision of her lying in the kitchen, murdered by his hand."

Sonny couldn't contain his giggles. "He killed himself for something he didn't even do. And you, Preacher, let him do it. This really is a classic. Too bad you won't be around to write this story, Ms. Meyer."

He turned to his silent partner. "I think it's time to wrap this up."

"Let me ask you one thing, first," said Burke.

"One request is customary for a condemmed man."

"Did you kill the other two girls?"

"Not me exactly. My friend here did the real work. I gave the directions and he took care of the terminations."

"Why'd you do it?"

"To protect Senator Steele. He's going to be our next President, you know. He's the only hope we have for this country."

"He was a client of the girls?"

"Yep, in the last two years. The Senator started his habit about then, switching girls every six months or so."

"Were they threatening him?"

"You could say so. Especially the first two. After getting rid of them we decided we should clean up the third one too. I think I've convinced the Senator to swear off his pleasures until after the elections. I have to take care of the Senator. The closer he gets, the more protection he needs. When he's elected President, I'll be right behind him, the power behind the throne. Too bad you won't be around to vote for him."

Flake lifted the pistol. Burke's nose wrinkled at the sudden smell of onions. His eyes flickered off and on like yellow traffic lights—warnings. He swayed with dizziness—the signs of a seizure. Not now, God, he prayed, harder than he'd ever prayed in his life. Not an epileptic seizure! Don't let me die now, not unconscious and in the dark. I've suffered enough. My sister Sarah. Carol Reese. Not Debbi, too. Don't make me die without facing it, like I've lived really. Afraid of life. Scared to confront it, refusing to risk anything, to get close to someone. Don't let me black out now, Lord.

From the edge of the void, Burke clawed his way back, through the tunnel threatening to close off in front of him, through the seizure, back to Debbi, back to fight.

Sonny's first shot missed and plowed into the wall behind Burke. Falling to the floor, Burke rolled backward toward Walt. He touched Walt's body and grabbed for his hand and found the gun Walt had used to kill himself. He grabbed the gun and fired wildly and the figure walking toward him slowed for a second. A third shot rang out and Burke felt the thump of a bullet in his right shoulder. He dropped the pistol as the bullet plowed into his flesh and the pain scorched through him. He heard the gun skid away from him on the floor and knew he would die before he could find it again in the darkness.

In a daze from pain and fear, he heard Debbi yelling to him, "In the car, Burke, in my purse!" Then he heard a thwump, thwump and he knew the big man had cracked Debbi on the head and she went silent. Knowing he had to move if he planned to survive, he pulled himself past Walt's body and another shot rang out and hit a body, but not his. This one landed in Walt's dead flesh. Burke braced himself, then flung himself out the window behind Walt and the glass shattered, but he couldn't feel anything now and the lacerations meant nothing to him.

He rolled off the porch into the mud and dragged himself toward the Volvo. Steps splashed behind him, but he was there now. He swung open the door, grabbed the purse and grasped the gun from the bottom of it.

Then he turned and flicked on the headlights of the Volvo. The lights pierced the darkness and froze Flake in his tracks. Burke saw the bangs in Flake's face and the memory electrocuted him. The memory flashed back into his mind, the memory of what happened during his epileptic blackout the night of Reese's murder.

For a split second everything stood still. He remembered what happened at Reese's house. He had regained consciousness that night, he had picked himself up off the ground and staggered back to her apartment door. He had started to ring the bell when two men—one with girlish bangs and the other much larger—suddenly flung open the door and raced out of Reese's condo. They had rushed by in the dark without noticing him pinned against the wall behind Reese's door. Too scared to continue, he had tottered off to the interstate, to hitchhike back to Cascade. Sonny Flake was one of those men.

Now, he fired a pistol point blank at the man wearing those girlish bangs. The shot popped through the rain and plowed through the bone which protected the left side of Flake's temple. Falling like a telephone pole axed by an errant car, Flake crashed backward into the mud.

Burke heard a car igniting behind him and he turned in time to see red tailights screeching onto the highway. He fired three shots at the fleeing car but it didn't stop. He thought for a minute he would chase it, but remembered Debbi was hurt inside.

He dropped the gun to the soggy ground and sloshed back into the cottage. Debbi lay slumped by the door. He pulled the blindfold off her head and she stared at him, her eyes gradually focusing.

"Are you O.K.?" he asked.

She reached up and wrapped her arms around his neck for an answer. He bent over and kissed the top of her head first, then lower to her cheeks wet with tears, then to her lips. She responded warmly to his tenderness and the kiss became a promise of a future together. Against the bleak night they huddled and Burke wanted the kiss to last forever, but it couldn't. The wail of an approaching siren interrupted it.

"Sounds like somone heard the shots," mumbled Debbi as the kiss ended.

"I don't know if that makes me glad or sad."

"A bit of both I think," said Debbi, squeezing him tighter.

He winced, feeling a throb in his wounded shoulder as the adrenalin settled down in his bloodstream.

"Are you hurt?" asked Debbi.

"Yeah, but it's not fatal, I don't think."

He inhaled deeply and squeezed Debbi once more, then stood. "Before anybody gets here, I want a few minutes with Walt." He helped her up and the two of them leaned on each other for a second. Debbi motioned him to the corner.

"You go to him, Burke. I'll wait on the porch."

"I want you with me," he said, not willing to leave her even for a second.

"I am with you," she comforted him. "But, I don't want to intrude on something that belongs to you."

"O.K.," he said, "I'll just need a minute." Burke dragged himself to Walt and eased down onto the floor. Gently, he took his friend's head in his lap and began to rock and sing, "Amazing grace, how sweet the sound, that saved a wretch like me. I once was lost, but now am found, was blind but now. . . ."

* * * * *

Outside, the rain suddenly stopped. The clouds began to break up. Staring up into the sky, Debbi listened to Burke's song. She stuck a strand of hair into her mouth and hugged herself. The melodic strains of the hymn wafting through the darkness comforted her and soothed her frayed nerves. Tonight she had almost died.

The hymn rolled out from the house. "'Twas grace that taught my heart to fear and grace my fears relieved. . . ." The words mixed in with the rocking of the ocean waves and the feathery touch of the wind blowing in her face. The moon peeped its bright face from behind the rushing clouds; the face of the moon smiled at her and the smile of the moon and the sound of the hymn stirred the unsettled yearnings of her spirit and offered them peace.

Debbi breathed a sigh of relief, glad for life and for the grace in Burke's song and for the grace she sought in her life. The moon glittered on her face and she smiled back. She wanted Burke to teach her how to believe.

* * * * *

Within minutes Broadus and Mays screeched to a stop and bounded out of their car, their guns drawn. Debbi squared her shoulders and greeted them professionally. "Officers," she said, holding her press credentials up in the glare of the police spotlight. "I'm Debbi Meyer from the *Independent*. Your prostitute homicide cases are solved."

"We'll see about that," nodded Mays as Broadus rushed by Debbi into the cottage. "Why don't we sit in the squad car and let you explain what's happened here?"

"Wait a minute," Debbi said, turning back into the house. "I need to bring a friend with me."

Mays led her in with his spotlight and Broadus stepped over to them. They followed Debbi into the bedroom where Burke sat on the floor beside Walt. For the second time that day, he had a friend's head in his lap and was saying goodbye. It wasn't any easier the second time around.

Debbi bent down and touched his shoulder. "Burke, it's time to go."

"I know," he sobbed. "I just wish I could take Walt home with me."

"He is home, Burke. This is his home. This is where he found his peace. He died at home. That's what he wanted." She gently coaxed Burke out of the corner, onto the porch and into the muddy yard.

In the yard, he took her hand and they splashed through the drive, into the spotlights of the police car, into the future.

"I've got a story to file," Debbi said.

"Will you tell them I'm innocent?" Burke asked.

"I knew it all the time."

CHAPTER

38

S itting at the table, Burke swallowed the last drop of his orange juice and focused on Bill and Barbara Metcalf. "What about the church, Burke?" asked Bill. "Will you come back and pastor us?"

Burke shrugged. "I don't know right now."

"Why wouldn't you come back? Everyone knows you're innocent."

Burke shook his head. "That's not the problem."

"What is it then?"

"I don't know, anger maybe. Anger at people who should have trusted me, but didn't. I don't feel like I should come back until I deal with that anger. Maybe time will help me sort out a few things. Then I'll know what to do next."

"But you'll miss it, won't you?" asked Barbara, as her eyes began to fill with tears.

Burke smiled. "Yeah, parts of it. I'll miss giving the children Tootsie Rolls on Sunday and the sound of the organ playing 'How Great Thou Art.' And I'll miss the Christmas Eve service when everybody's your friend and we light candles together." Burke smiled wider. "You know what I'll miss the most, Barbara?"

"What's that, Preacher?"

"I'll miss the hands, the hands I shake every Sunday as people rush out. Those hands always told me I wasn't alone—that other people needed what I was trying to share. I don't know if I realized it until now, but those hands kept coming back, week after week, Sunday after Sunday, they kept coming back to find something—no, to find someone they could reach out to. Those hands are why I preach, Bill, because they keep coming back."

"You'll be back, then," said Bill, motioning to Barbara and standing to leave.

"I hope I will."

"You will. I know it," he said, promising to check on him again soon.

Bill and Barbara left and Burke headed back to bed, still exhausted from the ordeal.

Two days had passed since Wednesday and he was still hurting and tired. Doctors had pulled the bullet out of his arm, wrapped his ribs, sewed three stitches over his right eye and and sent him home after 24 hours of observation. At home a whole parade of people had checked on him—Cody every day after work; his mom and dad from Birmingham on Thursday; Debbi on Thursday and Friday, but just for brief visits.

Now it was Saturday. Burke was glad for the time alone. The only one he really wanted to see was Debbi. They hadn't really had a chance to talk yet.

She was busy writing stories and Burke was busy too. Walt's dad and mom had asked him to say a word at Walt's funeral scheduled for Sunday, and he had spent hours considering his words. Plus, he had to deal with church members who appeared at all hours of the day at the Manse wanting to talk with him. Practically all of them had trooped by and the ones who came were repentant.

Margie Whitson brought him a peach cobbler and then talked for thirty minutes without stopping, making him pay a high price for the pie. The Mayor, after logically explaining why the church had voted to fire him, asked Burke to attend a special meeting Sunday evening when the church would reverse their decision. Burke didn't tell him he'd also attended the meeting in which he was voted out. Plopping into bed, he tried to shut out the parade of faces. He needed more time before he could face them all. The phone rang. Sighing, he picked it up and heard Jackie Broadus on the other end.

"I know you're tired," said Broadus, "but I wondered if you could stop by sometime this afternoon. You can pick up your Bible and we can go over your statement to make sure everything is cleared up. Would that be O.K., sir?"

Burke yawned. "Yeah, that'll be fine. Give me a couple of hours."

"See you then."

Burke hung up and called Debbi. She answered immediately.

"Debbi, this is Burke. Detective Broadus just called me. They're holding my Bible and want me to pick it up and answer a few questions. Want to drive with me? Maybe afterward we could get a bite to eat."

"Sure, why not?" she said.

"Good, see you in a few minutes."

An hour and a half later Debbi and Burke walked into the station room of Peachtree Street Precinct. Two uniformed patrolmen pushed by them with a handcuffed detainee as they opened the glass-paned doors and headed for the information desk. Guns were visible everywhere— under armpits in creaky leather holsters, on hips attached by bullet-filled belts, and behind locked racks on the walls.

"Sorta scary, isn't it?" Debbi said.

"Yeah, I'm glad I didn't end up here."

Jackie Broadus walked up. "Come into my office," she said, pointing them to a single metal desk parked to the right of the main walkway.

Debbi took the seat on the side and Burke accepted the one directly across from Broadus. Broadus knocked a California Lady out of a pack, and held it unlit between her fingers. She reached into her drawer and picked up a clear plastic bag. "Here's your Bible," she said, giving him the package.

Taking it, he rolled the bag over in his hands and inspected the Bible inside. "My mom gave this to me. I appreciate your taking care of it."

"No, problem. I appreciate your helping us find Reese's killer."

Burke nodded, "Where did you find the other guy, the one called Hock? I haven't seen much about that in the paper."

"No, hasn't much been printed about him. All the attention has been on you and Meyer and Flake. We picked him up right after sun-up. He was parked on a rural road about 30 miles from Litske's beach cottage. Strange though, he was just sitting there, not moving. A helicopter spotted the car and Mays and I went to pick him up."

"Is Hock as big as people say he is? We couldn't really see him at the cottage."

"He's huge!" exclaimed Jackie. "At least 6'8" and has to be 300 pounds. A giant really."

"But mentally handicapped?" Burke asked.

"Yeah, and you know the strangest part? He says he can't drive. But somehow he drove almost 30 miles. He denies it of course. Said he never went to Litske's place. Says Flake left him and told him he would pick him up later."

"Will his handicap keep him from standing trial?" Burke asked.

"Who knows? If the Senator hires him a good lawyer, they'll probably plead innocent by way of mental incompetence. Or they'll plea bargain the charge. With Flake dead most people will pin the blame on him and move on to other murders. Always a new one in Atlanta to keep people's attention."

"Think you can pin any of it on Steele?" asked Debbi.

"Probably not. He's too cagey for that. We don't have anything to connect him to the actual murders."

"But Flake said the Senator used these prostitues on a regular basis!" Burke complained.

"So, he used them. That doesn't prove he murdered them. We have absolutely no solid evidence to connect the Senator. We don't know that Flake and Hock weren't acting on their own. Flake certainly can't tell us anything and Hock can't remember from one day to the next. The Senator is pretty much scot-free. And, we have to assume his innocence until he's proven guilty."

"But we'll report his solicitation of prostitution," asserted Debbi, chewing on her hair.

"I doubt you'll even do that," said Jackie.

"Why not?"

Burke answered for Jackie. "Because the Senator's name in the book doesn't necessarily mean he had sex with her and the only other evidence we have is a female reporter and a preacher saying a dead man said he did."

"Precisely," agreed Jackie, standing up and stretching her long body backward. She reached out to shake hands, "We'll keep an eye on the Senator. If he slips, we'll nail him. Until then, I'm due for about four days' sleep. So, if you don't mind. . . ."

Burke stood too, with Debbi, and took Broadus' hand. "I want to thank you for getting there when you did," he said. "We were both pretty shook up. Plus, we didn't know that Hock wouldn't come back any second."

Jackie's eyes sparkled. "You were doing pretty well, if you ask me. You did our work for us."

"Maybe so, but we were at the end of our ropes when you showed up. Thanks."

"That's what we're paid for, Reverend Anderson." Jackie pivoted and walked away.

Burke grabbed Debbi's hand and they walked toward the door. A few feet short of the exit, the doors exploded inward, toward them. Chief Frank Conners and a retinue of staffers and reporters plowed into the precinct house, brushing past them, a swift current of people rushing by.

"That's the whole story as we've pieced it together over the last 48 hours," shouted Conners, his round face beet red from excitement. "The cases are closed. Sonny Flake and Senator Raymond Steele's bodyguard Hock are charged with the murders of the three prostitutes. We have no reason to suspect anyone else. The Reverend Anderson is no longer a suspect. But I think he'll have a hard time explaining why he was at the prostitute's house." The crowd laughed at the Chief's humor as they lunged ahead, following his bulky advance.

Backed up against the wall, Burke and Debbi watched them pass.

"Strange," said Burke, staring at Conners.

"What?"

"I've met him somewhere. Can't place it, but he looks awfully familiar."

"Probably from the news. He's been on television and in the paper a lot lately."

"Maybe so," said Burke, still unconvinced, but not able to place where he'd met Conners.

"Let's get out of here," urged Debbi, pulling on his arm. "I'm about to starve."

Burke grudgingly complied, peering back over his shoulder at Conners as he disappeared into his office.

* * * * *

Conners walked to his desk and dialed a private number.

"Conners here," he said, "Is the Senator available?"

"Just a moment."

Conners pulled his pipe out of his sport coat and slid it between his teeth.

"Steele here."

"Yeah, Senator. Conners. Just wanted you to know the prostitute cases are closed. I've taken care of everything on this end. It was a little dicey Wednesday night at Litske's cottage, and I'm sorry about Sonny, but at least I made it O.K. With Hock to blame, it looks like you and me are sitting pretty."

"Good, Frank. Great. You and Sonny do good work," beamed the Senator.

"Looks like I'll make retirement after all, huh, Raymond?"

"Absolutely, Frank, unless I need you in Washington. Either way, you'll be healthy and wealthy. You know I take good care of my friends. Bye now."

Both men dropped the phones onto their desks.

Pleased with the exchange, Conners pranced to his window and looked out at the courthouse across the street. The stars and stripes stretched out in the wind over the white-stoned building and flapped like a majestic bird. Watching the flag, Conners came to attention and saluted it with the precision of the good Marine he was. He whispered "Semper Fidelis, " and he meant it.

* * * * *

In his Cavalier, Burke pulled his Bible from the plastic bag and reverently laid it in his lap for inspection. Debbi watched as he opened it and thumbed through its pages.

"Where do we go from here, Burke?" she asked.

He noted the "we" in her question and was grateful for it. "I don't know exactly, but I know wherever I go, I want you with me."

"I can live with that," Debbi said, a wide smile capturing her face. "Wherever you go, I'll go with you. Sounds like a love song."

Burke turned to face her. "For me, I think it is," he said.

"I can live with that too," Debbi agreed softly, bending forward to kiss him. He met her kiss and lifted a hand to her face. After a few moments, he ended the kiss.

"Let's go home," he said, "We've got a lot to talk about." Debbi nooded in agreement.

Burke lifted the Bible from his lap, preparing to start the car. His eyes fell on the page opened in front of him and he saw some words underlined in red. "Someone has marked in my Bible!" he exclaimed.

Debbi leaned over and saw the markings too. "Who would have done that?" she asked. "The police?"

"No, don't think so," he said, scanning the pages to see if other verses were underlined. "You saw the plastic bag it was in. It's a serious offense if a policeman tampers with evidence."

"If not the police, then who?"

"Only one person could have done this." Burke stopped flipping the pages. His eyes widened and he leaned back against the seat, running his hands through his hair. "Carol Reese."

"You think so?"

"Who else?"

Burke held the Bible up where he could see it better and recited the red-lined passage. "Jesus said: 'Woman, where are they? Has no one condemned you?' 'No one sir.' 'Neither do I condemn you; Go and sin no more.'"

Debbi listened to him read. When he finished, neither of them spoke for several beats. Then Debbi asked, "You really think Reese marked those?"

"I can't imagine who else would have." Burke closed his eyes and in his imagination he saw Carol Reese searching through the Bible. In it, she found words she had read as a little girl and she read them again. This time the words were good to her and not harsh. The words grew wings and she flew on them. The words lifted her to the gates of heaven and she met God there and God spoke the glad word of love to her and she embraced the word and the sun came up on her face and God hugged her. Burke liked what he saw.

He opened his eyes and faced Debbi. "Maybe, in her last moments, a woman we called a sinner found her way to forgiveness."

Debbi placed her hand under the Bible and wrapped her fingers into Burke's. Little tears crawled to the edges of her eyes and waited. Her words gave them permission to fall. "If she could, then I can too."

Burke nodded. "If she could, then anybody can."